T0117898

Gulliver of Mars

Gulliver of Mars

Edwin L. Arnold

MINT EDITIONS

Gulliver of Mars was first published in 1905.

This edition published by Mint Editions 2020.

ISBN 9781513266565 | E-ISBN 9781513267005

Published by Mint Editions®

 MINT
EDITIONS
minteditionbooks.com

Publishing Director: Jennifer Newens
Project Manager: Gabrielle Maudiere
Design & Production: Rachel Lopez Metzger
Typesetting: Westchester Publishing Services

Chapter 1

Dare I say it? Dare I say that I, a plain, prosaic lieutenant in the republican service have done the incredible things here set out for the love of a woman—for a chimera in female shape; for a pale, vapid ghost of woman-loveliness? At times I tell myself I dare not: that you will laugh, and cast me aside as a fabricator; and then again I pick up my pen and collect the scattered pages, for I *must* write it—the pallid splendour of that thing I loved, and won, and lost is ever before me, and will not be forgotten. The tumult of the struggle into which that vision led me still throbs in my mind, the soft, lisping voices of the planet I ransacked for its sake and the roar of the destruction which followed me back from the quest drowns all other sounds in my ears! I must and will write—it relieves me; read and believe as you list.

At the moment this story commences I was thinking of grilled steak and tomatoes—steak crisp and brown on both sides, and tomatoes red as a setting sun!

Much else though I have forgotten, *that* fact remains as clear as the last sight of a well-remembered shore in the mind of some wave-tossed traveller. And the occasion which produced that prosaic thought was a night well calculated to make one think of supper and fireside, though the one might be frugal and the other lonely, and as I, Gulliver Jones, the poor foresaid Navy lieutenant, with the honoured stars of our Republic on my collar, and an undeserved snub from those in authority rankling in my heart, picked my way homeward by a short cut through the dismalness of a New York slum I longed for steak and stout, slippers and a pipe, with all the pathetic keenness of a troubled soul.

It was a wild, black kind of night, and the weirdness of it showed up as I passed from light to light or crossed the mouths of dim alleys leading Heaven knows to what infernal dens of mystery and crime even in this latter-day city of ours. The moon was up as far as the church steeples; large vapoury clouds scudding across the sky between us and her, and a strong, gusty wind, laden with big raindrops snarled angrily round corners and sighed in the parapets like strange voices talking about things not of human interest.

It made no difference to me, of course. New York in this year of grace is not the place for the supernatural be the time never so fit for witch-riding and the night wind in the chimney-stacks sound never so much like the last gurgling cries of throttled men. No! the world was very matter-of-fact, and particularly so to me, a poor younger son with five dollars in my purse by way of fortune, a packet of unpaid bills in my breastpocket, and round my neck a locket with a portrait therein of that dear buxom, freckled, stub-nosed girl away in a little southern seaport town whom I thought I loved with a magnificent affection. Gods! I had not even touched the fringe of that affliction.

Thus sauntering along moodily, my chin on my chest and much too absorbed in reflection to have any nice appreciation of what was happening about me, I was crossing in front of a dilapidated block of houses, dating back nearly to the time of the Pilgrim Fathers, when I had a vague consciousness of something dark suddenly sweeping by me—a thing like a huge bat, or a solid shadow, if such a thing could be, and the next instant there was a thud and a bump, a bump again, a half-stifled cry, and then a hurried vision of some black carpeting that flapped and shook as though all the winds of Eblis were in its folds, and then apparently disgorged from its inmost recesses a little man.

Before my first start of half-amused surprise was over I saw him by the flickering lamp-light clutch at space as he tried to steady himself, stumble on the slippery curb, and the next moment go down on the back of his head with a most ugly thud.

Now I was not destitute of feeling, though it had been my lot to see men die in many ways, and I ran over to that motionless form without an idea that anything but an ordinary accident had occurred. There he lay, silent and, as it turned out afterwards, dead as a door-nail, the strangest old fellow ever eyes looked upon, dressed in shabby sorrel-coloured clothes of antique cut, with a long grey beard upon his chin, pent-roof eyebrows, and a wizened complexion so puckered and tanned by exposure to Heaven only knew what weathers that it was impossible to guess his nationality.

I lifted him up out of the puddle of black blood in which he was lying, and his head dropped back over my arm as though it had been fixed to his body with string alone. There was neither heart-beat nor breath in him, and the last flicker of life faded out of that gaunt face even as I watched. It was not altogether a pleasant situation, and the only thing to do appeared to be to get the dead man into proper care (though little good it could do him now!) as speedily as possible. So, sending a chance passer-by into the main street for a cab, I placed him

EDWIN L. ARNOLD

into it as soon as it came, and there being nobody else to go, got in with him myself, telling the driver at the same time to take us to the nearest hospital.

"Is this your rug, captain?" asked a bystander just as we were driving off.

"Not mine," I answered somewhat roughly. "You don't suppose I go about at this time of night with Turkey carpets under my arm, do you? It belongs to this old chap here who has just dropped out of the skies on to his head; chuck it on top and shut the door!" And that rug, the very mainspring of the startling things which followed, was thus carelessly thrown on to the carriage, and off we went.

Well, to be brief, I handed in that stark old traveller from nowhere at the hospital, and as a matter of curiosity sat in the waiting-room while they examined him. In five minutes the house-surgeon on duty came in to see me, and with a shake of his head said briefly—

"Gone, sir—clean gone! Broke his neck like a pipe-stem. Most strange-looking man, and none of us can even guess at his age. Not a friend of yours, I suppose?"

"Nothing whatever to do with me, sir. He slipped on the pavement and fell in front of me just now, and as a matter of common charity I brought him in here. Were there any means of identification on him?"

"None whatever," answered the doctor, taking out his notebook and, as a matter of form, writing down my name and address and a few brief particulars, "nothing whatever except this curious-looking bead hung round his neck by a blackened thong of leather," and he handed me a thing about as big as a filbert nut with a loop for suspension and apparently of rock crystal, though so begrimed and dull its nature was difficult to speak of with certainty. The bead was of no seeming value and slipped unintentionally into my waistcoat pocket as I chatted for a few minutes more with the doctor, and then, shaking hands, I said goodbye, and went back to the cab which was still waiting outside.

It was only on reaching home I noticed the hospital porters had omitted to take the dead man's carpet from the roof of the cab when they carried him in, and as the cabman did not care about driving back to the hospital with it, and it could not well be left in the street, I somewhat reluctantly carried it indoors with me.

Once in the shine of my own lamp and a cigar in my mouth I had a closer look at that ancient piece of art work from heaven, or the other place, only knows what ancient loom.

A big, strong rug of faded Oriental colouring, it covered half the floor of my sitting-room, the substance being of a material more like camel's hair than anything else, and running across, when examined closely, were some dark fibres so long and fine that surely they must have come from the tail of Solomon's favourite black stallion itself. But the strangest thing about that carpet was its pattern. It was threadbare enough to all conscience in places, yet the design still lived in solemn, age-wasted hues, and, as I dragged it to my stove-front and spread it out, it seemed to me that it was as much like a star map done by a scribe who had lately recovered from *delirium tremens* as anything else. In the centre appeared a round such as might be taken for the sun, while here and there, "in the field," as heralds say, were lesser orbs which from their size and position could represent smaller worlds circling about it. Between these orbs were dotted lines and arrow-heads of the oldest form pointing in all directions, while all the intervening spaces were filled up with woven characters half-way in appearance between Runes and Cryptic-Sanskrit. Round the borders these characters ran into a wild maze, a perfect jungle of an alphabet through which none but a wizard could have forced a way in search of meaning.

Altogether, I thought as I kicked it out straight upon my floor, it was a strange and not unhandsome article of furniture—it would do nicely for the mess-room on the Carolina, and if any representatives of yonder poor old fellow turned up tomorrow, why, I would give them a couple of dollars for it. Little did I guess how dear it would be at any price!

Meanwhile that steak was late, and now that the temporary excitement of the evening was wearing off I fell dull again. What a dark, sodden world it was that frowned in on me as I moved over to the window and opened it for the benefit of the cool air, and how the wind howled about the roof tops. How lonely I was! What a fool I had been to ask for long leave and come ashore like this, to curry favour with a set of stubborn dunderheads who cared nothing for me—or Polly, and could not or would not understand how important it was to the best interests of the Service that I should get that promotion which alone would send me back to her an eligible wooer! What a fool I was not to have volunteered for some desperate service instead of wasting time like this! Then at least life would have been interesting; now it was dull as ditch-water, with wretched vistas of stagnant waiting between now and that joyful day when I could claim that dear, rosy-checked girl for my own. What a fool I had been!

"I wish, I wish," I exclaimed, walking round the little room, "I wish I were—"

While these unfinished exclamations were actually passing my lips I chanced to cross that infernal mat, and it is no more startling than true, but at my word a quiver of expectation ran through that gaunt web—a rustle of anticipation filled its ancient fabric, and one frayed corner surged up, and as I passed off its surface in my stride, the sentence still unfinished on my lips, wrapped itself about my left leg with extraordinary swiftness and so effectively that I nearly fell into the arms of my landlady, who opened the door at the moment and came in with a tray and the steak and tomatoes mentioned more than once already.

It was the draught caused by the opening door, of course, that had made the dead man's rug lift so strangely—what else could it have been? I made this apology to the good woman, and when she had set the table and closed the door took another turn or two about my den, continuing as I did so my angry thoughts.

"Yes, yes," I said at last, returning to the stove and taking my stand, hands in pockets, in front of it, "anything were better than this, any enterprise however wild, any adventure however desperate. Oh, I wish I were anywhere but here, anywhere out of this redtape-ridden world of ours! *I wish I were in the Planet Mars!*"

How can I describe what followed those luckless words? Even as I spoke the magic carpet quivered responsively under my feet, and an undulation went all round the fringe as though a sudden wind were shaking it. It humped up in the middle so abruptly that I came down sitting with a shock that numbed me for the moment. It threw me on my back and billowed up round me as though I were in the trough of a stormy sea. Quicker than I can write it lapped a corner over and rolled me in its folds like a chrysalis in a cocoon. I gave a wild yell and made one frantic struggle, but it was too late. With the leathery strength of a giant and the swiftness of an accomplished cigar-roller covering a "core" with leaf, it swamped my efforts, straightened my limbs, rolled me over, lapped me in fold after fold till head and feet and everything were gone—crushed life and breath back into my innermost being, and then, with the last particle of consciousness, I felt myself lifted from the floor, pass once round the room, and finally shoot out, point foremost, into space through the open window, and go up and up and up with a sound of rending atmospheres that seemed to tear like riven silk in one prolonged shriek under my head, and to close up in thunder astern until my reeling senses could stand it no longer, and time and space and circumstances all lost their meaning to me.

Chapter 2

How long that wild rush lasted I have no means of judging. It may have been an hour, a day, or many days, for I was throughout in a state of suspended animation, but presently my senses began to return and with them a sensation of lessening speed, a grateful relief to a heavy pressure which had held my life crushed in its grasp, without destroying it completely. It was just that sort of sensation though more keen which, drowsy in his bunk, a traveller feels when he is aware, without special perception, harbour is reached and a voyage comes to an end. But in my case the slowing down was for a long time comparative. Yet the sensation served to revive my scattered senses, and just as I was awakening to a lively sense of amazement, an incredible doubt of my own emotions, and an eager desire to know what had happened, my strange conveyance oscillated once or twice, undulated lightly up and down, like a woodpecker flying from tree to tree, and then grounded, bows first, rolled over several times, then steadied again, and, coming at last to rest, the next minute the infernal rug opened, quivering along all its borders in its peculiar way, and humping up in the middle shot me five feet into the air like a cat tossed from a schoolboy's blanket.

As I turned over I had a dim vision of a clear light like the shine of dawn, and solid ground sloping away below me. Upon that slope was ranged a crowd of squatting people, and a staid-looking individual with his back turned stood nearer by. Afterwards I found he was lecturing all those sitters on the ethics of gravity and the inherent properties of falling bodies; at the moment I only knew he was directly in my line as I descended, and him round the waist I seized, giddy with the light and fresh air, waltzed him down the slope with the force of my impetus, and, tripping at the bottom, rolled over and over recklessly with him sheer into the arms of the gaping crowd below. Over and over we went into the thickest mass of bodies, making a way through the people, until at last we came to a stop in a perfect mound of writhing forms and waving legs and arms. When we had done the mass disentangled itself and I was able to raise my head from the shoulder of someone on whom I had fallen, lifting him, or her—which was it?—into a sitting posture alongside of me at the same time, while the others rose about us like wheat-stalks after a storm, and edged shyly off, as well as they might.

Such a sleek, slim youth it was who sat up facing me, with a flush of gentle surprise on his face, and dapper hands that felt cautiously about his anatomy for injured places. He looked so quaintly rueful yet withal so good-tempered that I could not help bursting into laughter in spite of my own amazement. Then he laughed too, a sedate, musical chuckle, and said something incomprehensible, pointing at the same time to a cut upon my finger that was bleeding a little. I shook my head, meaning thereby that it was nothing, but the stranger with graceful solicitude took my hand, and, after examining the hurt, deliberately tore a strip of cloth from a bright yellow toga-like garment he was wearing and bound the place up with a woman's tenderness.

Meanwhile, as he ministered, there was time to look about me. Where was I? It was not the Broadway; it was not Staten Island on a Saturday afternoon. The night was just over, and the sun on the point of rising. Yet it was still shadowy all about, the air being marvellously tepid and pleasant to the senses. Quaint, soft aromas like the breath of a new world—the fragrance of unknown flowers, and the dewy scent of never-trodden fields drifted to my nostrils; and to my ears came a sound of laughter scarcely more human than the murmur of the wind in the trees, and a pretty undulating whisper as though a great concourse of people were talking softly in their sleep. I gazed about scarcely knowing how much of my senses or surroundings were real and how much fanciful, until I presently became aware the rosy twilight was broadening into day, and under the increasing shine a strange scene was fashioning itself.

At first it was an opal sea I looked on of mist, shot along its upper surface with the rosy gold and pinks of dawn. Then, as that soft, translucent lake ebbed, jutting hills came through it, black and crimson, and as they seemed to mount into the air other lower hills showed through the veil with rounded forest knobs till at last the brightening day dispelled the mist, and as the rosy-coloured gauzy fragments went slowly floating away a wonderfully fair country lay at my feet, with a broad sea glimmering in many arms and bays in the distance beyond. It was all dim and unreal at first, the mountains shadowy, the ocean unreal, the flowery fields between it and me vacant and shadowy.

Yet were they vacant? As my eyes cleared and day brightened still more, and I turned my head this way and that, it presently dawned upon me all the meadow coppices and terraces northwards of where I lay, all that blue and spacious ground I had thought to be bare and vacant, were alive with a teeming city of booths and tents; now I came

EDWIN L. ARNOLD

...as a whole town upon the slop...
...and branches still unwithered, th...
...hadows thronged with expectant...
... to and fro in lively streams—cha...
...and the tent doors in soft, gauzy, ...
...oth fascinating and perplexing.

...like a child at its first pantomime, diml...
...aw was novel, but more allured to the colour and
...than concerned with its exact meaning; and while
...ared and turned my finger was bandaged, and my new friend had
been lisping away to me without getting anything in turn but a shake
of the head. This made him thoughtful, and thereon followed a curious
incident which I cannot explain. I doubt even whether you will believe
it; but what am I to do in that case? You have already accepted the
episode of my coming, or you would have shut the covers before arriving
at this page of my modest narrative, and this emboldens me. I may
strengthen my claim on your credulity by pointing out the extraordinary
marvels which science is teaching you even on our own little world. To
quote a single instance: If any one had declared ten years ago that it
would shortly be practicable and easy for two persons to converse from
shore to shore across the Atlantic without any intervening medium,
he would have been laughed at as a possibly amusing but certainly
extravagant romancer. Yet that picturesque lie of yesterday is amongst
the accomplished facts of today! Therefore I am encouraged to ask your
indulgence, in the name of your previous errors, for the following and
any other instances in which I may appear to trifle with strict veracity.
There is no such thing as the impossible in our universe!

When my friendly companion found I could not understand him, he
looked serious for a minute or two, then shortened his brilliant yellow
toga, as though he had arrived at some resolve, and knelt down directly
in front of me. He next took my face between his hands, and putting his
nose within an inch of mine, stared into my eyes with all his might. At
first I was inclined to laugh, but before long the most curious sensations
took hold of me. They commenced with a thrill which passed all up my
body, and next all feeling save the consciousness of the loud beating of
my heart ceased. Then it seemed that boy's eyes were inside my head and
not outside, while along with them an intangible something pervaded
my brain. The sensation at first was like the application of ether to the
skin—a cool, numbing emotion. It was followed by a curious tingling

some dormant cells in my mind answer[...] and were filled and fertilised! My other [...] ly felt the vitalising of their companions, and for a[...] [ex]perienced extreme nausea and a headache such as comes[...] [...]y, though both passed swiftly off. I presume that in the f[uture] [we sh]all all obtain knowledge in this way. The Professors of a lat[er] [...] will perhaps keep shops for the sale of miscellaneous information, a[nd] we shall drop in and be inflated with learning just as the bicyclist gets his tire pumped up, or the motorist is recharged with electricity at so much per unit. Examinations will then become matters of capacity in the real meaning of that word, and we shall be tempted to invest our pocket-money by advertisements of "A cheap line in Astrology," "Try our double-strength, two-minute course of Classics," "This is remnant day for Trigonometry and Metaphysics," and so on.

My friend did not get as far as that. With him the process did not take more than a minute, but it was startling in its results, and reduced me to an extraordinary state of hypnotic receptibility. When it was over my instructor tapped with a finger on my lips, uttering aloud as he did so the words—

"Know none; know some; know little; know more!" again and again; and the strangest part of it is that as he spoke I did know at first a little, then more, and still more, by swift accumulation, of his speech and meaning. In fact, when presently he suddenly laid a hand over my eyes and then let go of my head with a pleasantly put question as to how I felt, I had no difficulty whatever in answering him in his own tongue, and rose from the ground as one gets from a hair-dresser's chair, with a vague idea of looking round for my hat and offering him his fee.

"My word, sir!" I said, in lisping Martian, as I pulled down my cuffs and put my cravat straight, "that was a quick process. I once heard of a man who learnt a language in the moments he gave each day to having his boots blacked; but this beats all. I trust I was a docile pupil?"

"Oh, fairly, sir," answered the soft, musical voice of the strange being by me; "but your head is thick and your brain tough. I could have taught another in half the time."

"Curiously enough," was my response, "those are almost the very words with which my dear old tutor dismissed me the morning I left college. Never mind, the thing is done. Shall I pay you anything?"

"I do not understand."

"Any honorarium, then? Some people understand one word and not the other." But the boy only shook his head in answer.

Strangely enough, I was not greatly surprised all this time either at the novelty of my whereabouts or at the hypnotic instruction in a new language just received. Perhaps it was because my head still spun too giddily with that flight in the old rug for much thought; perhaps because I did not yet fully realise the thing that had happened. But, anyhow, there is the fact, which, like so many others in my narrative, must, alas! remain unexplained for the moment. The rug, by the way, had completely disappeared, my friend comforting me on this score, however, by saying he had seen it rolled up and taken away by one whom he knew.

"We are very tidy people here, stranger," he said, "and everything found Lying about goes back to the Palace store-rooms. You will laugh to see the lumber there, for few of us ever take the trouble to reclaim our property."

Heaven knows I was in no laughing mood when I saw that enchanted web again!

When I had lain and watched the brightening scene for a time, I got up, and having stretched and shaken my clothes into some sort of order, we strolled down the hill and joined the light-hearted crowds that twined across the plain and through the streets of their city of booths. They were the prettiest, daintiest folk ever eyes looked upon, well-formed and like to us as could be in the main, but slender and willowy, so dainty and light, both the men and the women, so pretty of cheek and hair, so mild of aspect, I felt, as I strode amongst them, I could have plucked them like flowers and bound them up in bunches with my belt. And yet somehow I liked them from the first minute; such a happy, careless, light-hearted race, again I say, never was seen before. There was not a stain of thought or care on a single one of those white foreheads that eddied round me under their peaked, blossom-like caps, the perpetual smile their faces wore never suffered rebuke anywhere; their very movements were graceful and slow, their laughter was low and musical, there was an odour of friendly, slothful happiness about them that made me admire whether I would or no.

Unfortunately I was not able to live on laughter, as they appeared to be, so presently turning to my acquaintance, who had told me his name was the plain monosyllabic An, and clapping my hand on his shoulder as he stood lost in sleepy reflection, said, in a good, hearty way, "Hullo, friend Yellow-jerkin! If a stranger might set himself athwart the cheerful current of your meditations, may such a one ask how far 'tis to the nearest wine-shop or a booth where a thirsty man may get a mug of ale at a moderate reckoning?"

That gilded youth staggered under my friendly blow as though the hammer of Thor himself had suddenly lit upon his shoulder, and ruefully rubbing his tender skin, he turned on me mild, handsome eyes, answering after a moment, during which his native mildness struggled with the pain I had unwittingly given him—

"If your thirst be as emphatic as your greeting, friend Heavy-fist, it will certainly be a kindly deed to lead you to the drinking-place. My shoulder tingles with your good-fellowship," he added, keeping two arms'-lengths clear of me. "Do you wish," he said, "merely to cleanse a dusty throat, or for blue or pink oblivion?"

"Why," I answered laughingly, "I have come a longish journey since yesterday night—a journey out of count of all reasonable mileage—and I might fairly plead a dusty throat as excuse for a beginning; but as to the other things mentioned, those tinted forgetfulnesses, I do not even know what you mean."

"Undoubtedly you are a stranger," said the friendly youth, eyeing me from top to toe with renewed wonder, "and by your unknown garb one from afar."

"From how far no man can say—not even I—but from very far, in truth. Let that stay your curiosity for the time. And now to bench and ale-mug, on good fellow!—the shortest way. I was never so thirsty as this since our water-butts went overboard when I sailed the southern seas as a tramp apprentice, and for three days we had to damp our black tongues with the puddles the night-dews left in the lift of our mainsail."

Without more words, being a little awed of me, I thought, the boy led me through the good-humoured crowd to where, facing the main road to the town, but a little sheltered by a thicket of trees covered with gigantic pink blossoms, stood a drinking-place—a cluster of tables set round an open grass-plot. Here he brought me a platter of some light inefficient cakes which merely served to make hunger more self-conscious, and some fine aromatic wine contained in a triple-bodied flask, each division containing vintage of a separate hue. We broke our biscuits, sipped that mysterious wine, and talked of many things until at last something set us on the subject of astronomy, a study I found my dapper gallant had some knowledge of—which was not to be wondered at seeing he dwelt under skies each night set thick above his curly head

EDWIN L. ARNOLD

with tawny planets, and glittering constellations sprinkled through space like flowers in May meadows. He knew what worlds went round the sun, larger or lesser, and seeing this I began to question him, for I was uneasy in my innermost mind and, you will remember, so far had no certain knowledge of where I was, only a dim, restless suspicion that I had come beyond the ken of all men's knowledge.

Therefore, sweeping clear the board with my sleeve, and breaking the wafer cake I was eating, I set down one central piece for the sun, and, "See here!" I said, "good fellow! This morsel shall stand for that sun you have just been welcoming back with quaint ritual. Now stretch your starry knowledge to the utmost, and put down that tankard for a moment. If this be yonder sun and this lesser crumb be the outermost one of our revolving system, and this the next within, and this the next, and so on; now if this be so tell me which of these fragmentary orbs is ours—which of all these crumbs from the hand of the primordial would be that we stand upon?" And I waited with an anxiety a light manner thinly hid, to hear his answer.

It came at once. Laughing as though the question were too trivial, and more to humour my wayward fancy than aught else, that boy circled his rosy thumb about a minute and brought it down on the planet Mars!

I started and stared at him; then all of a tremble cried, "You trifle with me! Choose again—there, see, I will set the symbols and name them to you anew. There now, on your soul tell me truly which this planet is, the one here at our feet?" And again the boy shook his head, wondering at my eagerness, and pointed to Mars, saying gently as he did so the fact was certain as the day above us, nothing was marvellous but my questioning.

Mars! oh, dreadful, tremendous, unexpected! With a cry of affright, and bringing my fist down on the table till all the cups upon it leapt, I told him he lied—lied like a simpleton whose astronomy was as rotten as his wit—smote the table and scowled at him for a spell, then turned away and let my chin fall upon my breast and my hands upon my lap.

And yet, and yet, it might be so! Everything about me was new and strange, the crisp, thin air I breathed was new; the lukewarm sunshine new; the sleek, long, ivory faces of the people new! Yesterday—was it yesterday?—I was back there—away in a world that pines to know of other worlds, and one fantastic wish of mine, backed by a hideous, infernal chance, had swung back the doors of space and shot me—if that boy spoke true—into the outer void where never living man had been before: all my wits about me, all the horrible bathos of my earthly clothing on me, all my terrestrial hungers in my veins!

I sprang to my feet and swept my hands across my eyes. Was that a dream, or this? No, no, both were too real. The hum of my faraway city still rang in my ears: a swift vision of the girl I had loved; of the men I had hated; of the things I had hoped for rose before me, still dazing my inner eye. And these about me were real people, too; it was real earth; real skies, trees, and rocks—had the infernal gods indeed heard, I asked myself, the foolish wish that started from my lips in a moment of fierce discontent, and swept me into another sphere, another existence? I looked at the boy as though he could answer that question, but there was nothing in his face but vacuous wonder; I clapped my hands together and beat my breast; it was true; my soul within me said it was true; the boy had not lied; the djins had heard; I was just in the flesh I had; my common human hungers still unsatisfied where never mortal man had hungered before; and scarcely knowing whether I feared or not, whether to laugh or cry, but with all the wonder and terror of that great remove sweeping suddenly upon me I staggered back to my seat, and dropping my arms upon the table, leant my head heavily upon them and strove to choke back the passion which beset me.

EDWIN L. ARNOLD

Chapter 3

It was the light touch of the boy An upon my shoulder which roused me. He was bending down, his pretty face full of concernful sympathy, and in a minute said—knowing nothing of my thoughts, of course.

"It is the wine, stranger, the pink oblivion, it sometimes makes one feel like that until enough is taken; you stopped just short of what you should have had, and the next cup would have been delight—I should have told you."

"Ay," I answered, glad he should think so, "it was the wine, no doubt; your quaint drink, sir, tangled up my senses for the moment, but they are clearer now, and I am eager past expression to learn a little more of this strange country I have wandered into."

"I would rather," said the boy, relapsing again into his state of kindly lethargy, "that you learnt things as you went, for talking is work, and work we hate, but today we are all new and fresh, and if ever you are to ask questions now is certainly the time. Come with me to the city yonder, and as we go I will answer the things you wish to know;" and I went with him, for I was humble and amazed, and, in truth, at that moment, had not a word to say for myself.

All the way from the plain where I had awoke to the walls of the city stood booths, drinking-places, and gardens divided by labyrinths of canals, and embowered in shrubberies that seemed coming into leaf and flower as we looked, so swift was the process of their growth. These waterways were covered with skiffs being pushed and rowed in every direction; the cheerful rowers calling to each other through the leafy screens separating one lane from another till the place was full of their happy chirruping. Every booth and way-side halting-place was thronged with these delicate and sprightly people, so friendly, so gracious, and withal so purposeless.

I began to think we should never reach the town itself, for first my guide would sit down on a green stream-bank, his feet a-dangle in the clear water, and bandy wit with a passing boat as though there were nothing else in the world to think of. And when I dragged him out of that, whispering in his ear, "The town, my dear boy! the town! I am all agape to see it," he would saunter reluctantly to a booth a hundred yards further on and fall to eating strange confections or sipping coloured ines with chance acquaintances, till again I plucked him by the sleeve and said: "Seth, good comrade—was it not so you called your city just now?—take me to the gates, and I will be grateful to you," then on again down a flowery lane, aimless and happy, wasting my time and his, with placid civility I was led by that simple guide.

Wherever we went the people stared at me, as well they might, as I walked through them overtopping the tallest by a head or more. The drinking-cups paused half-way to their mouths; the jests died away upon their lips; and the blinking eyes of the drinkers shone with a momentary sparkle of wonder as their minds reeled down those many-tinted floods to the realms of oblivion they loved.

I heard men whisper one to another, "Who is he?"; "Whence does he come?"; "Is he a tribute-taker?" as I strolled amongst them, my mind still so thrilled with doubt and wonder that to me they seemed hardly more than painted puppets, the vistas of their lovely glades and the ivory town beyond only the fancy of a dream, and their talk as incontinent as the babble of a stream.

Then happily, as I walked along with bent head brooding over the incredible thing that had happened, my companion's shapely legs gave out, and with a sigh of fatigue he suggested we should take a skiff amongst the many lying about upon the margins and sail towards the town, "For," said he, "the breeze blows thitherward, and 'tis a shame to use one's limbs when Nature will carry us for nothing!"

"But have you a boat of your own hereabouts?" I queried; "for to tell the truth I came from home myself somewhat poorly provided with means to buy or barter, and if your purse be not heavier than mine we must still do as poor men do."

"Oh!" said An, "there is no need to think of that, no one here to hire or hire of; we will just take the first skiff we see that suits us."

"And what if the owner should come along and find his boat gone?"

"Why, what should he do but take the next along the bank, and the master of that the next again—how else could it be?" said the Martian, and shrugging my shoulders, for I was in no great mood to argue, we went down to the waterway, through a thicket of budding trees underlaid with a carpet of small red flowers filling the air with a scent of honey, and soon found a diminutive craft pulled up on the bank. There were some dainty cloaks and wraps in it which An took out and laid under a tree. But first he felt in the pouch of one for a sweetmeat which his fine nostrils, acute as a squirrel's, told him was there, and taking the lump out bit a piece from it, afterwards replacing it in the owner's pocket with the frankest simplicity.

Then we pushed off, hoisted the slender mast, set the smallest lug-sail that ever a sailor smiled at, and, myself at the helm, and that golden youth amidships, away we drifted under thickets of drooping canes tasselled with yellow catkin-flowers, up the blue alley of the water into the broader open river beyond with its rapid flow and crowding boats, the white city front now towering clear before us.

The air was full of sunshine and merry voices; birds were singing, trees were budding; only my heart was heavy, my mind confused. Yet why should I be sad, I said to myself presently? Life beat in my pulses; what had I to fear? This world I had tumbled into was new and strange, no doubt, but tomorrow it would be old and familiar; it discredited my manhood to sit brow-bent like that, so with an effort I roused myself.

"Old chap!" I said to my companion, as he sat astride of a thwart slowly chewing something sticky and eyeing me out of the corner of his eyes with vapid wonder, "tell me something of this land of yours, or something about yourself—which reminds me I have a question to ask. It is a bit delicate, but you look a sensible sort of fellow, and will take no offence. The fact is, I have noticed as we came along half your population dresses in all the colours of the rainbow—'fancy suitings' our tailors could call it at home—and this half of the census are undoubtedly men and women. The rub is that the other half, to which you belong, all dress alike in *yellow*, and I will be fired from the biggest gun on the Carolina's main deck if I can tell what sex you belong to! I took you for a boy in the beginning, and the way you closed with the idea of having a drink with me seemed to show I was dead on the right course. Then a little later on I heard you and a friend abusing our sex from an outside point of view in a way which was very disconcerting. This, and some other things, have set me all abroad again, and as fate seems determined to make us chums for this voyage—why—well, frankly, I should be glad to know if you be boy or girl? If you are as I am, no more nor less then—for I like you—there's my hand in comradeship. If you are otherwise, as those sleek outlines seem to promise—why, here's my hand again! But man or woman you must be—come, which is it?"

If I had been perplexed before, to watch that boy now was more curious than ever. He drew back from me with a show of wounded dignity, then bit his lips, and sighed, and stared, and frowned. "Come," I said laughingly, "speak! it engenders ambiguity to be so ambiguous of gender! 'Tis no great matter, yes or no, a plain answer will set us fairly in our friendship; if it is comrade, then comrade let it be; if maid, why, I shall not quarrel with that, though it cost me a likely messmate."

"You mock me."

"Not I, I never mocked any one."

"And does my robe tell you nothing?"

"Nothing so much; a yellow tunic and becoming enough, but nothing about it to hang a deduction on. Come! Are you a girl, after all?"

"I do not count myself a girl."

"Why, then, you are the most blooming boy that ever eyes were set upon; and though 'tis with some tinge of regret, yet cheerfully I welcome you into the ranks of manhood."

"I hate your manhood, send it after the maidhood; it fits me just as badly."

"But An, be reasonable; man or maid you must be."

"Must be; why?"

"Why?" Was ever such a question put to a sane mortal before? I stared at that ambiguous thing before me, and then, a little wroth to be played with, growled out something about Martians being all drunk or mad.

"'Tis you yourself are one or other," said that individual, by this time pink with anger, "and if you think because I am what I am you can safely taunt me, you are wrong. See! I have a sting," and like a thwarted child my companion half drew from the folds of the yellow tunic-dress the daintiest, most harmless-looking little dagger that was ever seen.

"Oh, if it comes to that," I answered, touching the Navy scabbard still at my hip, and regaining my temper at the sight of hers, "why, I have a sting also—and twice as long as yours! But in truth, An, let us not talk of these things; if something in what I have said has offended nice Martian scruples I am sorry, and will question no more, leaving my wonder for time to settle."

"No," said the other, "it was my fault to be hasty of offence; I am not so angered once a year. But in truth your question moves us yellow robes deeply. Did you not really know that we who wear this saffron tunic are slaves,—a race apart, despised by all."

"'Slaves,' no; how should I know it?"

"I thought you must understand a thing so fundamental, and it was that thought which made your questions seem unkind. But if indeed you have come so far as not to understand even this, then let me tell you once we of this garb were women—priestesses of the immaculate conceptions of humanity; guardians of those great hopes and longings which die so easily. And because we forgot our high station and took to aping another sex the gods deserted and men despised us, giving us, in the fierceness of their contempt, what we asked for. We are the slave ants of the nest, the work-bees of the hive, come, in truth, of those here who still be men and women of a sort, but toilers only; unknown in love, unregretted in death—those who dangle all children but their own—slaves cursed with the accomplishment of their own ambition."

There was no doubt poor An believed what she said, for her attitude was one of extreme dejection while she spoke, and to cheer her I laughed.

"Oh! come, it can't be as bad as that. Surely sometimes some of you win back to womanhood? You yourself do not look so far gone but what some deed of abnegation, some strong love if you could but conceive it would set you right again. Surely you of the primrose robes can sometimes love?"

Whereat unwittingly I troubled the waters in the placid soul of that outcast Martian! I cannot exactly describe how it was, but she bent her head silently for a moment or two, and then, with a sigh, lifting her eyes suddenly to mine, said quietly, "Yes, sometimes; sometimes—but very seldom," while for an instant across her face there flashed the summer lightning of a new hope, a single transient glance of wistful, timid entreaty; of wonder and delight that dared not even yet acknowledge itself.

Then it was my turn to sit silent, and the pause was so awkward that in a minute, to break it, I exclaimed—

"Let's drop personalities, old chap—I mean my dear Miss An. Tell me something about your people, and let us begin properly at the top: have you got a king, for instance?"

To this the girl, pulling herself out of the pleasant slough of her listlessness, and falling into my vein, answered—

"Both yes and no, sir traveller from afar—no chiefly, and yet perhaps yes. If it were no then it were so, and if yes then Hath were our king."

"A mild king I should judge by your uncertainty. In the place where I came from kings press their individualities somewhat more clearly on their subjects' minds. Is Hath here in the city? Does he come to your feasts today?"

An nodded. Hath was on the river, he had been to see the sunrise; even now she thought the laughter and singing down behind the bend might be the king's barge coming up citywards. "He will not be late," said my companion, "because the marriage-feast is set for tomorrow in the palace."

I became interested. Kings, palaces, marriage-feasts—why, here was something substantial to go upon; after all these gauzy folk might turn out good fellows, jolly comrades to sojourn amongst—and marriage-feasts reminded me again I was hungry.

"Who is it," I asked, with more interest in my tone, "who gets married?—is it your ambiguous king himself?"

Whereat An's purple eyes broadened with wonder: then as though she would not be uncivil she checked herself, and answered with smothered pity for my ignorance, "Not only Hath himself, but every one, stranger, they are all married tomorrow; you would not have them married one at a time, would you?"—this with inexpressible derision.

I said, with humility, something like that happened in the place I came from, asking her how it chanced the convenience of so many came to one climax at the same moment. "Surely, An, this is a marvel of arrangement. Where I dwelt wooings would sometimes be long or sometimes short, and all maids were not complacent by such universal agreement."

The girl was clearly perplexed. She stared at me a space, then said, "What have wooings long or short to do with weddings? You talk as if you did your wooing first and then came to marriage—we get married first and woo afterwards!"

"'Tis not a bad idea, and I can see it might lend an ease and certainty to the pastime which our method lacks. But if the woman is got first and sued subsequently, who brings you together? Who sees to the essential preliminaries of assortment?"

An, looking at my shoes as though she speculated on the remoteness of the journey I had come if it were measured by my ignorance, replied, "The urn, stranger, the urn does that—what else? How it may be in that out-fashioned region you have come from I cannot tell, but here—'tis so commonplace I should have thought you must have known it—we put each new year the names of all womenkind into an urn and the men draw for them, each town, each village by itself, and those they draw are theirs; is it conceivable your race has other methods?"

I told her it was so—we picked and chose for ourselves, beseeching the damsels, fighting for them, and holding the sun of romance was at its setting just where the Martians held it to rise. Whereat An burst out

EDWIN L. ARNOLD

laughing—a clear, ringing laugh that set all the light-hearted
nearest boats laughing in sympathy. But when the grotesquene
idea had somewhat worn off, she turned grave and asked me if
fancy did not lead to spite, envy, and bickerings. "Why, it seems to
she said, shaking her curly head, "such a plan might fire cities, deso.
plains, and empty palaces—"

"Such things have been."

"Ah! our way is much the better. See!" quoth that gentle philosopher.
"'Here,' one of our women would say, 'am I to-day, unwed, as free of
thought as yonder bird chasing the catkin down; tomorrow I shall be
married, with a whole summer to make love in, relieved at one bound
of all those uncertainties you acknowledge to, with nothing to do but
lie about on sunny banks with him whom chance sends me, come to
the goal of love without any travelling to get there.' Why, you must
acknowledge this is the perfection of ease."

"But supposing," I said, "chance dealt unkindly to you from your
nuptial urn, supposing the man was not to your liking, or another
coveted him?" To which An answered, with some shrewdness—

"In the first case we should do what we might, being no worse off
than those in your land who had played ill providence to themselves. In
the second, no maid would covet him whom fate had given to another,
it were too fatiguing, or if such a thing *did* happen, then one of them
would waive his claims, for no man or woman ever born was worth a
wrangle, and it is allowed us to barter and change a little."

All this was strange enough. I could not but laugh, while An laughed
at the lightest invitation, and thus chatting and deriding each other's
social arrangements we floated idly townwards and presently came
out into the main waterway perhaps a mile wide and flowing rapidly,
as streams will on the threshold of the spring, with brash or waste of
distant beaches riding down it, and every now and then a broken branch
or tree-stem glancing through waves whose crests a fresh wind lifted
and sowed in golden showers in the intervening furrows. The Martians
seemed expert upon the water, steering nimbly between these floating
dangers when they met them, but for the most part hugging the shore
where a more placid stream better suited their fancies, and for a time
all went well.

An, as we went along, was telling me more of her strange country,
pointing out birds or flowers and naming them to me. "Now that," she
said, pointing to a small grey owl who sat reflective on a floating log we

aching—"that is a bird of omen; cover your face and look

it is not well to watch it."

ereat I laughed. "Oh!" I answered, "so those ancient follies have

as far as this, have they? But it is no bird grey or black or white that

frighten folk where I come from; see, I will ruffle his philosophy for

n," and suiting the action to the words I lifted a pebble that happened

to lie at the bottom of the boat and flung it at that creature with the

melancholy eyes. Away went the owl, dipping his wings into the water

at every stroke, and as he went wailing out a ghostly cry, which even

amongst sunshine and glitter made one's flesh creep.

An shook her head. "You should not have done that," she said; "our

dead whom we send down over the falls come back in the body of

yonder little bird. But he has gone now," she added, with relief; "see, he

settles far up stream upon the point of yonder rotten bough; I would not

disturb him again if I were you—"

Whatever more An would have said was lost, for amidst a sound

of flutes and singing round the bend of the river below came a crowd

of boats decked with flowers and garlands, all clustering round a barge

barely able to move, so thick those lesser skiffs pressed upon it. So close

those wherries hung about that the garlanded rowers who sat at the

oars could scarcely pull, but, here as everywhere, it was the same good

temper, the same carelessness of order, as like a flowery island in the

dancing blue water the motley fleet came up.

I steered our skiff a space out from the bank to get a better view,

while An clapped her hands together and laughed. "It is Hath—he

himself and those of the palace with him. Steer a little nearer still,

friend—so! between yon floating rubbish flats, for those with Hath are

good to look at."

Nothing loth I made out into mid-stream to see that strange prince

go by, little thinking in a few minutes I should be shaking hands with

him, a wet and dripping hero. The crowd came up, and having the

advantage of the wind, it did not take me long to get a front place in

the ruck, whence I set to work, with republican interest in royalty, to

stare at the man who An said was the head of Martian society. He did

not make me desire to renounce my democratic principles. The royal

fellow was sitting in the centre of the barge under a canopy and on

a throne which was a mass of flowers, not bunched together as they

would have been with us, but so cunningly arranged that they rose from

the footstool to the pinnacle in a rhythm of colour, a poem in bud

and petals the like of which for harmonious beauty I could not h[...]
imagined possible. And in this fairy den was a thin, gaunt young m[...]
dressed in some sort of black stuff so nondescript that it amounte[...]
to little more than a shadow. I took it for granted that a substance of
bone and muscle was covered by that gloomy suit, but it was the face
above that alone riveted my gaze and made me return the stare he gave
me as we came up with redoubled interest. It was not an unhandsome
face, but ashy grey in colour and amongst the insipid countenances
of the Martians about him marvellously thoughtful. I do not know
whether those who had killed themselves by learning ever leave ghosts
behind, but if so this was the very ideal for such a one. At his feet I
noticed, when I unhooked my eyes from his at last, sat a girl in a loose
coral pink gown who was his very antipode. Princess Heru, for so she
was called, was resting one arm upon his knee at our approach and
pulling a blue convolvulus bud to pieces—a charming picture of dainty
idleness. Anything so soft, so silken as that little lady was never seen
before. Who am I, a poor quarter-deck loafer, that I should attempt
to describe what poet and painter alike would have failed to realise?
I know, of course, your stock descriptives: the melting eye, the coral
lip, the peachy cheek, the raven tress; but these were coined for mortal
woman—and this was not one of them. I will not attempt to describe
the glorious tenderness of those eyes she turned upon me presently;
the glowing radiance of her skin; the infinite grace of every action; the
incredible soul-searching harmony of her voice, when later on I heard
it—you must gather something of these things as I go—suffice it to
say that when I saw her there for the first time in the plenitude of her
beauty I fell desperately, wildly in love with her.

Meanwhile, even the most infatuated of mortals cannot stare for
ever without saying something. The grating of our prow against the
garlanded side of the royal barge roused me from my reverie, and
nodding to An, to imply I would be back presently, I lightly jumped
on to Hath's vessel, and, with the assurance of a free and independent
American voter, approached that individual, holding out my palm, and
saying as I did so,

"Shake hands, Mr. President!"

The prince came forward at my bidding and extending his hand for
mine. He bowed slow and sedately, in that peculiar way the Martians
have, a ripple of gratified civility passing up his flesh; lower and lower he
bowed, until his face was over our clasped hands, and then, with simple

tesy, he kissed my finger-tips! This was somewhat embarrassing. It is not like the procedure followed in Courts nearer to Washington than this one, as far as my reading went, and, withdrawing my fingers hastily, I turned to the princess, who had risen, and was eyeing her somewhat awkwardly, the while wondering what kind of salutation would be suitable in her case when a startling incident happened. The river, as said, was full of floating rubbish brought down from some far-away uplands by a spring freshet while the royal convoy was making slow progress upstream and thus met it all bow on. Some of this stuff was heavy timber, and when a sudden warning cry went up from the leading boats it did not take my sailor instinct long to guess what was amiss. Those in front shot side to side, those behind tried to drop back as, bearing straight down on the royal barge, there came a log of black wood twenty feet long and as thick as the mainmast of an old three-decker.

Hath's boat could no more escape than if it had been planted on a rocky pedestal, garlands and curtains trailing in the water hung so heavy on it. The gilded paddles of the slender rowers were so feeble—they had but made a half-turn from that great javelin's road when down it came upon them, knocking the first few pretty oarsmen head over heels and crackling through their oars like a bull through dry maize stalks. I sprang forward, and snatching a pole from a half-hearted slave, jammed the end into the head of the log and bore with all my weight upon it, diverting it a little, and thereby perhaps saving the ship herself, but not enough. As it flashed by a branch caught upon the trailing tapestry, hurling me to the deck, and tearing away with it all that finery. Then the great spar, tossing half its dripping length into the air, went plunging downstream with shreds of silk and flowers trailing from it, and white water bubbling in its rear.

When I scrambled to my feet all was ludicrous confusion on board. Hath still stood by his throne—an island in a sea of disorder—staring at me; all else was chaos. The rowers and courtiers were kicking and wallowing in the "waist" of the ship like fish newly shot out of a trawl net, but the princess was gone. Where was she? I brushed the spray from my eyes, and stared overboard. She was not in the bubbling blue water alongside. Then I glanced aft to where the log, now fifteen yards away, was splashing through the sunshine, and, as I looked, a fair arm came up from underneath and white fingers clutched convulsively at the sky. What man could need more? Down the barge I rushed, and dropping only my swordbelt, leapt in to her rescue. The gentle Martians were too numb to raise a hand in help; but it was not necessary. I had the tide with me, and gained at every stroke. Meanwhile that accursed tree, with poor Heru's skirts caught on a branch, was drowning her at its leisure; lifting her up as it rose upon the crests, a fair, helpless bundle, and then sousing her in its fall into the nether water, where I could see her gleam now and again like pink coral.

I redoubled my efforts and got alongside, clutching the rind of that old stump, and swimming and scrambling, at last was within reach of the princess. Thereon the log lifted her playfully to my arms, and when I had laid hold came down, a crushing weight, and forced us far into the clammy bosom of Martian sea. Again we came up, coughing and choking—I tugging furiously at that tangled raiment, and the lady, a mere lump of sweetness in my other arm—then down again with that log upon me and all the noises of Eblis in my ears. Up and down we went, over and over, till strength was spent and my ribs seemed breaking; then, with a last desperate effort, I got a knee against the stem, and by sheer strength freed my princess—the spiteful timber made a last ugly thrust at us as it rolled away—and we were free!

I turned upon my back, and, sure of rescue now, took the lady's head upon my chest, holding her sweet, white fists in mine the while, and, floating, waited for help.

It came only too quickly. The gallant Martians, when they saw the princess saved, came swiftly down upon us. Over the lapping of the water in my ears I heard their sigh—like cries of admiration and surprise, the rattle of spray on the canoe sides mingled with the splash of oars, the flitting shadows of their prows were all about us, and in less time than it takes to write we were hauled aboard, revived, and taken to Hath's barge. Again the prince's lips were on my fingertips; again the flutes and music struck up; and as I squeezed the water out of my hair, and tried to keep my eyes off the outline of Heru, whose loveliness shone through her damp, clinging, pink robe, as if that robe were but a gauzy fancy, I vaguely heard Hath saying wondrous things of my gallantry, and, what was more to the purpose, asking me to come with him and stay that night at the palace.

Chapter 4

They lodged me like a prince in a tributary country that first night. I was tired. 'Twas a stiff stage I had come the day before, and they gave me a couch whose ethereal softness seemed to close like the wings of a bird as I plunged at its touch into fathomless slumbers. But the next day had hardly broken when I was awake, and, stretching my limbs upon the piled silk of a legless bed upon the floor, found myself in a great chamber with a purple tapestry across the entrance, and a square arch leading to a flat terrace outside.

It was a glorious daybreak, making my heart light within me, the air like new milk, and the colours of the sunrise lay purple and yellow in bars across my room. I yawned and stretched, then rising, wrapped a silken quilt about me and went out into the flat terrace top, wherefrom all the city could be seen stretched in an ivory and emerald patchwork, with open, blue water on one side, and the Martian plain trending away in illimitable distance upon the other.

Directly underneath in the great square at the bottom of Hath's palace steps were gathered a concourse of people, brilliant in many-coloured dresses. They were sitting or lying about just as they might for all I knew have done through the warm night, without much order, save that where the black streaks of inlaid stone marked a carriageway across the square none were stationed. While I wondered what would bring so many together thus early, there came a sound of flutes—for these people can do nothing without piping like finches in a thicket in May—and from the storehouses half-way over to the harbour there streamed a line of carts piled high with provender. Down came the teams attended by their slaves, circling and wheeling into the open place, and as they passed each group those lazy, lolling beggars crowded round and took the dole they were too thriftless to earn themselves. It was strange to see how listless they were about the meal, even though Providence itself put it into their hands; to note how the yellow-girted slaves scudded amongst them, serving out the loaves, themselves had grown, harvested, and baked; slipping from group to group, rousing, exhorting, administering to a helpless throng that took their efforts without thought or thanks.

I stood there a long time, one foot upon the coping and my chin upon my hand, noting the beauty of the ruined town and wondering

EDWIN L. ARNOLD

how such a feeble race as that which lay about, b.
limpid sunshine, could have come by a city like this, c
ruins of its walls and buildings from the covetousness c
presently there was a rustle of primrose garments and my .
day before stood by me.

"Are you rested, traveller?" she questioned in that pretty voic
"Rested ambrosially, An."
"It is well; I will tell the Government and it will come up to wash
dress you, afterwards giving you breakfast."

"For the breakfast, damsel, I shall be grateful, but as for the washing
and dressing I will defend myself to the last gasp sooner than submit to
such administration."

"How strange! Do you never wash in your country?"

"Yes, but it is a matter left largely to our own discretion; so, my dear
girl, if you will leave me for a minute or two in quest of that meal you
have mentioned, I will guarantee to be ready when it comes."

Away she slipped, with a shrug of her rosy shoulders, to return presently,
carrying a tray covered with a white cloth, whereon were half a dozen
glittering covers whence came most fragrant odours of cooked things.

"Why, comrade," I said, sitting down and lifting lid by lid, for the
cold, sweet air outside had made me hungry, "this is better than was
hoped for; I thought from what I saw down yonder I should have to
trot behind a tumbril for my breakfast, and eat it on my heels amongst
your sleepy friends below."

An replied, "The stranger is a prince, we take it, in his own country,
and princes fare not quite like common people, even here."

"So," I said, my mouth full of a strange, unknown fish, and a cake
soft as milk and white as cotton in the pod. "Now that makes me feel
at home!"

"Would you have had it otherwise with us?"

"No! now I come to think of it, it is most natural things should be
much alike in all the corners of the universe; the splendid simplicity
that rules the spheres, works much the same, no doubt, upon one side
of the sun as upon the other. Yet, somehow—you can hardly wonder at
it—yesterday I looked to find your world, when I realised where I had
tumbled to, a world of djin and giants; of mad possibilities over realised,
and here I see you dwellers by the utterly remote little more marvellous
than if I had come amongst you on the introduction of a cheap tourist
ticket, and round some neglected corner of my own distant world!"

your meaning, sir."

urse you cannot. I was forgetting you did not know!
the stuff on yonder platter that looks like caked mud
nor fluke, and swells like breath of paradise, and let me
ou;" and while I sat and drank with that yellow servitor sitting
of me, I plied her with questions, just as a baby might who had
nto the world with a full-blown gift of speech. But though she
eady and willing enough to answer, and laughed gaily at my quaint
orance of simple things, yet there was little water in the well.

"Had they any kind of crafts or science; any cult of stars or figures?"
But again she shook her head, and said, "Hath might know, Hath
understood most things, but herself knew little of either." "Armies or
navies?" and again the Martian shrugged her shoulders, questioning in
turn—

"What for?"

"What for!" I cried, a little angry with her engaging dulness, "Why,
to keep that which the strong hand got, and to get more for those who
come next; navies to sweep yonder blue seas, and armies to ward what
they should bring home, or guard the city walls against all enemies,—for
I suppose, An," I said, putting down my knife as the cheering thought
came on me,—"I suppose, An, you have some enemies? It is not like
Providence to give such riches as you possess, such lands, such cities,
and not to supply the antidote in some one poor enough to covet them."

At once the girl's face clouded over, and it was obvious a tender
subject had been chanced upon. She waved her hand impatiently as
though to change the subject, but I would not be put off.

"Come," I said, "this is better than breakfast. It was the one thing—
this unknown enemy of yours—wanting to lever the dull mass of your
too peacefulness. What is he like? How strong? How stands the quarrel
between you? I was a soldier myself before the sea allured me, and love
horse and sword best of all things."

"You would not jest if you knew our enemy!"

"That is as it may be. I have laughed in the face of many a stronger
foe than yours is like to prove; but anyhow, give me a chance to judge.
Come, who is it that frightens all the blood out of your cheeks by a
bare mention and may not be laughed at even behind these substantial
walls?"

"First, then, you know, of course, that long ago this land of ours was
harried from the West."

"Not I."

"No!" said An, with a little warmth. "If it comes to that, you know nothing."

Whereat I laughed, and, saying the reply was just, vowed I would not interrupt again; so she went on saying how Hath—that interminable Hath!—would know it all better than she did, but long ago the land was overrun by a people from beyond the broad, blue waters outside; a people huge of person, hairy and savage, uncouth, unlettered, and poor An's voice trembled even to describe them; a people without mercy or compunction, dwellers in woods, eaters of flesh, who burnt, plundered, and destroyed all before them, and had toppled over this city along with many others in an ancient foray, the horrors of which, still burnt lurid in her people's minds.

"Ever since then," went on the girl, "these odious terrors of the outer land have been a nightmare to us, making hectic our pleasures, and filling our peace with horrid thoughts of what might be, should they chance to come again."

"'Tis unfortunate, no doubt, lady," I answered. "Yet it was long ago, and the plunderers are far away. Why not rise and raid them in turn? To live under such a nightmare is miserable, and a poet on my side of the ether has said—

"*He either fears his fate too much,*
Or his deserts are small,
Who will not put it to the touch,
To win or lose it all.'

It seems to me you must either bustle and fight again, or sit tamely down, and by paying the coward's fee for peace, buy at heavy price, indulgence from the victor."

"We," said An simply, and with no show of shame, "would rather die than fight, and so we take the easier way, though a heavy one it is. Look!" she said, drawing me to the broad window whence we could get a glimpse of the westward town and the harbour out beyond the walls. "Look! see yonder long row of boats with brown sails hanging loose reefed from every yard ranged all along the quay. Even from here you can make out the thin stream of porter slaves passing to and fro between them and the granaries like ants on a sunny path. Those are our tax-men's ships, they came yesterday from far out across the sea, as punctual as fate with the first day of spring, and two or three nights hence we trust will go again: and glad shall we be to see them start, although they leave scupper deep with our cloth, our corn, and gold."

"Is that what they take for tribute?"

"That and one girl—the fairest they can find."

"One—only one! 'Tis very moderate, all things considered."

"She is for the thither king, Ar-hap, and though only one as you say, stranger, yet he who loses her is apt sometimes to think her one too many lost."

"By Jupiter himself it is well said! If I were that man I would stir up heaven and hell until I got her back; neither man, nor beast, nor devil should stay me in my quest!" As I spoke I thought for a minute An's fingers trembled a little as she fixed a flower upon my coat, while there was something like a sigh in her voice as she said—

"The maids of this country are not accustomed, sir, to be so strongly loved."

By this time, breakfasted and rehabilitated, I was ready to go forth. The girl swung back the heavy curtain that served in place of door across the entrance of my chamber, and leading the way by a corridor and marble steps while I followed, and whether it was the Martian air or the meal I know not, but thinking mighty well of myself until we came presently onto the main palace stairs, which led by stately flights from the upper galleries to the wide square below.

As we passed into the full sunshine—and no sunshine is so crisply golden as the Martian—amongst twined flowers and shrubs and gay, quaint birds building in the cornices, a sleek youth rose slowly from where he had spread his cloak as couch upon a step and approaching asked—

"You are the stranger of yesterday?"

"Yes," I answered.

"Then I bring a message from Prince Hath, saying it would pleasure him greatly if you would eat the morning meal with him."

"Why," I answered, "it is very civil indeed, but I have breakfasted already."

"And so has Hath," said the boy, gently yawning. "You see I came here early this morning, but knowing you would pass sooner or later I thought it would save me the trouble if I lay down till you came—those quaint people who built these places were so prodigal of steps," and smiling apologetically he sank back on his couch and began toying with a leaf.

"Sweet fellow," I said, and you will note how I was getting into their style of conversation, "get back to Hath when you have rested, give him my most gracious thanks for the intended courtesy, but tell him the invitation should have started a week earlier; tell him from me, you nimble-footed messenger, that I will post-date his kindness and come tomorrow; say that meanwhile I pray him to send any ill news he has for me by you. Is the message too bulky for your slender shoulders?"

"No," said the boy, rousing himself slowly, "I will take it," and then he prepared to go. He turned again and said, without a trace of incivility, "But indeed, stranger, I wish you would take the message yourself. This is the third flight of stairs I have been up today."

Everywhere it was the same friendly indolence. Half the breakfasters were lying on coloured shawls in groups about the square; the other half were strolling off—all in one direction, I noticed—as slowly as could be towards the open fields beyond; no one was active or had anything to do save the yellow folk who flitted to and fro fostering the others, and doing the city work as though it were their only thought in life. There were no shops in that strange city, for there were no needs; some booths I saw indeed, and temple-like places, but hollow, and used for birds and beasts—things these lazy Martians love. There was no tramp of busy feet, for no one was busy; no clank of swords or armour in those peaceful streets, for no one was warlike; no hustle, for no one hurried; no wide-packed asses nodding down the lanes, for there was nothing to fill their packs with, and though a cart sometimes came by with a load of lolling men and maids, or a small horse, for horses they had, paced along, itself nearly as lazy as the master he bore, with trappings sewed over bits of coloured shell and coral, yet somehow it was all extraordinarily unreal. It was a city full of the ghosts of the life which once pulsed through its ways. The streets were peopled, the chatter of voices everywhere, the singing boys and laughing girls wandering, arms linked together, down the ways filled every echo with their merriment, yet somehow it was all so shallow that again and again I rubbed my eyes, wondering if I were indeed awake, or whether it were not a prolonged sleep of which the tomorrow were still to come.

"What strikes me as strangest of all, good comrade," I observed pleasantly to the tripping presence at my elbow, "is that these countrymen of yours who shirk to climb a flight of steps, and have palms as soft as rose petals, these wide ways paved with stones as hard as a usurer's heart."

An laughed. "The stones were still in their native quarries had it been left to us to seek them; we are like the conies in the ruins, sir, the inheritors of what other hands have done."

"Ay, and undone, I think, as well, for coming along I have noted axe chippings upon the walls, smudges of ancient fire and smoke upon the cornices."

An winced a little and stared uneasily at the walls, muttering below her breath something about trying to hide with flower garlands the marks they could not banish, but it was plain the conversation was not pleasing to her. So unpleasant was talk or sight of woodmen (Thither-folk, as she called them, in contradiction to the Hither people about us here), that the girl was clearly relieved when we were free of the town and out into the open playground of the people. The whole place down there was a gay, shifting crowd. The booths of yesterday, the arcades, the archways, were still standing, and during the night unknown hands had redecked them with flowers, while another day's sunshine had opened the coppice buds so that the whole place was brilliant past expression. And here the Hither folk were varying their idleness by a general holiday. They were standing about in groups, or lying ranked like new-plucked flowers on the banks, piping to each other through reeds as soft and melodious as running water. They were playing inconsequent games and breaking off in the middle of them like children looking for new pleasures. They were idling about the drinking booths, delicately stupid with quaint, thin wines, dealt out to all who asked; the maids were ready to chevy or be chevied through the blossoming thickets by anyone who chanced upon them, the men slipped their arms round slender waists and wandered down the paths, scarce seeming to care even whose waist it was they circled or into whose ear they whispered the remainder of the love-tale they had begun to some one else. And everywhere it was "Hi," and "Ha," and "So," and "See," as these quaint people called to one another, knowing each other as familiarly as ants of a nest, and by the same magic it seemed to me.

"An," I said presently, when we had wandered an hour or so through the drifting throng, "have these good countrymen of yours no other names but monosyllabic, nothing to designate them but these chirruping syllables?"

"Is it not enough?" answered my companion. "Once indeed I think we had longer names, but," she added, smiling, "how much trouble it saves to limit each one to a single sound. It is uncivil to one's neighbours to burden their tongues with double duty when half would do."

"But have you no patronymics—nothing to show the child comes of the same source as his father came?"

"We have no fathers."

"What! no fathers?" I said, starting and staring at her.

"No, nor mothers either, or at least none that we remember, for again, why should we? Mayhap in that strange district you come from you keep count of these things, but what have we to do with either when their initial duty is done. Look at that painted butterfly swinging on the honey-laden catkin there. What knows she of the mother who shed her life into a flowercup and forgot which flower it was the minute afterwards. We, too, are insects, stranger."

"And do you mean to say of this great concourse here, that every atom is solitary, individual, and can claim no kindred with another save the loose bonds of a general fraternity—a specious idea, horrible, impracticable!"

Whereat An laughed. "Ask the grasshoppers if it is impracticable; ask the little buzzing things of grass and leaves who drift hither and thither upon each breath of wind, finding kinsmen never but comrades everywhere—ask them if it is horrible."

This made me melancholy, and somehow set me thinking of the friends immeasurably distant I had left but yesterday.

What were they doing? Did they miss me? I was to have called for my pay this afternoon, and tomorrow was to have run down South to see that freckled lady of mine. What would she think of my absence? What would she think if she knew where I was? Gods, it was too mad, too absurd! I thrust my hands into my pockets in fierce desperation, and there they clutched an old dance programme and an out-of-date check for a New York ferry-boat. I scowled about on that sunny, helpless people, and laying my hand bitterly upon my heart felt in the breast-pocket beneath a packet of unpaid Boston tailors' bills and a note from my landlady asking if I would let her aunt do my washing while I was on shore. Oh! what would they all think of me? Would they brand me as a deserter, a poltroon, and a thief, letting my name presently sink down in shame and mystery in the shadowy realm of the forgotten? Dreadful thoughts! I would think no more.

Maybe An had marked my melancholy, for presently she led me to a stall where in fantastic vases wines of sorts I have described before were put out for all who came to try them. There was medicine here for every kind of dulness—not the gross cure which earthly wine effects, but so nicely proportioned to each specific need that one could regulate one's debauch to a hairbreadth, rising through all the gamut of satisfaction, from the staid contentment coming of that flask there to the wild extravagances of the furthermost vase. So my stripling told me, running her finger down the line of beakers carved with strange figures and cased in silver, each in its cluster of little attendant drinking-cups, like-coloured, and waiting round on the white napkins as the shore boats wait to unload a cargo round the sides of a merchant vessel.

"And what," I said, after curiously examining each liquor in turn, "what is that which stands alone there in the humble earthen jar, as though unworthy of the company of the others."

"Oh, that," said my friend, "is the most essential of them all—that is the wine of recovery, without which all the others were deadly poisons."

"The which, lady, looks as if it had a moral attaching to it."

"It may have; indeed I think it has, but I have forgotten. Prince Hath would know! Meanwhile let me give you to drink, great stranger, let me get you something."

"Well, then," I laughed, "reach me down an antidote to fate, a specific for an absent mistress, and forgetful friends."

"What was she like?" said An, hesitating a little and frowning.

"Nay, good friend," was my answer, "what can that matter to you?"

"Oh, nothing, of course," answered that Martian, and while she took from the table a cup and filled it with fluid I felt in the pouch of my sword-belt to see if by chance a bit of money was lying there, but there was none, only the pips of an orange poor Polly had sucked and laughingly thrown at me.

However, it did not matter. The girl handed me the cup, and I put my lips to it. The first taste was bitter and acrid, like the liquor of long-steeped wood. At the second taste a shiver of pleasure ran through me, and I opened my eyes and stared hard. The third taste grossness and heaviness and chagrin dropped from my heart; all the complexion of Providence altered in a flash, and a stupid irresistible joy, unreasoning, uncontrollable took possession of my fibre. I sank upon a mossy bank and, lolling my head, beamed idiotically on the lolling Martians all about me. How long I was like that I cannot say. The heavy minutes of sodden contentment slipped by unnoticed, unnumbered, till presently I felt the touch of a wine-cup at my lips again, and drinking of another liquor dulness vanished from my mind, my eyes cleared, my heart throbbed; a fantastic gaiety seized upon my limbs; I bounded to my feet, and seizing An's two hands in mine, swung that damsel round in a giddy dance, capering as never dancer danced before, till spent and weary I sank down again from sheer lack of breath, and only knew thereafter that An was sitting by me saying, "Drink! drink stranger, drink and forget!" and as a third time a cup was pressed to my lips, aches and pleasures, stupidness and joy, life itself, seemed slipping away into a splendid golden vacuity, a hazy episode of unconscious Elysium, indefinite, and unfathomable.

Chapter 5

When I woke, feeling as refreshed as though I had been dreaming through a long night, An, seeing me open-eyed, helped me to my feet, and when I had recovered my senses a little, asked if we should go on. I was myself again by this time, so willingly took her hand, and soon came out of the tangle into the open spaces. I must have been under the spell of the Martian wines longer than it seemed, for already it was late in the afternoon, the shadows of trees were lying deep and far-reaching over the motley crowds of people. Out here as the day waned they had developed some sort of method in their sports. In front of us was a broad, grassy course marked off with garlanded finger-posts, and in this space rallies of workfolk were taking part in all manner of games under the eyes of a great concourse of spectators, doing the Martians' pleasures for them as they did their labours. An led me gently on, leaning on my arm heavier, I thought, than she had done in the morning, and ever and anon turning her gazelle-like eyes upon me with a look I could not understand. As we sauntered forward I noticed all about lesser circles where the yellow-girted ones were drawing delighted laughter from good-tempered crowds by tricks of sleight-of-hand, and posturing, or tossing gilded cups and balls as though they were catering, as indeed they were, for outgrown children. Others fluted or sang songs in chorus to the slow clapping of hands, while others were doing I knew not what, sitting silent amongst silent spectators who every now and then burst out laughing for no cause that I could see. But An would not let me stop, and so we pushed on through the crowd till we came to the main enclosures where a dozen slaves had run a race for the amusement of those too lazy to race themselves, and were sitting panting on the grass.

To give them time to get their breath, perhaps, a man stepped out of the crowd dressed in a dark blue tunic, a strange vacuous-looking fellow, and throwing down a sheaf of javelins marched off a dozen paces, then, facing round, called out loudly he would give sixteen suits of "summer cloth" to any one who could prick him with a javelin from the heap.

"Why," I said in amazement, "this is the best of fools—no one could miss from such a distance."

"Ay but," replied my guide, "he is a gifted one, versed in mystics."

I was just going to say a good javelin, shod with iron, was a stronger argument than any mystic I had ever heard of could stand, when out of

EDWIN L. ARNOLD

the crowd stepped a youth, and amid the derisive cheers of his friends chose a reed from the bundle. He poised it in his hand a minute to get the middle, then turned on the living target. Whatever else they might be, these Martians were certainly beautiful as the daytime. Never had I seen such a perfect embodiment of grace and elegance as that boy as he stood there for a moment poised to the throw; the afternoon sunshine warm and strong on his bunched brown hair, a girlish flush of shyness on his handsome face, and the sleek perfection of his limbs, clear cut against the dusky background beyond. And now the javelin was going. Surely the mystic would think better of it at the last moment! No! the initiate held his ground with tight-shut lips and retrospective eyes, and even as I looked the weapon flew upon its errand.

"There goes the soul of a fool!" I exclaimed, and as the words were uttered the spear struck, or seemed to, between the neck and shoulder, but instead of piercing rose high into the air, quivering and flashing, and presently turning over, fell back, and plunged deep into the turf, while a low murmur of indifferent pleasure went round amongst the onlookers.

Thereat An, yawning gently, looked to me and said, "A strong-willed fellow, isn't he, friend?"

I hesitated a minute and then asked, "Was it *will* which turned that shaft?"

She answered with simplicity, "Why, of course—what else?"

By this time another boy had stepped out, and having chosen a javelin, tested it with hand and foot, then retiring a pace or two rushed up to the throwing mark and flung it straight and true into the bared bosom of the man. And as though it had struck a wall of brass, the shaft leapt back falling quivering at the thrower's feet. Another and another tried unsuccessfully, until at last, vexed at their futility, I said, "I have a somewhat scanty wardrobe that would be all the better for that fellow's summer suiting, by your leave I will venture a throw against him."

"It is useless," answered An; "none but one who knows more magic than he, or is especially befriended by the Fates can touch him through the envelope he has put on."

"Still, I think I will try."

"It is hopeless, I would not willingly see you fail," whispered the girl, with a sudden show of friendship.

"And what," I said, bending down, "would you give me if I succeeded?" Whereat An laughed a little uneasily, and, withdrawing her hand from mine, half turned away. So I pushed through the spectators and stepped into the ring. I went straight up to the pile of weapons, and having chosen one went over to the mystic. "Good fellow," I cried out ostentatiously, trying the sharpness of the javelin-point with my finger, "where are all of those sixteen summer suits of yours lying hid?"

"It matters nothing," said the man, as if he were asleep.

"Ay, but by the stars it does, for it will vex the quiet repose of your soul tomorrow if your heirs should swear they could not find them."

"It matters nothing," muttered the will-wrapped visionary.

"It will matter something if I take you at your word. Come, friend Purple-jerkin, will you take the council with your legs and run while there is yet time, or stand up to be thrown at?"

"I stand here immoveable in the confidence of my initiation."

"Then, by thunder, I will initiate you into the mysteries of a javelin-end, and your blood be on your head."

The Martians were all craning their necks in hushed eagerness as I turned to the casting-place, and, poising the javelin, faced the magician. Would he run at the last moment? I half hoped so; for a minute I gave him the chance, then, as he showed no sign of wavering, I drew my hand back, shook the javelin back till it bent like a reed, and hurled it at him.

The Martians' heads turned as though all on one pivot as the spear sped through the air, expecting no doubt to see it recoil as others had done. But it took him full in the centre of his chest, and with a wild wave of arms and a flutter of purple raiment sent him backwards, and down, and over and over in a shapeless heap of limbs and flying raiment, while a low murmur of awed surprise rose from the spectators. They crowded round him in a dense ring, as An came flitting to me with a startled face.

"Oh, stranger," she burst out, "you have surely killed him!" but more astounded I had broken down his guard than grieved at his injury.

"No," I answered smilingly; "a sore chest he may have tomorrow, but dead he is not, for I turned the lance-point back as I spun it, and it was the butt-end I threw at him!"

"It was none the less wonderful; I thought you were a common man, a prince mayhap, come but from over the hills, but now something tells me you are more than that," and she lapsed into thoughtful silence for a time.

Neither of us were wishful to go back amongst those who were raising the bruised magician to his legs, but wandered away instead

EDWIN L. ARNOLD

through the deepening twilight towards the city over meadows whose damp, soft fragrance loaded the air with sleepy pleasure, neither of us saying a word till the dusk deepened and the quick night descended, while we came amongst the gardened houses, the thousand lights of an unreal city rising like a jewelled bank before us, and there An said she would leave me for a time, meeting me again in the palace square later on, "To see Princess Heru read the destinies of the year."

"What!" I exclaimed, "more magic? I have been brought up on more substantial mental stuff than this."

"Nevertheless, I would advise you to come to the square," persisted my companion. "It affects us all, and—who knows?—may affect you more than any."

Therein poor An was unconsciously wearing the cloak of prophesy herself, and, shrugging my shoulders good-humouredly, I kissed her chin, little realising, as I let her fingers slip from mine, that I should see her no more.

Turning back alone, through the city, through ways twinkling with myriad lights as little lamps began to blink out amongst garlands and flower-decked booths on every hand, I walked on, lost in varying thoughts, until, fairly tired and hungry, I found myself outside a stall where many Martians stood eating and drinking to their hearts' content. I was known to none of them, and, forgetting past experience, was looking on rather enviously, when there came a touch upon my arm, and—

"Are you hungry, sir?" asked a bystander.

"Ay," I said, "hungry, good friend, and with all the zest which an empty purse lends to that condition."

"Then here is what you need, sir, even from here the wine smells good, and the fried fruit would make a mouse's eye twinkle. Why do you wait?"

"Why wait? Why, because though the rich man's dinner goes in at his mouth, the poor man must often be content to dine through his nose. I tell you I have nothing to get me a meal with."

The stranger seemed to speculate on this for a time, and then he said, "I cannot fathom your meaning, sir. Buying and selling, gold and money, all these have no meaning to me. Surely the twin blessings of an appetite and food abundant ready and free before you are enough."

"What! free is it—free like the breakfast served out this morning?"

"Why, of course," said the youth, with mild depreciation; "everything here is free. Everything is his who will take it, without exception. What else is the good of a coherent society and a Government if it cannot provide you with so rudimentary a thing as a meal?"

Whereat joyfully I undid my belt, and, without nicely examining the argument, marched into the booth, and there put Martian hospitality to the test, eating and drinking, but this time with growing wisdom, till I was a new man, and then, paying my leaving with a wave of the hand to the yellow-girted one who dispensed the common provender, I sauntered on again, caring little or nothing which way the road went, and soon across the current of my meditations a peal of laughter broke, accompanied by the piping of a flute somewhere close at hand, and the next minute I found myself amid a ring of light-hearted roisterers who were linking hands for a dance to the music a curly-headed fellow was making close by.

They made me join them! One rosey-faced damsel at the hither end of the chain drew up to me, and, without a word, slipped her soft, baby fingers into my hand; on the other side another came with melting eyes, breath like a bed of violets, and banked-up fun puckering her dainty mouth. What could I do but give her a hand as well? The flute began to gurgle anew, like a drinking spout in spring-time, and away we went, faster and faster each minute, the boys and girls swinging themselves in time to the tune, and capering presently till their tender feet were twinkling over the ground in gay confusion. Faster and faster till, as the infection of the dance spread even to the outside groups, I capered too. My word! if they could have seen me that night from the deck of the old Carolina, how they would have laughed—sword swinging, coat-tails flying—faster and faster, round and round we went, till limbs could stand no more; the gasping piper blew himself quite out, and the dance ended as abruptly as it commenced, the dancers melting away to join others or casting themselves panting on the turf.

Certainly these Martian girls were blessed with an ingratiating simplicity. My new friend of the violet-scented breath hung back a little, then after looking at me demurely for a minute or two, like a child that chooses a new playmate, came softly up, and, standing on tiptoe, kissed me on the cheek. It was not unpleasant, so I turned the other, whereon, guessing my meaning, without the smallest hesitation, she reached up again, and pressed her pretty mouth to my bronzed skin a second time. Then, with a little sigh of satisfaction, she ran an arm through mine, saying, "Comrade, from what country have you come? I never saw one quite like you before."

"From what country had I come?" Again the frown dropped down upon my forehead. Was I dreaming—was I mad? Where indeed had I come from? I stared back over my shoulder, and there, as if in answer to my thought—there, where the black tracery of flowering shrubs waved in the soft night wind, over a gap in the crumbling ivory ramparts, the sky was brightening. As I looked into the centre of that glow, a planet, magnified by the wonderful air, came swinging up, pale but splendid, and mapped by soft colours—green, violet, and red. I knew it on the minute, Heaven only knows how, but I knew it, and a desperate thrill of loneliness swept over me, a spasm of comprehension of the horrible void dividing us. Never did yearning babe stretch arms more wistfully to an unattainable mother than I at that moment to my mother earth. All her meanness and prosaicness was forgotten, all her imperfections and shortcomings; it was home, the one tangible thing in the glittering emptiness of the spheres. All my soul went into my eyes, and then I sneezed violently, and turning round, found that sweet damsel whose silky head nestled so friendly on my shoulder was tickling my nose with a feather she had picked up.

Womanlike, she had forgotten all about her first question, and now asked another, "Will you come to supper with me, stranger? 'Tis nearly ready, I think."

"To be able to say no to such an invitation, lady, is the first thing a young man should learn," I answered lightly; but then, seeing there was nothing save the most innocent friendliness in those hazel eyes, I went on, "but that stern rule may admit of variance. Only, as it chances, I have just supped at the public expense. If, instead, you would be a sailor's sweetheart for an hour, and take me to this show of yours—your princess's benefit, or whatever it is—I shall be obliged; my previous guide is hull down over the horizon, and I am clean out of my reckoning in this crowd."

By way of reply, the little lady, light as an elf, took me by the fingertips, and, gleefully skipping forward, piloted me through the mazes of her city until we came out into the great square fronting on the palace, which rose beyond it like a white chalk cliff in the dull light. Not a taper showed anywhere round its circumference, but a mysterious kind of radiance like sea phosphorescence beamed from the palace porch. All was in such deathlike silence that the nails in my "ammunition" boots made an unpleasant clanking as they struck on the marble pavement; yet, by the uncertain starlight, I saw, to my surprise, the whole square was thronged with Martians, all facing towards the porch, as still, as graven images, and as voiceless, for once, as though they had indeed been marble. It was strange to see them sitting there in the twilight, waiting for I knew not what, and my friend's voice at my elbow almost startled me as she said, in a whisper, "The princess knows you are in the crowd, and desires you to go up upon the steps near where she will be."

"Who brought her message?" I asked, gazing vaguely round, for none had spoken to us for an hour or more.

"No one," said my companion, gently pushing me up an open way towards the palace steps left clear by the sitting Martians. "It came direct from her to me this minute."

"But how?" I persisted.

"Nay," said the girl, "if we stop to talk like this we shall not be placed before she comes, and thus throw a whole year's knowledge out."

So, bottling my speculations, I allowed myself to be led up the first flight of worn, white steps to where, on the terrace between them and the next flight leading directly to the palace portico, was a flat, having a circle about twenty feet across, inlaid upon the marble with darker coloured blocks. Inside that circle, as I sat down close by it in the twilight, showed another circle, and then a final one in whose inmost middle stood a tall iron tripod and something atop of it covered by a cloth. And all round the outer circle were magic symbols—I started as I recognised the meaning of some of them—within these again the inner circle held what looked like the representations of planets, ending, as I have said, in that dished hollow made by countless dancers' feet, and its solitary tripod. Back again, I glanced towards the square where the great concourse—ten thousand of them, perhaps—were sitting mute and silent in the deepening shadows, then back to the magic circles, till the silence and expectancy of a strange scene began to possess me.

Shadow down below, star-dusted heaven above, and not a figure moving; when suddenly something like a long-drawn sigh came from the lips of the expectant multitude, and I was aware every eye had suddenly turned back to the palace porch, where, as we looked, a figure, wrapped in pale blue robes, appeared and stood for a minute, then stole down the steps with an eagerness in every movement holding us spellbound. I have seen many splendid pageants and many sights, each of which might be the talk of a lifetime, but somehow nothing ever so engrossing, so thrilling, as that ghostly figure in flowing robes stealing across the piazza in starlight and silence—the princess of a broken kingdom, the priestess of a forgotten faith coming to her station to perform a jugglery of which she knew not even the meaning. It was my versatile friend Heru, and with quick, incisive steps, her whole frame ambent for the time with the fervour of her mission, she came swiftly down to within a dozen yards of where I stood. Heru, indeed, but not the same princess as in the morning; an inspired priestess rather, her slim body wrapped in blue and quivering with emotion, her face ashine with Delphic fire, her hair loose, her feet bare, until at last when, as she stood within the limit of the magic circle, her white hands upon her breast, her eyes flashing like planets themselves in the starshine she looked so ghostly and unreal I felt for a minute I was dreaming.

Then began a strange, weird dance amongst the imagery of the rings, over which my earth planet was beginning to throw a haze of light. At first it was hardly more than a walk, a slow procession round the twin circumferences of the centred tripod. But soon it increased to an extraordinary graceful measure, a cadenced step without music or sound that riveted my eyes to the dancer. Presently I saw those mystic, twinkling feet of hers—as the dance became swifter—were performing a measured round amongst the planet signs—spelling out something, I knew not what, with quick, light touch amongst the zodiac figures, dancing out a soundless invocation of some kind as a dumb man might spell a message by touching letters. Quicker and quicker, for minute after minute, grew the dance, swifter and swifter the swing of the light blue drapery as the priestess, with eager face and staring eyes, swung panting round upon her orbit, and redder and redder over the city tops rose the circumference of the earth. It seemed to me all the silent multitude were breathing heavily as we watched that giddy dance, and whatever *they* felt, all my own senses seemed to be winding up upon that revolving figure as thread winds on a spindle.

"When will she stop?" I whispered to my friend under my breath.

"When the earth-star rests in the roof-niche of the temple it is climbing," she answered back.

"And then?"

"On the tripod is a globe of water. In it she will see the destiny of the year, and will tell us. The whiter the water stays, the better for us; it never varies from white. But we must not talk; see! she is stopping."

And as I looked back, the dance was certainly ebbing now with such smoothly decreasing undulations, that every heart began to beat calmer in response. There was a minute or two of such slow cessation, and then to say she stopped were too gross a description. Motion rather died away from her, and the priestess grounded as smoothly as a ship grounds in fine weather on a sandy bank. There she was at last, crouched behind the tripod, one corner of the cloth covering it grasped in her hand, and her eyes fixed on the shining round just poised upon the distant run.

Keenly the girl watched it slide into zenith, then the cloth was snatched from the tripod-top. As it fell it uncovered a beautiful and perfect globe of clear white glass, a foot or so in diameter, and obviously filled with the thinnest, most limpid water imaginable. At first it seemed to me, who stood near to the priestess of Mars, with that beaming sphere directly between us, and the newly risen world, that its smooth and flawless face was absolutely devoid of sign or colouring. Then, as the distant planet became stronger in the magnifying Martian air, or my eyes better accustomed to that sudden nucleus of brilliancy, a delicate and infinitely lovely network of colours came upon it. They were like the radiant prisms that sometimes flush the surface of a bubble more than aught else for a time. But as I watched that mosaic of yellow and purple creep softly to and fro upon the globe it seemed they slowly took form and meaning. Another minute or two and they had certainly congealed into a settled plan, and then, as I stared and wondered, it burst upon me in a minute that I was looking upon a picture, faithful in every detail, of the world I stood on; all its ruddy forests, its sapphire sea, both broad and narrow ones, its white peaked mountains, and unnumbered islands being mapped out with startling clearness for a spell upon that beaming orb.

Then a strange thing happened. Heru, who had been crouching in a tremulous heap by the tripod, rose stealthily and passed her hands a few times across the sphere. Colour and picture vanished at her touch like breath from a mirror. Again all was clear and pellucid.

"Now," said my companion, "now listen! For Heru reads the destiny; the whiter the globe stays the better for us—" and then I felt her hand tighten on mine with a startled grasp as the words died away upon her lips.

Even as the girl spoke, the sphere, which had been beaming in the centre of the silent square like a mighty white jewel, began to flush with angry red. Redder and redder grew the gleam—a fiery glow which

EDWIN L. ARNOLD

seemed curdling in the interior of the round as though it were filled with flame; redder and redder, until the princess, staring into it, seemed turned against the jet-black night behind, into a form of molten metal. A spasm of terror passed across her as she stared; her limbs stiffened; her frightened hands were clutched in front, and she stood cowering under that great crimson nucleus like one bereft of power and life, and lost to every sense but that of agony. Not a syllable came from her lips, not a movement stirred her body, only that dumb, stupid stare of horror, at the something she saw in the globe. What could I do? I could not sit and see her soul come out at her frightened eyes, and not a Martian moved a finger to her rescue; the red shine gleamed on empty faces, tier above tier, and flung its broad flush over the endless rank of open-mouthed spectators, then back I looked to Heru—that winsome little lady for whom, you will remember, I had already more than a passing fancy—and saw with a thrill of emotion that while she still kept her eyes on the flaming globe like one in a horrible dream her hands were slowly, very slowly, rising in supplication to *me!* It was not vanity. There was no mistaking the direction of that silent, imploring appeal.

Not a man of her countrymen moved, not even black Hath! There was not a sound in the world, it seemed, but the noisy clatter of my own shoenails on the marble flags. In the great red eye of that unholy globe the Martians glimmered like a picture multitude under the red cliff of their ruined palace. I glared round at them with contempt for a minute, then sprang forward and snatched the princess up. It was like pulling a flower up by the roots. She was stiff and stark when I lay hold of her, but when I tore her from the magic ground she suddenly gave a piercing shriek, and fainted in my arms.

Then as I turned upon my heels with her upon my breast my foot caught upon the cloths still wound about the tripod of the sphere. Over went that implement of a thousand years of sorcery, and out went the red fire. But little I cared—the princess was safe! And up the palace steps, amidst a low, wailing hum of consternation from the recovering Martians, I bore that bundle of limp and senseless loveliness up into the pale shine of her own porch, and there, laying her down upon a couch, watched her recover presently amongst her women with a varied assortment of emotions tingling in my veins.

Chapter 6

Beyond the first flutter of surprise, the Martians had shown no interest in the abrupt termination of the year's divinations. They melted away, a trifle more silently perhaps than usual, when I shattered the magic globe, but with their invariable indifference, and having handed the reviving Heru over to some women who led her away, apparently already half forgetful of the things that had just happened, I was left alone on the palace steps, not even An beside me, and only the shadow of a passerby now and then to break the solitude. Whereon a great loneliness took hold upon me, and, pacing to and fro along the ancient terrace with bent head and folded arms, I bewailed my fate. To and fro I walked, heedless and melancholy, thinking of the old world, that was so far and this near world so distant from me in everything making life worth living, thinking, as I strode gloomily here and there, how gladly I would exchange these poor puppets and the mockery of a town they dwelt in, for a sight of my comrades and a corner in the poorest wine-shop salon in New York or 'Frisco; idly speculating why, and how, I came here, as I sauntered down amongst the glistening, shell-like fragments of the shattered globe, and finding no answer. How could I? It was too fair, I thought, standing there in the open; there was a fatal sweetness in the air, a deadly sufficiency in the beauty of everything around falling on the lax senses like some sleepy draught of pleasure. Not a leaf stirred, the wide purple roof of the sky was unbroken by the healthy promise of a cloud from rim to rim, the splendid country, teeming with its spring-time richness, lay in rank perfection everywhere; and just as rank and sleek and passionless were those who owned it.

Why, even I, who yesterday was strong, began to come under the spell of it. But yesterday the spirit of the old world was still strong within me, yet how much things were now changing. The well-strung muscles loosening, the heart beating a slower measure, the busy mind drowsing off to listlessness. Was I, too, destined to become like these? Was the red stuff in my veins to be watered down to pallid Martian sap? Was ambition and hope to desert me, and idleness itself become laborious, while life ran to seed in gilded uselessness? Little did I guess how unnecessary my fears were, or of the incredible fairy tale of adventure into which fate was going to plunge me.

Still engrossed the next morning by these thoughts, I decided I

EDWIN L. ARNOLD

would go to Hath. Hath was a man—at least they said so—he might sympathise even though he could not help, and so, dressing finished, I went down towards the innermost palace whence for an hour or two had come sounds of unwonted bustle. Asking for the way occasionally from sleepy folk lolling about the corridors, waiting as it seemed for their breakfasts to come to them, and embarrassed by the new daylight, I wandered to and fro in the labyrinths of that stony ant-heap until I chanced upon a curtained doorway which admitted to a long chamber, high-roofed, ample in proportions, with colonnades on either side separated from the main aisle by rows of flowery figures and emblematic scroll-work, meaning I knew not what. Above those pillars ran a gallery with many windows looking out over the ruined city. While at the further end of the chamber stood three broad steps leading to a dais. As I entered, the whole place was full of bustling girls, their yellow garments like a bed of flowers in the sunlight trickling through the casements, and all intent on the spreading of a feast on long tables ranged up and down the hall. The morning light streamed in on the white cloths. It glittered on the glass and the gold they were putting on the trestles, and gave resplendent depths of colour to the ribbon bands round the pillars. All were so busy no one noticed me standing in the twilight by the door, but presently, laying a hand on a worker's shoulder, I asked who they banqueted for, and why such unwonted preparation?

"It is the marriage-feast tonight, stranger, and a marvel you did not know it. You, too, are to be wed."

"I had not heard of it, damsel; a paternal forethought of your Government, I suppose? Have you any idea who the lady is?"

"How should I know?" she answered laughingly. "That is the secret of the urn. Meanwhile, we have set you a place at the table-head near Princess Heru, and tonight you dip and have your chance like all of them; may luck send you a rosy bride, and save her from Ar-hap."

"Ay, now I remember; An told me of this before; Ar-hap is the sovereign with whom your people have a little difference, and shares unbidden in the free distribution of brides to-night. This promises to be interesting; depend on it I will come; if you will keep me a place where I can hear the speeches, and not forget me when the turtle soup goes round, I shall be more than grateful. Now to another matter. I want to get a few minutes with your President, Prince Hath. He concentrates the fluid intelligence of this sphere, I am told. Where can I find him?"

"He is drunk, in the library, sir!"

"My word! It is early in the day for that, and a singular conjunction of place and circumstance."

"Where," said the girl, "could he safer be? We can always fetch him if we want him, and sunk in blue oblivion he will not come to harm."

"A cheerful view, Miss, which is worthy of the attention of our reformers. Nevertheless, I will go to him. I have known men tell more truth in that state than in any other."

The servitor directed me to the library, and after desolate wanderings up crumbling steps and down mouldering corridors, sunny and lovely in decay, I came to the immense lumber-shed of knowledge they had told me of, a city of dead books, a place of dusty cathedral aisles stored with forgotten learning. At a table sat Hath the purposeless, enthroned in leather and vellum, snoring in divine content amongst all that wasted labour, and nothing I could do was sufficient to shake him into semblance of intelligence. So perforce I turned away till he should have come to himself, and wandering round the splendid litter of a noble library, presently amongst the ruck of volumes on the floor, amongst those lordly tomes in tattered green and gold, and ivory, my eye lit upon a volume propped up curiously on end, and going to it through the confusion I saw by the dried fruit rind upon the sticks supporting it, that the grave and reverend tome was set to catch a mouse! It was a splendid book when I looked more closely, bound as a king might bind his choicest treasure, the sweet-scented leather on it was no doubt frayed; the golden arabesques upon the covers had long since shed their eyes of inset gems, the jewelled clasp locking its learning up from vulgar gaze was bent and open. Yet it was a lordly tome with an odour of sanctity about it, and lifting it with difficulty, I noticed on its cover a red stain of mouse's blood. Those who put it to this quaint use of mouse-trap had already had some sport, but surely never was a mouse crushed before under so much learning. And while I stood guessing at what the book might hold within, Heru, the princess, came tripping in to me, and with the abrupt familiarity of her kind, laid a velvet hand upon my wrist, conned the title over to herself.

"What does it say, sweet girl?" I asked. "The matter is learned, by its feel," and that maid, pursing up her pretty lips, read the title to me—"The Secret of the Gods."

"The Secret of the Gods," I murmured. "Was it possible other worlds had struggled hopelessly to come within the barest ken of that great knowledge, while here the same was set to catch a mouse with?"

EDWIN L. ARNOLD

I said, "Silver-footed, sit down and read me a passage or two," and propping the mighty volume upon a table drew a bench before it and pulled her down beside me.

"Oh! a horrid, dry old book for certain," cried that lady, her pink fingertips falling as lightly on the musty leaves as almond petals on March dust. "Where shall I begin? It is all equally dull."

"Dip in," was my answer. "'Tis no great matter where, but near the beginning. What says the writer of his intention? What sets he out to prove?"

"He says that is the Secret of the First Great Truth, descended straight to him—"

"Many have said so much, yet have lied."

"He says that which is written in his book is through him but not of him, past criticism and beyond cavil. 'Tis all in ancient and crabbed characters going back to the threshold of my learning, but here upon this passage-top where they are writ large I make them out to say, '*Only the man who has died many times begins to live.*'"

"A pregnant passage! Turn another page, and try again; I have an inkling of the book already."

"'Tis poor, silly stuff," said the girl, slipping a hand covertly into my own. "Why will you make me read it? I have a book on pomatums worth twice as much as this."

"Nevertheless, dip in again, dear lady. What says the next heading?" And with a little sigh at the heaviness of her task, Heru read out: "*Sometimes the Gods themselves forget the answers to their own riddles.*"

"Lady, I knew it!

"All this is still preliminary to the great matter of the book, but the mutterings of the priest who draws back the curtains of the shrine—and here, after the scribe has left these two yellow pages blank as though to set a space of reverence between himself and what comes next—here speaks the truth, the voice, the fact of all life." But "Oh! Jones," she said, turning from the dusty pages and clasping her young, milk-warm hands over mine and leaning towards me until her blushing cheek was near to my shoulder and the incense of her breath upon me. "Oh! Gulliver Jones," she said. "Make me read no more; my soul revolts from the task, the crazy brown letters swim before my eyes. Is there no learning near at hand that would be pleasanter reading than this silly book of yours? What, after all," she said, growing bolder at the sound of her own voice, "what, after all, is the musty reticence of gods to the whispered secret of a maid? Jones, splendid stranger for whom all men stand aside and women look over shoulders, oh, let me be your book!" she whispered, slipping on to my knee and winding her arms round my neck till, through the white glimmer of her single vest, I could feel her heart beating against mine. "Newest and dearest of friends, put by this dreary learning and look in my eyes; is there nothing to be spelt out there?"

And I was constrained to do as she bid me, for she was as fresh as an almond blossom touched by the sun, and looking down into two swimming blue lakes where shyness and passion were contending— books easy enough, in truth, to be read, I saw that she loved me, with the unconventional ardour of her nature.

It was a pleasant discovery, if its abruptness was embarrassing, for she was a maid in a thousand; and half ashamed and half laughing I let her escalade me, throwing now and then a rueful look at the Secret of the Gods, and all that priceless knowledge treated so unworthily.

What else could I do? Besides, I loved her myself! And if there was a momentary chagrin at having yonder golden knowledge put off by this lovely interruption, yet I was flesh and blood, the gods could wait— they had to wait long and often before, and when this sweet interpreter was comforted we would have another try. So it happened I took her into my heart and gave her the answer she asked for.

For a long time we sat in the dusky grandeur of the royal library, my mind revolving between wonder and admiration of the neglected knowledge all about, and the stirrings of a new love, while Heru herself, lapsed again into Martian calm, lay half sleeping on my shoulder, but presently, unwinding her arms, I put her down.

"There, sweetheart," I whispered, "enough of this for the moment; tonight, perhaps, some more, but while we are here amongst all this lordly litter, I can think of nothing else." Again I bid her turn the pages, noting as she did so how each chapter was headed by the coloured configuration of a world. Page by page we turned of crackling parchment, until by chance, at the top of one, my eye caught a coloured round I could not fail to recognise—'twas the spinning button on the blue breast of the immeasurable that yesterday I inhabited. "Read here," I cried, clapping my finger upon the page midway down, where there were some signs looking like Egyptian writing. "Says this quaint dabbler in all knowledge anything of Isis, anything of Phra, of Ammon, of Ammon Top?"

"And who was Isis? who Ammon Top?" asked the lady.

"Nay, read," I answered, and down the page her slender fingers went awandering till at a spot of knotted signs they stopped. "Why, here is something about thy Isis," exclaimed Heru, as though amused at my perspicuity. "Here, halfway down this chapter of earth-history, it says," and putting one pink knee across the other to better prop the book she read:

"And the priests of Thebes were gone; the sand stood untrampled on the temple steps a thousand years; the wild bees sang the song of desolation in the ears of Isis; the wild cats littered in the stony lap of Ammon; ay, another thousand years went by, and earth was tilled of unseen hands and sown with yellow grain from Paradise, and the thin veil that separates the known from the unknown was rent, and men walked to and fro."

"Go on," I said.

"Nay," laughed the other, "the little mice in their eagerness have been before you—see, all this corner is gnawed away."

"Read on again," I said, "where the page is whole; those sips of knowledge you have given make me thirsty for more. There, begin where this blazonry of initialed red and gold looks so like the carpet spread by the scribe for the feet of a sovereign truth—what says he here?" And she, half pouting to be set back once more to that task, half wondering as she gazed on those magic letters, let her eyes run down the page, then began:

"And it was the Beginning, and in the centre void presently there came a nucleus of light: and the light brightened in the grey primeval morning and became definite and articulate. And from the midst of that natal splendour, behind which was the Unknowable, the life came hitherward; from the midst of that nucleus undescribed, undescribable, there issued presently the primeval sigh that breathed the breath of life into all things. And that sigh thrilled through the empty spaces of the illimitable: it breathed the breath of promise over the frozen hills of the outside planets where the night-frost had lasted without beginning: and the waters of ten thousand nameless oceans, girding nameless planets, were stirred, trembling into their depth. It crossed the illimitable spaces where the herding aerolites swirl forever through space in the wake of careering world, and all their whistling wings answered to it. It reverberated through the grey wastes of vacuity, and crossed the dark oceans of the Outside, even to the black shores of the eternal night beyond.

"And hardly had echo of that breath died away in the hollow of the heavens and the empty wombs of a million barren worlds, when the light brightened again, and drawing in upon itself became definite and took form, and therefrom, at the moment of primitive conception, there came—"

And just then, as she had read so far as that, when all my faculties were aching to know what came next—whether this were but the idle scribbling of a vacuous fool, or something else—there rose the sound of soft flutes and tinkling bells in the corridors, as seneschals wandered piping round the palace to call folk to meals, a smell of roast meat and grilling fish as that procession lifted the curtains between the halls, and—

"Dinner!" shouted my sweet Martian, slapping the covers of The Secret of the Gods together and pushing the stately tome headlong from the table. "Dinner! 'Tis worth a hundred thousand planets to the hungry!"

Nothing I could say would keep her, and, scarcely knowing whether to laugh or to be angry at so unseemly an interruption, but both being purposeless I dug my hands into my pockets, and somewhat sulkily refusing Heru's invitation to luncheon in the corridor (Navy rations had not fitted my stomach for these constant debauches of gossamer food), strolled into the town again in no very pleasant frame of mind.

Chapter 7

It was only at moments like these I had any time to reflect on my circumstances or that giddy chance which had shot me into space in this fashion, and, frankly, the opportunities, when they did come, brought such an extraordinary depressing train of thought, I by no means invited them. Even with the time available the occasion was always awry for such reflection. These dainty triflers made sulking as impossible amongst them as philosophy in a ballroom. When I stalked out like that from the library in fine mood to moralise and apostrophise heaven in a way that would no doubt have looked fine upon these pages, one sprightly damsel, just as the gloomy rhetoric was bursting from my lips, thrust a flower under my nose whose scent brought on a violent attack of sneezing, her companions joining hands and dancing round me while they imitated my agony. Then, when I burst away from them and rushed down a narrow arcade of crumbling mansions, another stopped me in mid-career, and taking the honey-stick she was sucking from her lips, put it to mine, like a pretty, playful child. Another asked me to dance, another to drink pink oblivion with her, and so on. How could one lament amongst all this irritating cheerfulness?

An might have helped me, for poor An was intelligent for a Martian, but she had disappeared, and the terrible vacuity of life in the planet was forced upon me when I realised that possessing no cognomen, no fixed address, or rating, it would be the merest chance if I ever came across her again.

Looking for my friendly guide and getting more and more at sea amongst a maze of comely but similar faces, I made chance acquaintance with another of her kind who cheerfully drank my health at the Government's expense, and chatted on things Martian. She took me to see a funeral by way of amusement, and I found these people floated their dead off on flower-decked rafts instead of burying them, the send-offs all taking place upon a certain swift-flowing stream, which carried the dead away into the vast region of northern ice, but more exactly whither my informant seemed to have no idea. The voyager on this occasion was old, and this brought to my mind the curious fact that I had observed few children in the city, and no elders, all, except perhaps Hath, being in a state of sleek youthfulness. My new friend explained the peculiarity by declaring Martians ripened with extraordinary rapidity from infancy to the equivalent of about twenty-five years of age, with us, and then remained at that period however long they might live; Only when they died did their accumulated seasons come upon them; the girl turning pale, and wringing her pretty hands in sympathetic concern when I told her there was a land where decrepitude was not so happily postponed. The Martians, she said, arranged their calendar by the varying colours of the seasons, and loved blue as an antidote to the generally red and rusty character of their soil.

Discussing such things as these we lightly squandered the day away, and I know of nothing more to note until the evening was come again: that wonderful purple evening which creeps over the outer worlds at sunset, a seductive darkness gemmed with ten thousand stars riding so low in the heaven they seem scarcely more than mast high. When that hour was come my friend tiptoed again to my cheek, and then, pointing to the palace and laughingly hoping fate would send me a bride "as soft as catkin and as sweet as honey," slipped away into the darkness.

Then I remembered all on a sudden this was the connubial evening of my sprightly friends—the occasion when, as An had told me, the Government constituted itself into a gigantic matrimonial agency, and, with the cheerful carelessness of the place, shuffled the matrimonial pack anew, and dealt a fresh hand to all the players. Now I had no wish to avail myself of a sailor's privilege of a bride in every port, but surely this game would be interesting enough to see, even if I were but a disinterested spectator. As a matter of fact I was something more than that, and had been thinking a good deal of Heru during the day. I do not know whether I actually aspired to her hand—that were a large order, even if there had been no suspicion in my mind she was already bespoke in some vague way by the invisible Hath, most abortive of princes. But she was undeniably a lovely girl; the more one thought of her the more she grew upon the fancy, and then the preference she had shown myself was very gratifying. Yes, I would certainly see this quaint ceremonial, even if I took no leading part in it.

The great centre hall of the palace was full of a radiant light bringing up its ruined columns and intruding creepers to the best effect when I entered. Dinner also was just being served, as they would say in another, and alas! very distant place, and the whole building thronged with folk. Down the centre low tables with room for four hundred people were ranged, but they looked quaint enough since but two hundred were sitting there, all brand-new bachelors about to be turned into brand new

EDWIN L. ARNOLD

Benedicts, and taking it mightily calmly it seemed. Across the hall-top was a raised table similarly arranged and ornamented; and entering into the spirit of the thing, and little guessing how stern a reality was to come from the evening, I sat down in a vacant place near to the dais, and only a few paces from where the pale, ghost-eyed Hath was already seated.

Almost immediately afterwards music began to buzz all about the hall—music of the kind the people loved which always seemed to me as though it were exuding from the tables and benches, so disembodied and difficult it was to locate; all the sleepy gallants raised their flower-encircled heads at the same time, seizing their wine-cups, already filled to the brim, and the door at the bottom of the hall opening, the ladies, preceded by one carrying a mysterious vase covered with a glittering cloth, came in.

Now, being somewhat thirsty, I had already drunk half the wine in my beaker, and whether it was that draught, drugged as all Martian wines are, or the sheer loveliness of the maids themselves, I cannot say, but as the procession entered, and, dividing, circled round under the colonnades of the hall, a sensation of extraordinary felicity came over me—an emotion of divine contentment purged of all grossness—and I stared and stared at the circling loveliness, gossamer-clad, flower-girdled, tripping by me with vapid delight. Either the wine was budding in my head, or there was little to choose from amongst them, for had any of those ladies sat down in the vacant place beside me, I should certainly have accepted her as a gift from heaven, without question or cavil. But one after another they slipped by, modestly taking their places in the shadows until at last came Princess Heru, and at the sight of her my soul was stirred.

She came undulating over the white marble, the loveliness of her fairy person dimmed but scarcely hidden by a robe of softest lawn in colour like rose-petals, her eyes aglitter with excitement and a charming blush upon her face.

She came straight up to me, and, resting a dainty hand upon my shoulder, whispered, "Are you come as a spectator only, dear Mr. Jones, or do you join in our custom tonight?"

"I came only as a bystander, lady, but the fascination of the opportunity is deadly—"

"And have you any preference?"—this in the softest little voice from somewhere in the nape of my neck. "Strangers sometimes say there are fair women in Seth."

"None—till you came; and now, as was said a long time ago, 'All is dross that is not Helen.' Dearest lady," I ran on, detaining her by the fingertips and gazing up into those shy and star-like eyes, "must I indeed put all the hopes your kindness has roused in me these last few days to a shuffle in yonder urn, taking my chance with all these lazy fellows? In that land whereof I was, we would not have had it so, we loaded our dice in these matters, a strong man there might have a willing maid though all heaven were set against him! But give me leave, sweet lady, and I will ruffle with these fellows; give me a glance and I will barter my life for your billet when it is drawn, but to stand idly by and see you won by a cold chance, I cannot do it."

That lady laughed a little and said, "Men make laws, dear Jones, for women to keep. It is the rule, and we must not break it." Then, gently tugging at her imprisoned fingers and gathering up her skirts to go, she added, "But it might happen that wit here were better than sword." Then she hesitated, and freeing herself at last slipped from my side, yet before she was quite gone half turned again and whispered so low that no one but I could hear it, "A golden pool, and a silver fish, and a line no thicker than a hair!" and before I could beg a meaning of her, had passed down the hall and taken a place with the other expectant damsels.

"A golden pool," I said to myself, "a silver fish, and a line of hair." What could she mean? Yet that she meant something, and something clearly of importance, I could not doubt. "A golden pool, and a silver fish—" I buried my chin in my chest and thought deeply but without effect while the preparations were made and the fateful urn, each maid having slipped her name tablet within, was brought down to us, covered in a beautiful web of rose-coloured tissue, and commenced its round, passing slowly from hand to hand as each of those handsome, impassive, fawn-eyed gallants lifted a corner of the web in turn and helped themselves to fate.

"A golden pool," I muttered, "and a silver fish"—so absorbed in my own thoughts I hardly noticed the great cup begin its journey, but when it had gone three or four places the glitter of the lights upon it caught my eye. It was of pure gold, round-brimmed, and circled about with a string of the blue convolvulus, which implies delight to these people. Ay! and each man was plunging his hand into the dark and taking in his turn a small notch-edged mother-of-pearl billet from it that flashed soft and silvery as he turned it in his hand to read the name engraved

EDWIN L. ARNOLD

in unknown characters thereon. "Why," I said, with a start, "surely *this* might be the golden pool and these the silver fish—but the hair-fine line?" And again I meditated deeply, with all my senses on the watch.

Slowly the urn crept round, and as each man took a ticket from it, and passed it, smiling, to the seneschal behind him, that official read out the name upon it, and a blushing damsel slipped from the crowd above, crossing over to the side of the man with whom chance had thus lightly linked her for the brief Martian year, and putting her hands in his they kissed before all the company, and sat down to their places at the table as calmly as country folk might choose partners at a village fair in hay-time.

But not so with me. Each time a name was called I started and stared at the drawer in a way which should have filled him with alarm had alarm been possible to the peace-soaked triflers, then turned to glance to where, amongst the women, my tender little princess was leaning against a pillar, with drooping head, slowly pulling a convolvulus bud to pieces. None drew, though all were thinking of her, as I could tell in my fingertips. Keener and keener grew the suspense as name after name was told and each slim white damsel skipped to the place allotted her. And all the time I kept muttering to myself about that "golden pool," wondering and wondering until the urn had passed half round the tables and was only some three men up from me—and then an idea flashed across my mind. I dipped my fingers in the scented water-basin on the table, drying them carefully on a napkin, and waiting, outwardly as calm as any, yet inwardly wrung by those tremors which beset all male creation in such circumstances.

And now at last it was my turn. The great urn, blazing golden, through its rosy covering, was in front, and all eyes on me. I clapped a sunburnt hand upon its top as though I would take all remaining in it to myself and stared round at that company—only her herself I durst not look at! Then, with a beating heart, I lifted a corner of the web and slipped my hand into the dark inside, muttering to myself as I did so, "A golden pool, and a silver fish, and a line no thicker than a hair." I touched in turn twenty perplexing tablets and was no whit the wiser, and felt about the sides yet came to nothing, groping here and there with a rising despair, until as my fingers, still damp and fine of touch, went round the sides a second time, yes! there was something, something in the hollow of the fluting, a thought, a thread, and yet enough. I took it unseen, lifting it with infinite forbearance, and the end was weighted, the other tablets slipped and rattled as from their midst, hanging to that one fine virgin hair, up came a pearly billet. I doubted no longer, but snapped the thread, and showed the tablet, heard Heru's name, read from it amongst the soft applause of that luxurious company with all the unconcern I could muster.

There she was in a moment, lip to lip with me, before them all, her eyes more than ever like planets from her native skies, and only the quick heave of her bosom, slowly subsiding like a ground swell after a storm, remaining to tell that even Martian blood could sometimes beat quicker than usual! She sat down in her place by me in the simplest way, and soon everything was as merry as could be. The main meal came on now, and as far as I could see those Martian gallants had extremely good appetites, though they drank at first but little, wisely remembering the strength of their wines. As for me, I ate of fishes that never swam in earthly seas, and of strange fowl that never flapped a way through thick terrestrial air, ate and drank as happy as a king, and falling each moment more and more in love with the wonderfully beautiful girl at my side who was a real woman of flesh and blood I knew, yet somehow so dainty, so pink and white, so unlike other girls in the smoothness of her outlines, in the subtle grace of each unthinking attitude, that again and again I looked at her over the rim of my tankard half fearing she might dissolve into nothing, being the half-fairy which she was.

Presently she asked, "Did that deed of mine, the hair in the urn, offend you, stranger?"

"Offend me, lady!" I laughed. "Why, had it been the blackest crime that ever came out of a perverse imagination it would have brought its own pardon with it; I, least of all in this room, have least cause to be offended."

"I risked much for you and broke our rules."

"Why, no doubt that was so, but 'tis the privilege of your kind to have some say in this little matter of giving and taking in marriage. I only marvel that your countrywomen submit so tamely to the quaintest game of chance I ever played at.

"Ay, and it is women's nature no doubt to keep the laws which others make, as you have said yourself. Yet this rule, lady, is one broken with more credit than kept, and if you have offended no one more than me, your penance is easily done."

"But I have offended some one," she said, laying her hand on mine with gentle nervousness in its touch, "one who has the power to hurt, and enough energy to resent. Hath, up there at the cross-table, have I offended deeply tonight, for he hoped to have me, and would have compelled any other man to barter me for the maid chance assigned to him; but of you, somehow, he is afraid—I have seen him staring at you, and changing colour as though he knew something no one else knows—"

"Briefly, charming girl," I said, for the wine was beginning to sing in my head, and my eyes were blinking stupidly—"briefly, Hath hath thee not, and there's an end of it. I would spit a score of Haths, as these figs are spit on this golden skewer, before I would relinquish a hair of your head to him, or to any man," and as everything about the great hall began to look gauzy and unreal through the gathering fumes of my confusion, I smiled on that gracious lady, and began to whisper I know not what to her, and whisper and doze, and doze—

I know not how long afterwards it was, whether a minute or an hour, but when I lifted my head suddenly from the lady's shoulder all the place was in confusion, every one upon their feet, the talk and the drinking ceased, and all eyes turned to the far doorway where the curtains were just dropping again as I looked, while in front of them were standing three men.

These newcomers were utterly unlike any others—a frightful vision of ugly strength amidst the lolling loveliness all about. Low of stature, broad of shoulder, hairy, deep-chested, with sharp, twinkling eyes, set far back under bushy eyebrows, retreating foreheads, and flat noses in faces tanned to a dusky copper hue by exposure to every kind of weather that racks the extreme Martian climate they were so opposite to all about me, so quaint and grim amongst those mild, fair-skinned folk, that at first I thought they were but a disordered creation of my fancy.

I rubbed my eyes and stared and blinked, but no! they were real men, of flesh and blood, and now they had come down with as much stateliness as their bandy legs would admit of, into the full glare of the lights to the centre table where Hath sat. I saw their splendid apparel, the great strings of rudely polished gems hung round their hairy necks and wrists, the cunningly dyed skins of soft-furred animals, green and red and black, wherewith their limbs were swathed, and then I heard some one by me whisper in a frightened tone, "The envoys from over seas."

"Oh," I thought sleepily to myself, "so these are the ape-men of the western woods, are they? Those who long ago vanquished my white-skinned friends and yearly come to claim their tribute. Jove, what hay they must have made of them! How those peach-skinned girls must have screamed and the downy striplings by them felt their dimpled knees knock together, as the mad flood of barbarians came pouring over from the forest, and long ago stormed their citadels like a stream of red lava, as deadly, as irresistible, as remorseless!" And I lay asprawl upon my arms on the table watching them with the stupid indifference I thought I could so well afford.

Meanwhile Hath was on foot, pale and obsequious like others in the presence of those dread ambassadors, but more collected, I thought. With the deepest bows he welcomed them, handing them drink in a golden State cup, and when they had drunk (I heard the liquor running down their great throats, in the frightened hush, like water in a runnel on a wet day), they wiped their fierce lips upon their furry sleeves, and the leader began reciting the tribute for the year. So much corn, so much wine—and very much it was—so many thousands ells of cloth and webbing, and so much hammered gold, and sinah and lar, precious metal of which I knew nothing as yet; and ever as he went growling through the list in his harsh animal voice, he refreshed his memory with a coloured stick whereon a notch was made for every item, the woodmen not having come as yet, apparently, to the gentler art of written signs and symbols. Longer and longer that caravan of unearned wealth stretched out before my fancy, but at last it was done, or all but done, and the head envoy, passing the painted stick to a man behind, folded his bare, sinewy arms, upon which the red fell bristles as it does upon a gorilla's, across his ample chest, and, including us all in one general scowl, turned to Hath as he said—

"All this for Ar-hap, the wood-king, my master and yours; all this, and the most beautiful woman here tonight at your tables!"

"An item," I smiled stupidly to myself, for indeed I was very sleepy and had no nice perception of things, "which shows his majesty with the two-pronged name is a jolly fellow after all, and knows wealth is incomplete without the crown and priming of all riches. I wonder how the Martian boys will like this postscript," and chin on hand, and eyes that would hardly stay open, I watched to see what would happen next. There was a little conversation between the prince and the ape-man; then I saw Hath the traitor point in my direction and say—

EDWIN L. ARNOLD

"Since you ask and will be advised, then, mighty sir, there can be no doubt of it, the most beautiful woman here tonight is undoubtedly she who sits yonder by him in blue."

"A very pretty compliment!" I thought, too dull to see what was coming quickly, "and handsome of Hath, all things considered."

And so I dozed and dozed, and then started, and stared! Was I in my senses? Was I mad, or dreaming? The drunkenness dropped from me like a mantle; with a single, smothered cry I came to myself and saw that it was all too true. The savage envoy had come down the hall at Hath's vindictive prompting, had lifted my fair girl to her feet, and there, even as I looked, had drawn her, white as death, into the red circle of his arm, and with one hand under her chin had raised her sweet face to within an inch of his, and was staring at her with small, ugly eyes.

"Yes," said the enjoy, more interestedly than he had spoken yet, "it will do; the tribute is accepted—for Ar-hap, my master!" And taking shrinking Heru by the wrist, and laying a heavy hand upon her shoulder, he was about to lead her up the hall.

I was sober enough then. I was on foot in an instant, and before all the glittering company, before those simpering girls and pale Martian youths, who sat mumbling their fingers, too frightened to lift their eyes from off their half-finished dinners, I sprang at the envoy. I struck him with my clenched fist on the side of his bullet head, and he let go of Heru, who slipped insensible from his hairy chest like a white cloud slipping down the slopes of a hill at sunrise, and turned on me with a snort of rage. We stared at each other for a minute, and then I felt the wine fumes roaring in my head; I rushed at him and closed. It was like embracing a mountain bull, and he responded with a hug that made my ribs crackle. For a minute we were locked together like that, swinging here and there, and then getting a hand loose, I belaboured him so unmercifully that he put his head down, and that was what I wanted. I got a new hold of him as we staggered and plunged, roaring the while like the wild beasts we were, the teeth chattering in the Martian heads as they watched us, and then, exerting all my strength, lifted him fairly from his feet and with supreme effort swung him up, shoulder high, and with a mighty heave hurled him across the tables, flung that ambassador, whom no Martian dared look upon, crashing and sprawling through the gold and silver of the feast, whirled him round with such a splendid send that bench and trestle, tankards and flagons, chairs and cloths and candelabras all went down into thundering chaos with him, and the envoy only stayed when his sacred person came to harbour amongst the westral odds and ends, the soiled linen, and dirty platters of our wedding feast.

I remember seeing him there on hands and knees, and then the liquor I had had would not be denied. In vain I drew my hands across my drooping eyelids, in vain I tried to master my knees that knocked together. The spell of the love-drink that Heru, blushing, had held to my lips was on me. Its soft, overwhelming influence rose like a prismatic fog between me and my enemy, everything again became hazy and dreamlike, and feebly calling on Heru, my chin dropped upon my chest, my limbs relaxed, and I slipped down in drowsy oblivion before my rival.

EDWIN L. ARNOLD

Chapter 8

They must have carried me, still under the influence of wine fumes, to the chamber where I slept that night, for when I woke the following morning my surroundings were familiar enough, though a glorious maze of uncertainties rocked to and fro in my mind.

Was it a real feast we had shared in overnight, or only a quaint dream? Was Heru real or only a lovely fancy? And those hairy ruffians of whom a horrible vision danced before my waking eyes, were they fancy too? No, my wrists still ached with the strain of the tussle, the quaint, sad wine taste was still on my lips—it was all real enough, I decided, starting up in bed; and if it was real where was the little princess? What had they done with her? Surely they had not given her to the ape-men—cowards though they were they could not have been cowards enough for that. And as I wondered a keen, bright picture of the hapless maid as I saw her last blossomed before my mind's eye, the ambassadors on either side holding her wrists, and she shrinking from them in horror while her poor, white face turned to me for rescue in desperate pleading—oh! I must find her at all costs; and leaping from bed I snatched up those trousers without which the best of heroes is nothing, and had hardly got into them when there came the patter of light feet without and a Martian, in a hurry for once, with half a dozen others behind him, swept aside the curtains of my doorway.

They peeped and peered all about the room, then one said, "Is Princess Heru with you, sir?"

"No," I answered roughly. "Saints alive, man, do you think I would have you tumbling in here over each other's heels if she were?"

"Then it must indeed have been Heru," he said, speaking in an awed voice to his fellows, "whom we saw carried down to the harbour at daybreak by yonder woodmen," and the pink upon their pretty cheeks faded to nothing at the suggestion.

"What!" I roared, "Heru taken from the palace by a handful of men and none of you infernal rascals—none of you white-livered abortions lifted a hand to save her—curse on you a thousand times. Out of my way, you churls!" And snatching up coat and hat and sword I rushed furiously down the long, marble stairs just as the short Martian night was giving place to lavender-coloured light of morning. I found my way somehow down the deserted corridors where the air was heavy with aromatic vapours; I flew by curtained niches and chambers where amongst mounds of half-withered flowers the Martian lovers were slowly waking. Down into the banquethall I sped, and there in the twilight was the litter of the feast still about—gold cups and silver, broken bread and meat, the convolvulus flowers all turning their pallid faces to the rosy daylight, making pools of brightness between the shadows. Amongst the litter little sapphire-coloured finches were feeding, twittering merrily to themselves as they hopped about, and here and there down the long tables lay asprawl a belated reveller, his empty oblivion-phial before him, his curly head upon his arms, dreaming perhaps of last night's feast and a neglected bride dozing dispassionate in some distant chamber. But Heru was not there and little I cared for twittering finches or sighing damsels. With hasty feet I rushed down the hall out into the cool, sweet air of the planet morning.

There I met one whom I knew, and he told me he had been among the crowd and had heard the woodmen had gone no farther than the river gate, that Heru was with them beyond a doubt. I would not listen to more. "Good!" I shouted. "Get me a horse and just a handful of your sleek kindred and we will pull the prize from the bear's paw even yet! Surely," I said, turning to a knot of Martian youths who stood listening a few steps away, "surely some of you will come with me at this pinch? The big bullies are very few; the sea runs behind them; the maid in their clutch is worth fighting for; it needs but one good onset, five minutes' gallantry, and she is ours again. Think how fine it will look to bring her back before yon sleepy fellows have found their weapons. You, there, with the blue tunic! you look a proper fellow, and something of a heart should beat under such gay wrappings, will you come with me?"

But blue-mantle, biting his thumbs, murmured he had not breakfasted yet and edged away behind his companions. Wherever I looked eyes dropped and timid hands fidgeted as their owners backed off from my dangerous enthusiasm. There was obviously no help to be had from them, and meantime the precious moments were flying, so with a disdainful glance I turned on my heels and set off alone as hard as I could go for the harbour.

But it was too late. I rushed through the marketplace where all was silent and deserted; I ran on to the wharves beyond and they were empty save for the litter and embers of the fires Ar-hap's men had made during their stay; I dashed out to the landing-place, and there at the hythe the last boat-loads of the villains were just embarking, two boatloads of them twenty yards from shore, and another still upon the beach. This latter was careening over as a dusky group of men lifted aboard to a heap of tumbled silks and stuffs in the stern such a sweet piece of insensible merchandise as no man, I at least of all, could mistake. It was Heru herself, and the rogues were ladling her on board like so much sandal-wood or cotton sheeting. I did not wait for more, but out came my sword, and yielding to a reckless impulse, for which perhaps last night's wine was as much to blame as anything, I sprang down the steps and leapt aboard of the boat just as it was pushed off upon the swift tide. Full of Bersark rage, I cut one brawny copper-coloured thief down, and struck another with my fist between the eyes so that he went headlong into the water, sinking like lead, and deep into the great target of his neighbour's chest I drove my blade. Had there been a man beside me, had there been but two or three of all those silken triflers, too late come on the terraces above to watch, we might have won. But all alone what could I do? That last red beast turned on my blade, and as he fell dragged me half down with him. I staggered up, and tugging the metal from him turned on the next.

At that moment the cause of all the turmoil, roused by the fighting, came to herself, and sitting up on the piled plunder in the boat stared round for a moment with a childish horror at the barbarians whose prize she was, then at me, then at the dead man at my feet whose blood was welling in a red tide from the wound in his breast. As the full meaning of the scene dawned upon her she started to her feet, looking wonderfully beautiful amongst those dusky forms, and extending her hands to me began to cry in the most piteous way. I sprang forward, and as I did so saw an ape-man clap his hairy paw over her mouth and face—it was like an eclipse of the moon by a red earth-shadow, I thought at the moment—and drag her roughly back, but that was about the last I remembered. As I turned to hit him standing on the slippery thwart, another rogue crept up behind and let drive with a club he had in hand. The cudgel caught me sideways on the head, a glancing shot. I can recall a blaze of light, a strange medley of sounds in my ears, and then, clutching at a pile of stuffs as I fell, a tall bower of spray rising on either hand, and the cool shock of the blue sea as I plunged headlong in—but nothing after that!

How long after I know not, but presently a tissue of daylight crept into my eyes, and I awoke again. It was better than nothing perhaps, yet it was a poor awakening. The big sun lay low down, and the day was all but done; so much I guessed as I rocked in that light with an undulating movement, and then as my senses returned more fully, recognised with a start of wonder that I was still in the water, floating on a swift current into the unknown on an air-filled pile of silken stuffs which had been pulled down with me from the boat when I got my ganging from yonder rascal's mace. It was a wet couch, sodden and chilly, but as the freshening evening wind blew on my face and the darkening water lapped against my forehead I revived more fully.

Where had we come to? I turned an aching neck, and all along on both sides seemed to stretch steep, straight coasts about a mile or so apart, in the shadow of the setting sun black as ebony. Between the two the hampered water ran quickly, with, away on the right, some shallow sandy spits and islands covered with dwarf bushes—chilly, inhospitable-looking places they seemed as I turned my eyes upon them; but he who rides helpless down an evening tide stands out for no great niceties of landing-place; could I but reach them they would make at least a drier bed than this of mine, and at that thought, turning over, I found all my muscles as stiff as iron, the sinews of my neck and forearms a mass of agonies and no more fit to swim me to those reedy swamps, which now, as pain and hunger began to tell, seemed to wear the aspects of paradise.

With a groan I dropped back upon my raft and watched the islands slipping by, while over my feet the southern sky darkened to purple. There was no help there, but glancing round away on the left and a few furlongs from me, I noticed on the surface of the water two converging strands of brightness, an angle the point of which seemed to be coming towards me. Nearer it came and nearer, right across my road, until I could see a black dot at the point, a head presently developed, then as we approached the ears and antlers of a swimming stag. It was a huge beast as it loomed up against the glow, bigger than any mortal stag ever was—the kind of fellow-traveller no one would willingly accost, but even if I had wished to get out of its path I had no power to do so.

Closer and closer we came, one of us drifting helplessly, and the other swimming strongly for the islands. When we were about a furlong apart the great beast seemed to change its course, mayhap it took the wreckage on which I floated for an outlying shoal, something on which it could rest a space in that long swim. Be this as it may, the beast came hurtling down on me lip deep in the waves, a mighty brown head with pricked ears that flicked the water from them now and then, small bright eyes set far back, and wide palmated antlers on a mighty forehead, like the dead branches of a tree. What that Martian mountain elk had hoped for can only be guessed, what he met with was a tangle of floating finery carrying a numbed traveller on it, and with a snort of disappointment he turned again.

It was a poor chance, but better than nothing, and as he turned I tried to throw a strand of silk I had unwound from the sodden mass over his branching tines. Quick as thought the beast twisted his head aside and tossed his antlers so that the try was fruitless. But was I to lose my only chance of shore? With all my strength I hurled myself upon him, missing my clutch again by a hair's-breadth and going headlong into the salt furrow his chest was turning up. Happily I kept hold of the web, for the great elk then turned back, passing between me and the ruck of stuff and getting thereby the silk under his chin, and as I came gasping to the top once more round came that dainty wreckage over his back, and I clutched it, and sooner than it takes to tell I was towing to the shore as perhaps no one was ever towed before.

The big beast dragged the ruck like withered weed behind him, bellowing all the time with a voice which made the hills echo all round; and then, when he got his feet upon the shallows, rose dripping and mountainous, a very cliff of black hide and limb against the night shine, and with a single sweep of his antlers tore the webbing from me, who lay prone and breathless in the mud, and, thinking it was his enemy, hurled the limp bundle on the beach, and then, having pounded it with his cloven feet into formless shreds, bellowed again victoriously and went off into the darkness of the forests.

Chapter 9

I landed, stiff enough as you will guess, but pleased to be on shore again. It was a melancholy neighbourhood of low islands, overgrown with rank grass and bushes, salt water encircling them, and inside sandy dunes and hummocks with shallow pools, gleaming ghostly in the retreating daylight, while beyond these rose the black bosses of what looked like a forest. Thither I made my way, plunging uncomfortably through shallows, and tripping over blackened branches which, lying just below the surface, quivered like snakes as the evening breeze ruffled each surface, until the ground hardened under foot, and presently I was standing, hungry and faint but safe, on dry land again.

The forest was so close to the sea, one could not advance without entering it, and once within its dark arcades every way looked equally gloomy and hopeless. I struggled through tangles night made more and more impenetrable each minute, until presently I could go no further, and where a dense canopy of trees overhead gave out for a minute on the edge of a swampy hollow, I determined to wait for daylight.

Never was there a more wet or weary traveller, or one more desperately lonely than he who wrapped himself up in the miserable insufficiency of his wet rags, and without fire or supper crept amongst the exposed roots of a tree growing out of a bank, and prepared to hope grimly for morning.

Round and round meanwhile was drawn the close screen of night, till the clearing in front was blotted out, and only the tree-tops, black as rugged hills one behind the other, stood out against the heavy purple of the circlet of sky above. As the evening deepened the quaintest noises began on every hand—noises so strange and bewildering that as I cowered down with my teeth chattering, and stared hard into the impenetrable, they could be likened to nothing but the crying of all the souls of dead things since the beginning. Never was there such an infernal chorus as that which played up the Martian stars. Down there in front, where hummock grass was growing, some beast squeaked continuously, till I shouted at him, then he stopped a minute, and began again in entirely another note. Away on the hills two rival monsters were calling to each other in tones so hollow they seemed as I listened to penetrate through me, and echo out of my heart again. Far overhead, gigantic bats were flitting, the shadow of their wings dimming a dozen universes at once, and crying to each other in shrill tones that rent the air like tearing silk.

As I listened to those vampires discussing their infernal loves under the stars, from a branch right overhead broke such a deathly howl from the throat of a wandering forest cat that everything else was hushed for a moment. All about a myriad insects were making night giddy with their ghostly fires, while underground and from the labyrinths of matted roots came quaint sounds of rustling snakes and forest pigs, and all the lesser things that dig and scratch and growl.

Yet I was desperately sleepy, my sword hung heavy as lead at my side, my eyelids drooped, and so at last I dozed uneasily for an hour or two. Then, all on a sudden, I came wide awake with a shock. The night was quieter now; away in the forest depth strange noises still arose, but close at hand was a strange hush, like the hush of expectation, and, listening wonderingly, I was aware of slow, heavy footsteps coming up from the river, now two or three steps together, then a pause, then another step or two, and as I bent towards the approaching thing, staring into the darkness, my strained senses were conscious of another approach, as like as could be, coming from behind me. On they came, making the very ground quake with their weight, till I judged that both were about on the edge of the clearing, two vast rat-like shadows, but as big as elephants, and bringing a most intolerable smell of sour slime with them. There, on the edge of the amphitheatre, each for the first time appeared to become aware of the other's presence—the footsteps stopped dead. I could hear the water dripping from the fur of those giant brutes amongst the shadows and the deep breathing of the one nearest me, a scanty ten paces off, but not another sound in the stillness.

Minute after minute passed, yet neither moved. A half-hour grew to a full hour, and that hour lengthened amid the keenest tension till my ears ached with listening, and my eyes were sore with straining into the blackness. At last I began to wonder whether those earth-shaking beasts had not been an evil dream, and was just venturing to stretch out a cramped leg, and rally myself upon my cowardice, when, without warning, at my elbow rose the most ear-piercing scream of rage that ever came from a living throat. There was a sweeping rush in the darkness which I could feel but not see, and with a shock the two gladiators met in the midst of the arena. Over and over they went screaming and struggling, and slipping and plunging. I could hear them tearing at each other, and the sharp cries of pain, first one and then another gave as claw or tooth got home, and all the time, though the ground was quaking under their struggles and the air full of horrible uproar, not a thing was to be seen. I did not even know what manner of beasts they were who rocked and rolled and tore at each other's throats, but I heard their teeth snapping, and their fierce breath in the pauses of the struggle, and could but wait in a huddle amongst the roots until it was over. To and fro they went, now at the far side of the dark clearing, now so close that hot drops of blood from their jaws fell on my face like rain in the darkness. It seemed as though the fight would never end, but presently there was more of worrying in it and less of snapping; it was clear one or the other had had enough and as I marked this those black shadows came gasping and struggling towards me. There was a sudden sharp cry, a desperate final tussle—before which strong trees snapped and bushes were flattened out like grass, not twenty yards away—and then for a minute all was silent.

One of them had killed, and as I sat rooted to the spot I was forced to listen while his enemy tore him up and ate him. Many a banquet have I been at, but never an uglier one than that. I sat in the darkness while the unknown thing at my feet ripped the flesh from his half-dead rival in strips, and across the damp night wind came the reek of that abominable feast—the reek of blood and spilt entrails—until I turned away my face in loathing, and was nearly starting to my feet to venture a rush into the forest shadows. But I was spellbound, and remained listening to the heavy munch of blood-stained jaws until presently I was aware other and lesser feasters were coming. There was a twinkle of hungry eyes all about the limits of the area, the shine of green points of envious fire that circled round in decreasing orbits, as the little foxes and jackals came crowding in. One fellow took me for a rock, so still I sat, putting his hot, soft paws upon my knee for a space, and others passed me so near I could all but touch them.

The big beast had taken himself off by this time, and there must have been several hundreds of these newcomers. A merry time they had of it; the whole place was full of the green, hurrying eyes, and amidst the snap of teeth and yapping and quarrelling I could hear the flesh being torn from the red bones in every direction. One wolf-like individual brought a mass of hot liver to eat between my feet, but I gave him a kick, and sent him away much to his surprise. Gradually, however, the sound of this unholy feast died away, and, though you may hardly believe it, I fell off into a doze. It was not sleep, but it served the purpose, and when in an hour or two a draught of cool air roused me, I awoke, feeling more myself again.

Slowly morning came, and the black wall of forest around became full of purple interstices as the east brightened. Those glimmers of light between bough and trunk turned to yellow and red, the day-shine presently stretched like a canopy from point to point of the treetops on either side of my sleeping-place, and I arose.

All my limbs were stiff with cold, my veins emptied by hunger and wounds, and for a space I had not even strength to move. But a little rubbing softened my cramped muscles presently and limping painfully down to the place of combat, I surveyed the traces of that midnight fight. I will not dwell upon it. It was ugly and grim; the trampled grass, the giant footmarks, each enringing its pool of curdled blood; the broken bushes, the grooved mud-slides where the unknown brutes had slid in deadly embrace; the hollows, the splintered boughs, their ragged points tufted with skin and hair— all was sickening to me. Yet so hungry was I that when I turned towards the odious remnants of the vanquished—a shapeless mass of abomination—my thoughts flew at once to breakfasting! I went down and inspected the victim cautiously—a huge rat-like beast as far as might be judged from the bare uprising ribs—all that was left of him looking like the framework of a schooner yacht. His heart lay amongst the offal, and my knife came out to cut a meal from it, but I could not do it. Three times I essayed the task, hunger and disgust contending for mastery; three times turned back in loathing. At last I could stand the sight no more, and, slamming the knife up again, turned on my heels, and fairly ran for fresh air and the shore, where the sea was beginning to glimmer in the light a few score yards through the forest stems. There, once more out on the open, on a pebbly beach, I stripped, spreading my things out to dry on the stones, and laying myself down with the lapping of the waves in my ears, and the first yellow sunshine thawing my limbs, tried to piece together the hurrying events of the last few days.

What were my gay Martians doing? Lazy dogs to let me, a stranger, be the only one to draw sword in defence of their own princess! Where was poor Heru, that sweet maiden wife? The thought of her in the hands of the ape-men was odious. And yet was I not mad to try to rescue, or even to follow her alone? If by any chance I could get off this beast-haunted place and catch up with the ravishers, what had I to look for from them except speedy extinction, and that likely enough by the most painful process they were acquainted with?

The other alternative of going back empty handed was terribly ignominious. I had lectured the amiable young manhood of Seth so soundly on the subject of gallantry, and set them such a good example on two occasions, that it would be bathos to saunter back, hands in pockets, and confess I knew nothing of the lady's fate and had been daunted by the first night alone in the forest. Besides, how dull it would be in that beautiful, tumble-down old city without Heru, with no expectation day by day of seeing her sylph-like form and hearing the merry tinkle of her fairy laughter as she scoffed at the unknown learning collected by her ancestors in a thousand laborious years. No! I would go on for certain. I was young, in love, and angry, and before those qualifications difficulties became light.

Meanwhile, the first essential was breakfast of some kind. I arose, stretched, put on my half-dried clothes, and mounting a low hummock on the forest edge looked around. The sun was riding up finely into the sky, and the sea to the eastward shone for leagues and leagues in the loveliest azure. Where it rippled on my own beach and those of the low islands noted over night, a wonderful fire of blue and red played on the sands as though the broken water were full of living gems. The sky was full of strange gulls with long, forked tails, and a lovely little flying lizard with transparent wings of the palest green—like those of a grasshopper—was flitting about picking up insect stragglers.

All this was very charming, but what I kept saying to myself was "Streaky rashers and hot coffee: rashers and coffee and rolls," and, indeed, had the gates of Paradise themselves opened at that moment I fear my first look down the celestial streets within would have been for a restaurant. They did not, and I was just turning away disconsolate when my eye caught, ascending from behind the next bluff down the beach, a thin strand of smoke rising into the morning air.

It was nothing so much in itself—a thin spiral creeping upwards mast-high, then flattening out into a mushroom head—but it meant everything to me. Where there was fire there must be humanity, and where there was humanity—ay, to the very outlayers of the universe— there must be breakfast. It was a splendid thought; I rushed down the hillock and went gaily for that blue thread amongst the reeds. It was not two hundred yards away, and soon below me was a tiny bay with bluest water frilling a silver beach, and in the midst of it a fire on a hearth dancing round a pot that simmered gloriously. But of an owner there was nothing to be seen. I peered here and there on the shore, but nothing moved, while out to sea the water was shining like molten metal with not a dot upon it!—what did it matter? I laughed as, pleased and hungry, I slipped down the bank and strode across the sands; it pleased Fate to play bandy with me, and if it sent me supperless to bed, why, here was restitution in the way of breakfast. I took up a morsel of the stuff in the kettle on a handy stick and found it good—indeed, I knew it at once as a very dainty mess made from the roots of a herb the Martians greatly liked; An had piled my platter with it when we supped that night in the market-place of Seth, and the sweet white stuff had melted into my corporal essence, it seemed, without any gross intermediate process of digestion. And here I was again, hungry, sniffing the fragrant breath of a full meal and not a soul in sight—I should have been a fool not to have eaten. So thinking, down I sat, taking the pot from its place, and when it was a little cool plunging my hands into it and feasting with as good an appetite as ever a man had before.

It was gloriously ambrosial, and deeper and deeper I went, with the tall stalk of the smoke in front growing from the hearth-stones like some strange new plant, the pleasant sunshine on my back, and never a thought for anything but the task in hand. Deeper and deeper, oblivious of all else, until to get the very last drops I lifted the pipkin up and putting back my head drank in that fashion.

It was only when with a sigh of pleasure I lowered it slowly again that over the rim as it sank there dawned upon me the vision of a Martian standing by an empty canoe on the edge of the water and regarding me with calm amazement. I was, in fact, so astonished that for a minute the empty pot stood still before my face, and over its edge we stared at each other in mute surprise, then with all the dignity that might be I laid the vessel down between my feet and waited for the newcomer to speak. She was a girl by her yellow garb, a fisherwoman, it seemed, for in the prow of her craft was piled a net upon which the scales of fishes were twinkling—a Martian, obviously, but something more robust than most of them, a savour of honest work about her sunburnt face which my pallid friends away yonder were lacking in, and when we had stared at each other for a few moments in silence she came forward a step or two and said without a trace of fear or shyness, "Are you a spirit, sir?

"Why," I answered, "about as much, no more and no less, than most of us."

"Aye," she said. "I thought you were, for none but spirits live here upon this island; are you for good or evil?"

"Far better for the breakfast of which I fear I have robbed you, but wandering along the shore and finding this pot boiling with no owner, I ventured to sample it, and it was so good my appetite got the better of manners."

The girl bowed, and standing at a respectful distance asked if I would like some fish as well; she had some, but not many, and if I would eat she would cook them for me in a minute—it was not often, she added lightly, she had met one of my kind before. In fact, it was obvious that simple person did actually take me for a being of another world, and was it for me to say she was wrong? So adopting a dignity worthy of my reputation I nodded gravely to her offer. She fetched from the boat four little fishes of the daintiest kind imaginable. They were each about as big as a hand and pale blue when you looked down upon them, but so clear against the light that every bone and vein in their bodies could be traced. These were wrapped just as they were in a broad, green leaf and then the Martian, taking a pointed stick, made a hollow in the white ashes, laid them in side by side, and drew the hot dust over again.

While they cooked we chatted as though the acquaintance were the most casual thing in the world, and I found it was indeed an island we were on and not the mainland, as I had hoped at first. Seth, she told me, was far away to the eastward, and if the woodmen had gone by in their ships they would have passed round to the north-west of where we were.

I spent an hour or two with that amiable individual, and, it is to be hoped, sustained the character of a spiritual visitant with considerable dignity. In one particular at least, that, namely, of appetite, I did honour to my supposed source, and as my entertainer would not hear of payment in material kind, all I could do was to show her some conjuring tricks, which greatly increased her belief in my supernatural origin, and to teach her some new hitches and knots, using her fishing-line as a means of illustration, a demonstration which called from her the natural observation that we must be good sailors "up aloft" since we knew so much about cordage, then we parted.

She had seen nothing of the woodmen, though she had heard they had been to Seth and thought, from some niceties of geographical calculation which I could not follow, they would have crossed to the north, as just stated, of her island. There she told me, with much surprise at my desire for the information, how I might, by following

EDWIN L. ARNOLD

the forest track to the westward coast, make my way to a fishing village, where they would give me a canoe and direct me, since such was my extraordinary wish, to the place where, if anywhere, the wild men had touched on their way home.

She filled my wallet with dried honey-cakes and my mouth with sugar plums from her little store, then down on her knees went that poor waif of a worn-out civilisation and kissed my hands in humble farewell, and I, blushing to be so saluted, and after all but a sailor, got her by the rosy fingers and lifted her up shoulder high, and getting one hand under her chin and the other behind her head kissed her twice upon her pretty cheeks; and so, I say, we parted.

Chapter 10

Off into the forest I went, feeling a boyish elation to be so free nor taking heed or count of the reckless adventure before me. The Martian weather for the moment was lovely and the many-coloured grass lush and soft under foot. Mile after mile I went, heeding the distance lightly, the air was so elastic. Now pressing forward as the main interest of my errand took the upper hand, and remembrance of poor Heru like a crushed white flower in the red grip of those cruel ravishers came upon me, and then pausing to sigh with pleasure or stand agape—forgetful even of her—in wonder of the unknown loveliness about me.

And well might I stare! Everything in that forest was wonderful! There were plants which turned from colour to colour with the varying hours of the day. While others had a growth so swift it was dangerous to sit in their neighbourhood since the long, succulent tendrils clambering from the parent stem would weave you into a helpless tangle while you gazed, fascinated, upon them. There were plants that climbed and walked; sighing plants who called the winged things of the air to them with a noise so like to a girl sobbing that again and again I stopped in the tangled path to listen. There were green bladder-mosses which swam about the surface of the still pools like gigantic frog-broods. There were on the ridges warrior trees burning in the vindictiveness of a long forgotten cause—a blaze of crimson scimitar thorns from root to topmost twig; and down again in the cool hollows were lady-bushes making twilight of the green gloom with their cloudy ivory blossoms and filling the shadows with such a heavy scent that head and heart reeled with fatal pleasure as one pushed aside their branches. Every river-bed was full of mighty reeds, whose stems clattered together when the wind blew like swords on shields, and every now and then a bit of forest was woven together with the ropey stems of giant creepers till no man or beast could have passed save for the paths which constant use had kept open through the mazes.

All day long I wandered on through those wonderful woodlands, and in fact loitered so much over their infinite marvels that when sundown came all too soon there was still undulating forest everywhere, vistas of fairy glades on every hand, peopled with incredible things and echoing with sounds that excited the ears as much as other things fascinated the eyes, but no sign of the sea or my fishing village anywhere.

It did not matter; a little of the Martian leisureliness was getting into my blood: "If not today, why then tomorrow," as An would have said; and with this for comfort I selected a warm, sandy hollow under the roots of a big tree, made my brief arrangements for the night, ate some honey cakes, and was soon sleeping blissfully.

I woke early next morning, after many hours of interrupted dreams, and having nothing to do till the white haze had lifted and made it possible to start again, rested idly a time on my elbow and watched the sunshine filter into the recesses.

Very pretty it was to see the thick canopy overhead, by star-light so impenetrable, open its chinks and fissures as the searching sun came upon it; to see the pin-hole gaps shine like spangles presently, the spaces broaden into lesser suns, and even the thick leafage brighten and shine down on me with a soft sea-green radiance. The sunward sides of the tree-stems took a glow, and the dew that ran dripping down their mossy sides trickled blood-red to earth. Elsewhere the shadows were still black, and strange things began to move in them—things we in our middle-aged world have never seen the likeness of: beasts half birds, birds half creeping things, and creeping things which it seemed to me passed through lesser creations down to the basest life that crawls without interruption or division.

It was not for me, a sailor, to know much of such things, yet some I could not fail to notice. On one grey branch overhead, jutting from a tree-stem where a patch of velvet moss made in the morning glint a fairy bed, a wonderful flower unfolded. It was a splendid bud, ivory white, cushioned in leaves, and secured to its place by naked white roots that clipped the branch like fingers of a lady's hand. Even as I looked it opened, a pale white star, and hung pensive and inviting on its mossy cushion. From it came such a ravishing odour that even I, at the further end of the great scale of life, felt my pulses quicken and my eyes brighten with cupidity. I was in the very act of climbing the tree, but before I could move hand or foot two things happened, whether you take my word for them or no.

Firstly, up through a glade in the underwood, attracted by the odour, came an ugly brown bird with a capacious beak and shining claws. He perched near by, and peeped and peered until he made out the flower pining on her virgin stem, whereat off he hopped to her branch and there, with a cynical chuckle, strutted to and fro between her and the main stem like an ill genius guarding a fairy princess.

Surely Heaven would not allow him to tamper with so chaste a bud! My hand reached for a stone to throw at him when happened the second thing. There came a gentle pat upon the woodland floor, and from a tree overhead dropped down another living plant like to the one above yet not exactly similar, a male, my instincts told me, in full solitary blossom like her above, cinctured with leaves, and supported by half a score of thick white roots that worked, as I looked, like the limbs of a crab. In a twinkling that parti-coloured gentleman vegetable near me was off to the stem upon which grew his lady love; running and scrambling, dragging the finery of his tasselled petals behind, it was laughable to watch his eagerness. He got a grip of the tree and up he went, "hand over hand," root over root. I had just time to note others of his species had dropped here and there upon the ground, and were hurrying with frantic haste to the same destination when he reached the fatal branch, and was straddling victoriously down it, blind to all but love and longing. That ill-omened bird who stood above the maiden-flower let him come within a stalk's length, so near that the white splendour of his sleeping lady gleamed within arms' reach, then the great beak was opened, the great claws made a clutch, the gallant's head was yanked from his neck, and as it went tumbling down the maw of the feathered thing his white legs fell spinning through space, and lay knotting themselves in agony upon the ground for a minute or two before they relaxed and became flaccid in the repose of death. Another and another vegetable suitor made for that fatal tryst, and as each came up the snap of the brown bird's beak was all their obsequies. At last no more came, and then that Nemesis of claws and quills walked over to the girl-flower, his stomach feathers ruffled with repletion, the green blood of her lovers dripping from his claws, and pulled her golden heart out, tore her white limbs one from the other, and swallowed her piecemeal before my very eyes! Then up in wrath I jumped and yelled at him till the woods echoed, but too late to stay his sacrilege.

By this time the sun was bathing everything in splendour, and turning away from the wonders about me, I set off at best pace along the well-trodden path which led without turning to the west coast village where the canoes were.

It proved far closer than expected. As a matter of fact the forest in this direction grew right down to the water's edge; the salt-loving trees actually overhanging the waves—one of the pleasantest sights in nature—and thus I came right out on top of the hamlet before there

EDWIN L. ARNOLD

had been an indication of its presence. It occupied two sides of a pretty little bay, the third side being flat land given over to the cultivation of an enormous species of gourd whose characteristic yellow flowers and green, succulent leaves were discernible even at this distance.

I branched off along the edge of the surf and down a dainty little flowery path, noticing meanwhile how the whole bay was filled by hundreds of empty canoes, while scores of others were drawn up on the strand, and then the first thing I chanced upon was a group of people—youthful, of course, with the eternal Martian bloom—and in the splendid simplicity of almost complete nakedness. My first idea was that they were bathing, and fixing my eyes on the tree-tops with great propriety, I gave a warning cough. At that sound instead of getting to cover, or clothes, all started up and stood staring for a time like a herd of startled cattle. It was highly embarrassing; they were right in the path, a round dozen of them, naked and so little ashamed that when I edged away modestly they began to run after me. And the farther they came forward the more I retired, till we were playing a kind of game of hide-and-seek round the tree-stems. In the middle of it my heel caught in a root and down I went very hard and very ignominiously, whereon those laughing, light-hearted folk rushed in, and with smiles and jests helped me to my feet.

"Was I the traveller who had come from Seth?"

"Yes."

"Oh, then that was well. They had heard such a traveller was on the road, and had come a little way down the path, as far as might be without fatigue, to meet him."

"Would I eat with them?" these amiable strangers asked, pushing their soft warm fingers into mine and ringing me round with a circle. "But firstly might they help me out of my clothes? It was hot, and these things were cumbersome." As to the eating, I was agreeable enough seeing how casual meals had been with me lately, but my clothes, though Heaven knows they were getting horribly ragged and travel-stained, I clung to desperately.

My new friends shrugged their dimpled shoulders and, arguments being tedious, at once squatted round me in the dappled shade of a big tree and produced their stores of never failing provisions. After a pleasant little meal taken thus in the open and with all the simplicity Martians delight in, we got to talking about those yellow canoes which were bobbing about on the blue waters of the bay.

"Would you like to see where they are grown?" asked an individual basking by my side.

"Grown!" I answered with incredulity. "Built, you mean. Never in my life did I hear of growing boats."

"But then, sir," observed the girl as she sucked the honey out of the stalk of an azure convolvulus flower and threw the remains at a butterfly that sailed across the sunshine, "you know so little! You have come from afar, from some barbarous and barren district. Here we undoubtedly grow our boats, and though we know the Thither folk and such uncultivated races make their craft by cumbrous methods of flat planks, yet we prefer our own way, for one thing because it saves trouble," and as she murmured that all-sufficient reason the gentle damsel nodded reflectively.

But one of her companions, more lively for the moment, tickled her with a straw until she roused, and then said, "Let us take the stranger to the boat garden now. The current will drift us round the bay, and we can come back when it turns. If we wait we shall have to row in both directions, or even walk," and again planetary slothfulness carried the day.

So down to the beach we strolled and launched one of the golden-hued skiffs upon the pretty dancing wavelets just where they ran, lipped with jewelled spray, on the shore, and then only had I a chance to scrutinise their material. I patted that one we were upon inside and out. I noted with a seaman's admiration its lightness, elasticity, and supreme sleekness, its marvellous buoyancy and fairy-like "lines," and after some minutes' consideration it suddenly flashed across me that it was all of gourd rind. And as if to supply confirmation, the flat land we were approaching on the opposite side of the bay was covered by the characteristic verdure of these plants with a touch here and there of splendid yellow blossoms, but all of gigantic proportions.

"Ay," said a Martian damsel lying on the bottom, and taking and kissing my hand as she spoke, in the simple-hearted way of her people, "I see you have guessed how we make our boats. Is it the same in your distant country?"

"No, my girl, and what's more, I am a bit uneasy as to what the fellows on the Carolina will say if they ever hear I went to sea in a hollowed-out pumpkin, and with a young lady—well, dressed as you are—for crew. Even now I cannot imagine how you get your ships so trim and shapely—there is not a seam or a patch anywhere, it looks as if you had run them into a mould."

"That's just what we have done, sir, and now you will witness the moulds at work, for here we are," and the little skiff was pulled ashore and the Martians and I jumped out on the shelving beach, hauled our boat up high and dry, and there right over us, like great green umbrellas, spread the fronds of the outmost garden of this strangest of all ship-building yards. Briefly, and not to make this part of my story too long, those gilded boys and girls took me ashore, and chattering like finches in the evening, showed how they planted their gourd seed, nourished the gigantic plants as they grew with brackish water and the burnt ashes; then, when they flowered, mated the male and female blossoms, glorious funnels of golden hue big enough for one to live in; and when the young fruit was of the bigness of an ordinary bolster, how they slipped it into a double mould of open reed-work something like the two halves of a walnut-shell; and how, growing day by day in this, it soon took every curve and line they chose to give it, even the hanging keel below, the strengthened bulwarks, and tall prow-piece. It was so ingenious, yet simple; and I confess I laughed over my first skiff "on the stalk," and fell to bantering the Martians, asking whether it was a good season for navies, whether their Cunarders were spreading nicely, if they could give me a pinch of barge seed, or a yacht in bud to show to my friends at home.

But those lazy people took the matter seriously enough. They led me down green alleys arched over with huge melon-like leaves; they led me along innumerable byways, making me peep and peer through the chequered sunlight at ocean-growing craft, that had budded twelve months before, already filling their moulds to the last inch of space. They told me that when the growing process was sufficiently advanced, they loosened the casing, and cutting a hole into the interior of each giant fruit, scooped out all its seed, thereby checking more advance, and throwing into the rind strength that would otherwise have gone to reproductiveness. They said each fruit made two vessels, but the upper half was always best and used for long salt-water journeys, the lower piece being but for punting or fishing on their lakes. They cut them in half while still green, scraped out the light remaining pulp when dry, and dragged them down with the minimum of trouble, light as feathers, tenacious as steel plate, and already in the form and fashion of dainty craft from five to twenty feet in length, when the process was completed.

By the time we had explored this strangest of ship-building yards, and I had seen last year's crop on the stocks being polished and fitted with seats and gear, the sun was going down; and the Martian twilight, owing to the comparative steepness of the little planet's sides, being brief, we strolled back to the village, and there they gave me harbourage for the night, ambrosial supper, and a deep draught of the wine of Forgetfulness, under the gauzy spell of which the real and unreal melted into the vistas of rosy oblivion, and I slept.

Chapter 11

With the new morning came fresh energy and a spasm of conscience as I thought of poor Heru and the shabby sort of rescuer I was to lie about with these pretty triflers while she remained in peril.

So I had a bath and a swim, a breakfast, and, to my shame be it acknowledged, a sort of farewell merry-go-round dance on the yellow sands with a dozen young persons all light-hearted as the morning, beautiful as the flowers that bound their hair, and in the extremity of statuesque attire.

Then at last I got them to give me a sea-going canoe, a stock of cakes and fresh water; and with many parting injunctions how to find the Woodman trail, since I would not listen to reason and lie all the rest of my life with them in the sunshine, they pushed me off on my lonely voyage.

"Over the blue waters!" they shouted in chorus as I dipped my paddle into the diamond-crested wavelets. "Six hours, adventurous stranger, with the sun behind you! Then into the broad river behind the yellow sand-bar. But not the black northward river! Not the strong, black river, above all things, stranger! For that is the River of the Dead, by which many go but none come back. Goodbye!" And waving them adieu, I sternly turned my eyes from delights behind and faced the fascination of perils in front.

In four hours (for the Martians had forgotten in their calculations that my muscles were something better than theirs) I "rose" the further shore, and then the question was, Where ran that westward river of theirs?

It turned out afterwards that, knowing nothing of their tides, I had drifted much too far to northward, and consequently the coast had closed up the estuary mouth I should have entered. Not a sign of an opening showed anywhere, and having nothing whatever for guidance I turned northward, eagerly scanning an endless line of low cliffs, as the day lessened, for the promised sand-bar or inlet.

About dusk my canoe, flying swiftly forward at its own sweet will, brought me into a bight, a bare, desolate-looking country with no vegetation save grass and sedge on the near marshes and stony hills rising up beyond, with others beyond them mounting step by step to a long line of ridges and peaks still covered in winter snow.

The outlook was anything but cheering. Not a trace of habitation had been seen for a long time, not a single living being in whose neighbourhood I could land and ask the way; nothing living anywhere but a monstrous kind of sea-slug, as big as a dog, battening on the waterside garbage, and gaunt birds like vultures who croaked on the mud-flats, and half-spread wings of funereal blackness as they gambolled here and there. Where was poor Heru? Where pink-shouldered An? Where those wild men who had taken the princess from us? Lastly, but not least, where was I?

All the first stars of the Martian sky were strange to me, and my boat whirling round and round on the current confused what little geography I might otherwise have retained. It was a cheerless look out, and again and again I cursed my folly for coming on such a fool's errand as I sat, chin in hand, staring at a landscape that grew more and more depressing every mile. To go on looked like destruction, to go back was almost impossible without a guide; and while I was still wondering which of the two might be the lesser evil, the stream I was on turned a corner, and in a moment we were upon water which ran with swift, oily smoothness straight for the snow-ranges now beginning to loom unpleasantly close ahead.

By this time the night was coming on apace, the last of the evil-looking birds had winged its way across the red sunset glare, and though it was clear enough in mid-river under the banks, now steep and unclimbable, it was already evening.

And with the darkness came a wondrous cold breath from off the ice-fields, blowing through my lowland wrappings as though they were but tissue. I munched a bit of honey-cake, took a cautious sip of wine, and though I will not own I was frightened, yet no one will deny that the circumstances were discouraging.

Standing up in the frail canoe and looking around, at the second glance an object caught my eye coming with the stream, and rapidly overtaking me on a strong sluice of water. It was a raft of some sort, and something extra-ordinarily like a sitting Martian on it! Nearer and nearer it came, bobbing to the rise and fall of each wavelet with the last icy sunlight touching it up with reds and golds, nearer and nearer in the deadly hush of that forsaken region, and then at last so near it showed quite plainly on the purple water, a raft with some one sitting under a canopy.

With a thrill of delight I waved my cap aloft and shouted—

"Ship-ahoy! Hullo, messmate, where are we bound to?"

But never an answer came from that swiftly-passing stranger, so again I hailed—

"Put up your helm, Mr. Skipper; I have lost my bearings, and the chronometer has run down," but without a pause or sound that strange craft went slipping by.

That silence was more than I could stand. It was against all sea courtesies, and the last chance of learning where I was passing away. So, angrily the paddle was snatched from the canoe bottom, and roaring out again—

"Stop, I say, you d——lubber, stop, or by all the gods I will make you!" I plunged the paddle into the water and shot my little craft slantingly across the stream to intercept the newcomer. A single stroke sent me into mid-stream, a second brought me within touch of that strange craft. It was a flat raft, undoubtedly, though so disguised by flowers and silk trailers that its shape was difficult to make out. In the centre was a chair of ceremony bedecked with greenery and great pale buds, hardly yet withered—oh, where had I seen such a chair and such a raft before?

And the riddle did not long remain unanswered. Upon that seat, as I swept up alongside and laid a sunburnt hand upon its edge, was a girl, and another look told me she was dead!

Such a sweet, pallid, Martian maid, her fair head lolling back against the rear of the chair and gently moving to and fro with the rise and fall of her craft. Her face in the pale light of the evening like carved ivory, and not less passionless and still; her arms bare, and her poor fingers still closed in her lap upon the beautiful buds they had put into them. I fairly gasped with amazement at the dreadful sweetness of that solitary lady, and could hardly believe she was really a corpse! But, alas! there was no doubt of it, and I stared at her, half in admiration and half in fear; noting how the last sunset flush lent a hectic beauty to her face for a moment, and then how fair and ghostly she stood out against the purpling sky; how her light drapery lifted to the icy wind, and how dreadfully strange all those soft-scented flowers and trappings seemed as we sped along side by side into the country of night and snow.

Then all of a sudden the true meaning of her being there burst upon me, and with a start and a cry I looked around. *We were flying swiftly down that river of the dead they had told me of that has no outlet and no returning!*

With frantic haste I snatched up a paddle again and tried to paddle against the great black current sweeping us forward. I worked until the perspiration stood in beads on my forehead, and all the time I worked the river, like some black snake, hissed and twined, and that pretty lady rode cheerily along at my side. Overhead stars of unearthly brilliancy were coming out in the frosty sky, while on either hand the banks were high and the shadows under them black as ink. In those shadows now and then I noticed with a horrible indifference other rafts were travelling, and presently, as the stream narrowed, they came out and joined us, dead Martians, budding boys and girls; older voyagers with their age quickening upon them in the Martian manner, just as some fruit only ripens after it falls; yellow-girt slaves staring into the night in front, quite a merry crew all clustered about I and that gentle lady, and more far ahead and more behind, all bobbing and jostling forward as we hurried to the dreadful graveyard in the Martian regions of eternal winter none had ever seen and no one came to! I cried aloud in my desolation and fear and hid my face in my hands, while the icy cliffs mocked my cry and the dead maid, tripping alongside, rolled her head over, and stared at me with stony, unseeing eyes.

Well, I am no fine writer. I sat down to tell a plain, unvarnished tale, and I will not let the weird horror of that ride get into my pen. We careened forward, I and those lost Martians, until pretty near on midnight, by which time the great light-giving planets were up, and never a chance did Fate give me all that time of parting company with them. About midnight we were right into the region of snow and ice, not the actual polar region of the planet, as I afterwards guessed, but one of those long outliers which follow the course of the broad waterways almost into fertile regions, and the cold, though intense, was somewhat modified by the complete stillness of the air.

It was just then that I began to be aware of a low, rumbling sound ahead, increasing steadily until there could not be any doubt the journey was nearly over and we were approaching those great falls An had told me of, over which the dead tumble to perpetual oblivion. There was no opportunity for action, and, luckily, little time for thought. I remember clapping my hand to my heart as I muttered an imperfect prayer, and laughing a little as I felt in my pocket, between it and that organ, an envelope containing some corn-plaster and a packet of unpaid tailors' bills. Then I pulled out that locket with poor forgotten Polly's photograph, and while I was still kissing it fervently, and the dead girl on my right was jealously nudging my canoe with the corner of her raft, we plunged into a narrow gully as black as hell, shot round a sharp

EDWIN L. ARNOLD

corner at a tremendous pace, and the moment afterwards entered a lake in the midst of an unbroken amphitheatre of cliffs gleaming in soft light all round.

Even to this moment I can recall the blue shine of those terrible ice crags framing the weird picture in on every hand, and the strange effect upon my mind as we passed out of the darkness of the gully down which we had come into the sepulchral radiance of that place. But though it fixed with one instantaneous flash its impression on my mind forever, there was no time to admire it. As we swept on to the lake's surface, and a glance of light coming over a dip in the ice walls to the left lit up the dead faces and half-withered flowers of my fellow-travellers with startling distinctness, I noticed with a new terror at the lower end of the lake towards which we were hurrying the water suddenly disappeared in a cloud of frosty spray, and it was from thence came the low, ominous rumble which had sounded up the ravine as we approached. It was the fall, and beyond the stream dropped down glassy step after step, in wild pools and rapids, through which no boat could live for a moment, to a black cavern entrance, where it was swallowed up in eternal night.

I *would* not go that way! With a yell such as those solitudes had probably never heard since the planet was fashioned out of the void, I seized the paddle again and struck out furiously from the main current, with the result of postponing the crisis for a time, and finding myself bobbing round towards the northern amphitheatre, where the light fell clearest from planets overhead. It was like a great ballroom with those constellations for tapers, and a ghastly crowd of Martians were doing cotillions and waltzes all about me on their rafts as the troubled water, icy cold and clear as glass, eddied us here and there in solemn confusion. On the narrow beaches at the cliff foot were hundreds of wrecked voyagers—the wall-flowers of that ghostly assembly-room— and I went jostling and twirling round the circle as though looking for a likely partner, until my brain spun and my heart was sick.

For twenty minutes Fate played with me, and then the deadly suck of the stream got me down again close to where the water began to race for the falls. I vowed savagely I would not go over them if it could be helped, and struggled furiously.

On the left, in shadow, a narrow beach seemed to lie between the water and the cliff foot; towards it I fought. At the very first stroke I fouled a raft; the occupant thereof came tumbling aboard and nearly swamped me. But now it was a fight for life, so him I seized without ceremony by clammy neck and leg and threw back into the water. Then another playful Martian butted the behind part of my canoe and set it spinning, so that all the stars seemed to be dancing giddily in the sky. With a yell I shoved him off, but only to find his comrades were closing round me in a solid ring as we sucked down to the abyss at ever-increasing speed.

Then I fought like a fury, hacking, pushing, and paddling shorewards, crying out in my excitement, and spinning and bumping and twisting ever downwards. For every foot I gained they pushed me on a yard, as though determined their fate should be mine also.

They crowded round me in a compact circle, their poor flower-girt heads nodding as the swift current curtsied their crafts. They hemmed me in with desperate persistency as we spun through the ghostly starlight in a swirling mass down to destruction! And in a minute we were so close to the edge of the fall I could see the water break into ridges as it felt the solid bottom give way under it. We were so close that already the foremost rafts, ten yards ahead, were tipping and their occupants one by one waving their arms about and tumbling from their funeral chairs as they shot into the spray veil and went out of sight under a faint rainbow that was arched over there, the symbol of peace and the only lovely thing in that gruesome region. Another minute and I must have gone with them. It was too late to think of getting out of the tangle then; the water behind was heavy with trailing silks and flowers. We were jammed together almost like one huge float and in that latter fact lay my one chance.

On the left was a low ledge of rocks leading back to the narrow beach already mentioned, and the ledge came out to within a few feet of where the outmost boat on that side would pass it. It was the only chance and a poor one, but already the first rank of my fleet was trembling on the brink, and without stopping to weigh matters I bounded off my own canoe on to the raft alongside, which rocked with my weight like a tea-tray. From that I leapt, with such hearty good-will as I had never had before, on to a second and third. I jumped from the footstool of one Martian to the knee of another, steadying myself by a free use of their nodding heads as I passed. And every time I jumped a ship collapsed behind me. As I staggered with my spring into the last and outermost boat the ledge was still six feet away, half hidden in a smother of foam, and the rim of the great fall just under it. Then I drew all my sailor agility together and just as the little vessel was going bow up over the

EDWIN L. ARNOLD

edge I leapt from her—came down blinded with spray on the ledge, rolled over and over, clutched frantically at the frozen soil, and was safe for the moment, but only a few inches from the vortex below!

As soon as I picked myself up and got breath, I walked shorewards and found, with great satisfaction, that the ledge joined the shelving beach, and so walked on in the blue obscurity of the cliff shadow back from the falls in the bare hope that the beach might lead by some way into the gully through which we had come and open country beyond. But after a couple of hundred yards this hope ended as abruptly as the spit itself in deep water, and there I was, as far as the darkness would allow me to ascertain, as utterly trapped as any mortal could be.

I will not dwell on the next few minutes, for no one likes to acknowledge that he has been unmanned even for a space. When those minutes were over calmness and consideration returned, and I was able to look about.

All the opposite cliffs, rising sheer from the water, were in light, their cold blue and white surfaces rising far up into the black starfields overhead. Looking at them intently from this vantage-point I saw without at first understanding that along them horizontally, tier above tier, were rows of objects, like—like—why, good Heavens, they were like men and women in all sorts of strange postures and positions! Rubbing my eyes and looking again I perceived with a start and a strange creepy feeling down my back that they *were* men and women!—hundreds of them, thousands, all in rows as cormorants stand upon sea-side cliffs, myriads and myriads now I looked about, in every conceivable pose and attitude but never a sound, never a movement amongst the vast concourse.

Then I turned back to the cliffs behind me. Yes! they ere there too, dimmer by reason of the shadows, but there for certain, from the snowfields far above down, down—good Heavens! to the very level where I stood. There was one of them not ten yards away half in and half out of the ice wall, and setting my teeth I walked over and examined him. And there was another further in behind as I peered into the clear blue depth, another behind that one, another behind him—just like cherries in a jelly.

It was startling and almost incredible, yet so many wonderful things had happened of late that wonders were losing their sharpness, and I was soon examining the cliff almost as coolly as though it were only some trivial geological "section," some new kind of petrified sea-urchins which had caught my attention and not a whole nation in ice, a huge amphitheatre of fossilised humanity which stared down on me.

The matter was simple enough when you came to look at it with philosophy. The Martians had sent their dead down here for many thousand years and as they came they were frozen in, the bands and zones in which they sat indicating perhaps alternating seasons. Then after Nature had been storing them like that for long ages some upheaval happened, and this cleft and lake opened through the heart of the preserve. Probably the river once ran far up there where the starlight was crowning the blue cliffs with a silver diadem of light, only when this hollow opened did it slowly deepen a lower course, spreading out in a lake, and eventually tumbling down those icy steps lose itself in the dark roots of the hills. It was very simple, no doubt, but incredibly weird and wonderful to me who stood, the sole living thing in that immense concourse of dead humanity.

Look where I would it was the same everywhere. Those endless rows of frozen bodies lying, sitting, or standing stared at me from every niche and cornice. It almost seemed, as the light veered slowly round, as though they smiled and frowned at times, but never a word was there amongst those millions; the silence itself was audible, and save the dull low thunder of the fall, so monotonous the ear became accustomed to and soon disregarded it, there was not a sound anywhere, not a rustle, not a whisper broke the eternal calm of that great caravansary of the dead.

The very rattle of the shingle under my feet and the jingle of my navy scabbard seemed offensive in the perfect hush, and, too awed to be frightened, I presently turned away from the dreadful shine of those cliffs and felt my way along the base of the wall on my own side. There was no means of escape that way, and presently the shingle beach itself gave out as stated, where the cliff wall rose straight from the surface of the lake, so I turned back, and finding a grotto in the ice determined to make myself as comfortable as might be until daylight came.

Chapter 12

Fortunately there was a good deal of broken timber thrown up at "high-water" mark, and with a stack of this at the mouth of the little cave a pleasant fire was soon made by help of a flint pebble and the steel back of my sword. It was a hearty blaze and lit up all the near cliffs with a ruddy jumping glow which gave their occupants a marvellous appearance of life. The heat also brought off the dull rime upon the side of my recess, leaving it clear as polished glass, and I was a little startled to see, only an inch or so back in the ice and standing as erect as ever he had been in life, the figure of an imposing grey clad man. His arms were folded, his chin dropped upon his chest, his robes of the finest stuff, the very flowers they had decked his head with frozen with immortality, and under them, round his crisp and iron-grey hair, a simple band of gold with strange runes and figures engraved upon it.

There was something very simple yet stately about him, though his face was hidden and as I gazed long and intently the idea got hold of me that he had been a king over an undegenerate Martian race, and had stood waiting for the Dawn a very, very long time.

I wished a little that he had not been quite so near the glassy surface of the ice down which the warmth was bringing quick moisture drops. Had he been back there in the blue depths where others were sitting and crouching it would have been much more comfortable. But I was a sailor, and misfortune makes strange companions, so I piled up the fire again, and lying down presently on the dry shingle with my back to him stared moodily at the blaze till slowly the fatigues of the day told, my eyelids dropped and, with many a fitful start and turn, at length I slept.

It was an hour before dawn, the fire had burnt low and I was dreaming of an angry discussion with my tailor in New York as to the sit of my last new trousers when a faint sound of moving shingle caught my quick seaman ear, and before I could raise my head or lift a hand, a man's weight was on me—a heavy, strong man who bore me down with irresistible force. I felt the slap of his ice-cold hand upon my throat and his teeth in the back of my neck! In an instant, though but half awake, with a yell of surprise and anger I grappled with the enemy, and exerting all my strength rolled him over. Over and over we went struggling towards the fire, and when I got him within a foot or so of it I came out on top, and, digging my knuckles into his throttle, banged his head upon the stony floor in reckless rage, until all of a sudden it seemed to me he was done for. I relaxed my grip, but the other man never moved. I shook him again, like a terrier with a rat, but he never resented it. Had I killed him? How limp and cold he was! And then all of a sudden an uneasy feeling came upon me. I reached out, and throwing a handful of dried stuff upon the embers the fire danced gaily up into the air, and the blaze showed me I was savagely holding down to the gravel and kneeling on the chest of that long-dead king from my grotto wall!

It was the man out of the ice without a doubt. There was the very niche he had fallen from under the influence of the fire heat, the very recess, exactly in his shape in every detail, whence he had stood gazing into vacuity all those years. I left go my hold, and after the flutter in my heart had gone down, apologetically set him up against the wall of the cavern whence he had fallen; then built up the fire until twirling flames danced to the very roof in the blue light of dawn, and hobgoblin shadows leapt and capered about us. Then once more I sat down on the opposite side of the blaze, resting my chin upon my hands, and stared into the frozen eyes of that grim stranger, who, with his chin upon his knees, stared back at me with irresistible, remorseless steadfastness.

He was as fresh as if he had died but yesterday, yet by his clothing and something in his appearance, which was not that of the Martian of to-day, I knew he might be many thousand years old. What things he had seen, what wonders he knew! What a story might be put into his mouth if I were a capable writer gifted with time and imagination instead of a poor outcast, ill-paid lieutenant whose literary wit is often taxed hardly to fill even a log-book entry! I stared at him so long and hard, and he at me through the blinking flames, that again I dozed—and dozed—and dozed again until at last when I woke in good earnest it was daylight.

By this time hunger was very aggressive. The fire was naught but a circlet of grey ashes; the dead king, still sitting against the cave-side, looked very blue and cold, and with an uncomfortable realisation of my position I shook myself together, picked up and pocketed without much thought the queer gold circlet that had dropped from his forehead, and went outside to see what prospect of escape the new day had brought.

It was not much. Upriver there was not the remotest chance. Not even a Niagara steamer could have forged back against the sluice coming down from the gulch there. Looking round, the sides of the icy amphitheatre—just lighting up now with glorious gold and crimson glimmers of morning—were as steep as a wall face; only back towards the falls was there a possibility of getting out of the dreadful trap, so thither I went, after a last look at the poor old king, along my narrow beach with all the eagerness begotten of a final chance. Up to the very brink it looked hopeless enough, but, looking downwards when that was reached, instead of a sheer drop the slope seemed to be a wild "staircase" of rocks and icy ledges with here and there a little patch of sand on a cornice, and far below, five hundred feet or so, a good big spread of gravel an acre or two in extent close by where the river plunged out of sight into the nethermost cavern mouth.

It was so hopeless up above it, it could not possibly be worse further down, and there was the ugly black flood running into the hole to trust myself to as a last resource; so slipping and sliding I began the descent.

Had I been a schoolboy with a good breakfast ahead the incident might have been amusing enough. The travelling was mostly done on the seat of my trousers, which consequently became caked with mud and glacial loam. Some was accomplished on hands and knees, with now and then a bit down a snow slope, in good, honest head-over-heels fashion. The result was a fine appetite for the next meal when it should please providence to send it, and an abrupt arrival on the bottom beach about five minutes after leaving the upper circles.

I came to behind a cluster of breast-high rocks, and before moving took a look round. Judge then of my astonishment and delight at the second glance to perceive about a hundred yards away a brown object, looking like an ape in the half light, meandering slowly up the margin of the water towards me. Every now and then it stopped, stooping down to pick up something or other from the scum along the torrent, and it was the fact that these trifles, whatever they were, were put into a wallet by the vision's side—not into his mouth—which first made me understand with a joyful thrill that it was a *man* before me—a real, living man in this huge chamber of dead horrors! Then again it flashed across my mind in a luminous moment that where one man could come, or go, or live, another could do likewise, and never did cat watch mouse with more concentrated eagerness than I that quaint, bent-shouldered thing hobbling about in the blue morning shadows where all else was silence.

Nearer and nearer he came, till so close face and garb were discernible, and then there could no longer be any doubt, it was a woodman, an old man, with grizzled monkey-face, stooping gait, and a shaggy fur cloak, utterly unlike the airy garments of my Hither folk, who now stood before me. It gave me quite a start to recognise him there, for it showed I was in a new land, and since he was going so cheerfully about his business, whatever it might chance to be, there must be some way out of this accursed pit in which I had fallen. So very cautiously I edged out, taking advantage of all the cover possible until we were only twenty yards apart, and then suddenly standing up, and putting on the most affable smile, I called out—

"Hullo, mess-mate!"

The effect was electrical. That quaint old fellow sprang a yard into air as though a spring had shot him up. Then, coming down, he stood transfixed at his full height as stiff as a ramrod, staring at me with incredible wonder. He looked so funny that in spite of hunger and loneliness I burst out laughing, whereat the woodman, suddenly recovering his senses, turned on his heels and set off at his best pace in the opposite direction. This would never do! I wanted him to be my guide, philosopher, and friend. He was my sole visible link with the outside world, so after him I went at tip-top speed, and catching him up in fifty yards along the shingle laid hold of his nether garments. Whereat the old fellow stopping suddenly I shot clean over his back, coming down on my shoulder in the gravel.

But I was much younger than he, and in a minute was in chase again. This time I laid hold of his cloak, and the moment he felt my grip he slipped the neck-thongs and left me with only the mangy garment in my hands. Again we set off, dodging and scampering with all our might upon that frozen bit of beach. The activity of that old fellow was marvellous, but I could not and would not lose him. I made a rush and grappled him, but he tossed his head round and slipped away once more under my arm, as though he had been brought up by a Chinese wrestler. Then he got on one side of a flat rock, I the other, and for three or four minutes we waltzed round that slab in the most insane manner.

But by this time we were both pretty well spent—he with age and I with faintness from my long fast, and we came presently to a standstill.

After glaring at me for a time, the woodman gasped out as he struggled for breath—

"Oh, mighty and dreadful spirit! Oh, dweller in primordial ice, say from which niche of the cliffs has the breath of chance thawed you?"

EDWIN L. ARNOLD

"Never a niche at all, Mr. Hunter-for-Haddocks'-Eyes," I answered as soon as I could speak. "I am just a castaway wrecked last night on this shore of yours, and very grateful indeed will I be if you can show me the way to some breakfast first, and afterwards to the outside world."

But the old fellow would not believe. "Spirits such as you," he said sullenly, "need no food, and go whither they will by wish alone."

"I tell you I am not a spirit, and as hungry as I don't particularly want to be again. Here, look at the back of my trousers, caked three inches deep in mud. If I were a spirit, do you think I would slide about on my coat-tails like that? Do you think that if I could travel by volition I would slip down these infernal cliffs on my pants' seat as I have just done? And as for materialism—look at this fist; it punched you just now! Surely there was nothing spiritual in that knock?"

"No," said the savage, rubbing his head, "it was a good, honest rap, so I must take you at your word. If you are indeed man, and hungry, it will be a charity to feed you; if you are a spirit, it will at least be interesting to watch you eat; so sit down, and let's see what I have in my wallet."

So cross legged we squatted opposite each other on the table rock, and, feeling like another Sindbad the Sailor, I watched my new friend fumble in his bag and lay out at his side all sorts of odds and ends of string, fish-hooks, chewing-gum, material for making a fire, and so on, until at last he came to a package (done up, I noted with delight, in a broad, green leaf which had certainly been growing that morning), and unrolling it, displayed a lump of dried meat, a few biscuits, much thicker and heavier than the honey-cakes of the Hither folk, and something that looked and smelt like strong, white cheese.

He signed to me to eat, and you may depend upon it I was not slow in accepting the invitation. That tough biltong tasted to me like the tenderest steak that ever came from a grill; the biscuits were ambrosial; the cheese melted in my mouth as butter melts in that of the virtuous; but when the old man finished the quaint picnic by inviting me to accompany him down to the waterside for a drink, I shook my head. I had a great respect for dead queens and kings, I said, but there were too many of them up above to make me thirsty this morning; my respect did not go to making me desire to imbibe them in solution!

Afterwards I chanced to ask him what he had been picking up just now along the margin, and after looking at me suspiciously for a minute he asked—

"You are not a thief?" On being reassured on that point he continued: "And you will not attempt to rob me of the harvest for which I venture into this ghost-haunted glen, which you and I alone of living men have seen?"

"No." Whatever they were, I said, I would respect his earnings.

"Very well, then," said the old man, "look here! I come hither to pick up those pretty trifles which yonder lords and ladies have done with," and plunging his hand into another bag he brought out a perfect fistful of splendid gems and jewels, some set and some unset. "They wash from the hands and wrists of those who have lodgings in the crevices of the falls above," he explained. "After a time the beach here will be thick with them. Could I get up whence you came down, they might be gathered by the sackful. Come! there is an eddy still unsearched, and I will show you how they lie."

It was very fascinating, and I and that old man set to work amongst the gravels, and, to be brief, in half an hour found enough glittering stuff to set up a Fifth Avenue jeweller's shop. But to tell the truth, now that I had breakfasted, and felt manhood in my veins again, I was eager to be off, and out of the close, death-tainted atmosphere of that valley. Consequently I presently stood up and said—

"Look here, old man, this is fine sport no doubt, but just at present I have a big job on hand—one which will not wait, and I must be going. See, luck and young eyes have favoured me; here is twice as much gold and stones as you have got together—it is all yours without a question if you will show me the way out of this den and afterwards put me on the road to your big city, for thither I am bound with an errand to your king, Ar-hap."

The sight of my gems, backed, perhaps, with the mention of Ar-hap's name, appealed to the old fellow; and after a grunt or two about "losing a tide" just when spoil was so abundant, he accepted the bargain, shouldered his belongings, and led me towards the far corner of the beach.

It looked as if we were walking right against the towering ice wall, but when we were within a yard or two of it a narrow cleft, only eighteen inches wide, and wonderfully masked by an ice column, showed to the left, and into this we squeezed ourselves, the entrance by which we had come appearing to close up instantly we had gone a pace or two, so perfectly did the ice walls match each other.

It was the most uncanny thoroughfare conceivable—a sheer, sharp crack in the blue ice cliffs extending from where the sunlight shone in a dazzling golden band five hundred feet overhead to where bottom was touched in blue obscurity of the ice-foot. It was so narrow we had to travel sideways for the most part, a fact which brought my face close against the clear blue glass walls, and enabled me from time to time to see, far back in those translucent depths, more and more and evermore frozen Martians waiting in stony silence for their release.

But the fact of facts was that slowly the floor of the cleft trended upwards, whilst the sky strip appeared to come downwards to meet it. A mile, perhaps, we growled and squeezed up that wonderful gully; then with a feeling of incredible joy I felt the clear, outer air smiting upon me.

In my hurry and delight I put my head into the small of the back of the puffing old man who blocked the way in front and forced him forward, until at last—before we expected it—the cleft suddenly ended, and he and I tumbled headlong over each other on to a glittering, frozen snowslope; the sky azure overhead, the sunshine warm as a tepid bath, and a wide prospect of mountain and plain extending all around.

So delightful was the sudden change of circumstances that I became quite boyish, and seizing the old man in my exuberance by the hands, dragged him to his feet, and danced him round and round in a circle, while his ancient hair flapped about his head, his skin cloak waved from his shoulders like a pair of dusky wings and half-eaten cakes, dried flesh, glittering jewels, broken diadems, and golden finger-rings were flung in an arc about us. We capered till fairly out of breath, and then, slapping him on the back shoulder, I asked whose land all this was about us.

He replied that it was no one's, all waste from verge to verge.

"What!" was my exclamation. "All ownerless, and with so much treasure hidden hereabout! Why, I shall annex it to my country, and you and I will peg out original settlers' claims!" And, still excited by the mountain air, I whipped out my sword, and in default of a star-spangled banner to plant on the newly-acquired territory, traced in gigantic letters on the snow-crust—U.S.A.

"And now," I added, wiping the rime off my blade with the lappet of my coat, "let us stop capering about here and get to business. You have promised to put me on the way to your big city."

"Come on then," said the little man, gathering up his property. "This white hillside leads to nowhere; we must get into the valley first, and then you shall see your road." And right well that quaint barbarian kept his promise.

Chapter 13

I t was half a day's march from those glittering snow-fields into the low country, and when that was reached I found myself amongst quite another people.

The land was no longer fat and flowery, giving every kind of produce for the asking, but stony for the most part, and, where we first came on vegetation, overgrown by firs, with a pine which looked to me like a species which went to make the coal measures in my dear but distant planet. More than this I cannot say, for there are no places in the world like mess-room and quarter-deck for forgetting school learning. Instead of the glorious wealth of parti-coloured vegetation my eyes had been accustomed to lately, here they rested on infertile stretches of marshland intersected by moss-covered gravel shoots, looking as though they had been pushed into the plains in front of extinct glaciers coming down from the region behind us. On the low hills away from the sea those sombre evergreen forests with an undergrowth of moss and red lichens were more variegated with light foliage, and indeed the pines proved to be but a fringe to the Arctic ice, giving way rapidly to more typical Martian vegetation each mile we marched to the southward.

As for the inhabitants, they seemed, like my guide, rough, uncouth fellows, but honest enough when you came to know them. An introduction, however, was highly desirable. I chanced upon the first native as he was gathering reindeer-moss. My companion was some little way behind at the moment, and when the gentle aborigine saw the stranger he stared hard for a moment, then, turning on his heels, with extraordinary swiftness flung at me half a pound of hard flint stone. Had his aim been a little more careful this humble narrative had never appeared on the Broadway bookstalls. As it was, the pebble, missing my head by an inch or two, splintered into a hundred fragments on a rock behind, and while I was debating whether a revengeful rush at the slinger or a strategic advance to the rear were more advisable, my guide called out to his countryman—

"Ho! you base prowler in the morasses; you eater of unclean vegetation, do you not see this is a ghost I am conducting, a dweller in the ice cliffs, a spirit ten thousand years old? Put by your sling lest he wither you with a glance." And, very reasonably, surprised, the aborigine did as he was bid and cautiously advanced to inspect me.

EDWIN L. ARNOLD

The news soon spread over the countryside that my jewel-hunter was bringing a live "spook" along with him, considerable curiosity mixed with an awe all to my advantage characterising the people we met thereafter. Yet the wonder was not so great as might have been expected, for these people were accustomed to meeting the tags of lost races, and though they stared hard, their interest was chiefly in hearing how, when, and where I had been found, whether I bit or kicked, or had any other vices, and if I possessed any commercial value.

My guide's throat must have ached with the repetition of the narrative, but as he made the story redound greatly to his own glory, he put up cheerfully with the hoarseness. In this way, walking and talking alternately, we travelled during daylight through a country which slowly lost its rugged features and became more and more inhabited, the hardy people living in scattered villages in contradiction to the debased city-loving Hither folk.

About nightfall we came to a sea-fishers' hamlet, where, after the old man had explained my exalted nature and venerable antiquity, I was offered shelter for the night.

My host was the headman, and I must say his bearing towards the supernatural was most unaffected. If it had been an Avenue hotel I could not have found more handsome treatment than in that reed-thatched hut. They made me wash and rest, and then were all agog for my history; but that I postponed, contenting myself with telling them I had been lately in Seth, and had come thence to see them via the ice valley—to all of which they listened with the simplicity of children. Afterwards I turned on them, and openly marvelled that so small a geographical distance as there was between that land and this could make so vast a human difference. "The truth, O dweller in blue shadows of primordial ice, is," said the most intelligent of the Thither folk as we sat over fried deer-steak in his hut that evening, "we who are *men*, not Peri-zad, not overstayed fairies like those you have been amongst, are newcomers here on this shore. We came but a few generations ago from where the gold curtains of the sun lie behind the westward pine-trees, and as we came we drove, year by year, those fays, those spent triflers, back before us. All this land was theirs once, and more and more towards our old home. You may still see traces of harbours dug and cities built thousands of years ago, when the Hither folk were living men and women—not their shadows. The big water outside stops us for a space, but," he added, laughing gruffly and taking a draught of a strong beer he had been heating by the fire, "King Ar-hap has their pretty noses between his fingers; he takes tribute and girls while he gets ready—they say he is nearly ready this summer, and if he is, it will not be much of an excuse he will need to lick up the last of those triflers, those pretences of manhood."

Then we fell to talking of Ar-hap, his subjects and town, and I learned the tides had swept me a long way to the northward of the proper route between the capitals of the two races, that day they carried me into the Dead-Men's Ice, as these entertainers of mine called the northern snows. To get back to the place previously aimed at, where the woodmen road came out on the seashore, it was necessary to go either by boat, a roundabout way through a maze of channels, "as tangled as the grass roots in autumn"; or, secondly, by a couple of days' marching due southward across the base of the great peninsula we were on, and so strike blue water again at the long-sought-for harbour.

As I lay dozing and dreaming on a pile of strange furs in the corner of the hut that evening I made up my mind for the land journey tomorrow, having had enough for the moment of nautical Martian adventures; and this point settled, fell again to wondering what made me follow so reckless a quest in the way I was doing; asking myself again and again what was gazelle-eyed Heru to me after all, and why should it matter even as much as the value of a brass waist-coat button whether Hath had her or Ar-hap? What a fool I was to risk myself day by day in quaint and dangerous adventures, wearing out good Government shoe-leather in other men's quarrels, all for a silly slip of royal girlhood who, by this time, was probably making herself comfortable and forgetting both Hath and me in the arms of her rough new lord.

And from Heru my mind drifted back dreamily to poor An, and Seth, the city of fallen magnificence, where the spent masters of a strange planet now lived on sufferance—the ghosts of their former selves. Where was An, where the revellers on the morning—so long ago it seemed!—when first that infernal rug of mine translated a chance wish into a horrible reality and shot me down here, a stranger and an outcast? Where was the magic rug itself? Where my steak and tomato supper? Who had eaten it? Who was drawing my pay? If I could but find the rug when I got back to Seth, gods! but I would try if it would not return whence I had come, and as swiftly, out of all these silly coils and adventuring.

EDWIN L. ARNOLD

So musing, presently the firelight died down, and bulky forms of hide-wrapped woodmen sleeping on the floor slowly disappeared in obscurity like ranges of mountains disappearing in the darkness of night. All those uncouth forms, and the throb of the sea outside, presently faded upon my senses, and I slept the heavy sleep of one whose wakefulness gives way before an imperious physical demand. All through the long hours of the night, while the waves outside champed upon the gravels, and the woodmen snored and grunted uneasily as they simultaneously dreamt of the day's hunting and digested its proceeds, I slept; and then when dawn began to break I passed from that heavy stupor into another and lighter realm, wherein fancy again rose superior to bodily fatigue, and events of the last few days passed in procession through my mind.

I dreamt I was lunching at a fashionable seaside resort with Polly at my side, and An kept bringing us melons, which grew so monstrous every time a knife was put into them that poor Polly screamed aloud. I dreamt I was afloat on a raft, hotly pursued by my tailor, whose bare and shiny head—may Providence be good to him!—was garlanded with roses, while in his fist was a bunch of unpaid bills, the which he waved aloft, shouting to me to stop. And thus we danced down an ink-black river until he had chiveyed me into the vast hall of the Admiralty, where a fearsome Secretary, whose golden teeth rattled and dropped from his head with mingled cold and anger, towered above me as he asked why I was absent from my ship without leave. And I was just mumbling out excuses while stooping to pick up his golden dentistry, when some one stirring in the hut aroused me. I started up on my elbow and looked around. Where was I? For a minute all was confused and dark. The heavy mound-like forms of sleeping men, the dim outlines of their hunting gear upon the walls, the pale sea beyond, half seen through the open doorway, just turning livid in the morning light; and then as my eyes grew more accustomed to the obscurity, and my stupid senses returned, I recognised the surroundings, and, with a sigh, remembered yesterday's adventures.

However, it would never do to mope; so, rising silently and picking a way through human lumber on the floor, I went out and down to the water's edge, where "shore-going" clothes, as we sailors call them, were slipped off, and I plunged into the sea for a swim.

It was a welcome dip, for I needed the plunge physically and intellectually, but it came to an abrupt conclusion. The Thither folk apparently had never heard of this form of enjoyment; to them water stood for drinking or drowning, nothing else, and since one could not drink the sea, to be in it meant, even for a ghost, to drown. Consequently, when the word went round the just rousing villages that "He-on-foot-from-afar" was adrift in the waves, rescue parties were hurriedly organised, a boat launched, and, in spite of all my kicking and shouting (which they took to be evidence of my semi-moribund condition), I was speedily hauled out by hairy and powerful hands, pungent herbs burnt under my nose, and my heels held high in the air in order that the water might run out of me. It was only with the greatest difficulty those rough but honest fellows were eventually got to believe me saved.

The breakfast I made of grilled deer flesh and a fish not unlike salmon, however, convinced them of my recovery, and afterward we parted very good friends; for there was something in the nature of those rugged barbarians just coming into the dawn of civilisation that won my liking far more than the effete gentleness of others across the water.

When the time of parting came they showed no curiosity as to my errand, but just gave me some food in a fish-skin bag, thrust a heavy stone-headed axe into my hand, "in case I had to talk to a thief on the road," and pointed out on the southern horizon a forked mountain, under which, they said, was the harbour and high-road to King Ar-hap's capital. Then they hugged me to their hairy chests in turn, and let me go with a traveller's blessing.

There I was again, all alone, none but my thoughts for companions, and nothing but youth to excuse the folly in thus venturing on a reckless quest!

However, who can gainsay that same youth? The very spice of danger made my steps light and the way pleasant. For a mile or two the track was plain enough, through an undulating country gradually becoming more and more wooded with vegetation, changing rapidly from Alpine to sub-tropical. The air also grew warmer, and when the dividing ridge was crossed and a thick forest entered, the snows and dreadful region of Deadmen's Ice already seemed leagues and leagues away.

Probably a warm ocean current played on one side of the peninsula, while a cold one swept the other, but for scientific aspects of the question I cared little in my joy at being anew in a soft climate, amongst beautiful flowers and vivid life again. Mile after mile slipped quickly by as I strode along, whistling "Yankee Doodle" to myself and revelling in the change. At one place I met a rough-looking Martian woodcutter, who wanted to fight until he found I also wanted to, when he turned very civil and as talkative as a solitary liver often is when his tongue gets started. He particularly desired to know where I came from, and, as in the case with so many other of his countrymen, took it for granted, and with very little surprise, that I was either a spirit or an inhabitant of another world. With this idea in his mind he gave me a curious piece of information, which, unfortunately, I was never able to follow up.

"I don't think you can be a spirit," he said, critically eyeing my clothes, which were now getting ragged and dirty beyond description. "They are finer-looking things than you, and I doubt if their toes come through their shoes like yours do. If you are a wanderer from the stars, you are not like that other one we have down yonder," and he pointed to the southward.

"What!" I asked, pricking my ears in amazement, "another wanderer from the outside world! Does he come from the earth?"—using the word An had given me to signify my own planet.

"No, not from there; from the one that burns blue in evening between sun and sea. Men say he worked as a stoker or something of the kind when he was at home, and got trifling with a volcano tap, and was lapped in hot mud, and blown out here. My brother saw him about a week ago."

"Now what you say is down right curious. I thought I had a monopoly of that kind of business in this sphere of yours. I should be tremendously interested to see him."

"No you wouldn't," briefly answered the woodman. "He is the stupidest fool ever blown from one world to another—more stupid to look at than you are. He is a gaseous, wavey thing, so glum you can't get two words a week out of him, and so unstable that you never know when you are with him and when the breeze has drifted him somewhere else."

I could but laugh and insist, with all respect to the woodcutter, such an individual were worth the knowing however unstable his constitution; at which the man shrugged his shoulders and changed the conversation, as though the subject were too trivial to be worth much consideration.

This individual gave me the pleasure of his company until nearly sundown, and finding I took an interest in things of the forest, pointed out more curious plants and trees than I have space to mention. Two of them, however, cling to my memory very tenaciously. One was a very Circe amongst plants, the horrible charm of which can never be forgotten. We were going down a glade when a most ravishing odour fell upon my nostrils. It was heavenly sweet yet withal there lurked an incredibly, unexpressibly tempting spice of wickedness in it. The moment he caught that ambrosial invitation in the air my woodman spit fiercely on the ground, and taking a plug of wool from his pouch stuffed his nostrils up. Then he beckoned me to come away. But the odour was too ravishing, I was bound to see whence it arose, and finding me deaf to all warnings, the man reluctantly turned aside down the enticing trail. We pushed about a hundred yards through bushes until we came to a little arena full in sunshine where there were neither birds nor butterflies, but a death-like hush upon everything. Indeed, the place seemed shunned in spite of the sodden loveliness of that scent which monopolised and mounted to my brain until I was beginning to be drunk with the sheer pleasure of it. And there in the centre of the space stood a plant not unlike a tree fern, about six feet high, and crowned by one huge and lovely blossom. It resembled a vast passion-flower of incredible splendour. There were four petals, with points resting on the ground, each six feet long, ivory-white inside, exquisitely patterned with glittering silver veins. From the base of these rose upright a gauzy veil of azure filaments of the same length as the petals, wirelike, yet soft as silk, and inside them again rested a chalice of silver holding a tiny pool of limpid golden honey. Circe, indeed! It was from that cup the scent arose, and my throat grew dry with longing as I looked at it; my eyes strained through the blue tendrils towards that liquid nectar, and my giddy senses felt they must drink or die! I glanced at the woodman with a smile of drunken happiness, then turned tottering legs towards the blossom. A stride up the smooth causeway of white petals, a push through the azure haze, and the wine of the wood enchantress would be mine—molten amber wine, hotter and more golden than the sunshine; the fire of it was in my veins, the recklessness of intoxication was on me, life itself as nothing compared to a sip from that chalice, my lips must taste or my soul would die, and with trembling hand and strained face I began to climb.

But the woodman pulled me back.

"Back, stranger!" he cried. "Those who drink there never live again."

"Blessed oblivion! If I had a thousand lives the price were still too cheap," and once more I essayed to scramble up.

But the man was a big fellow, and with nostrils plugged, and eyes averted from the deadly glamour, he seized me by the collar and threw me back. Three times I tried, three times he hurled me down, far too faint and absorbed to heed the personal violence. Then standing between us, "Look," he said, "look and learn."

He had killed a small ape that morning, meaning later on to take its fur for clothing, and this he now unslung from his shoulder, and hitching the handle of his axe into the loose skin at the back of its neck, cautiously advanced to the witch plant, and gently hoisted the monkey over the blue palings. The moment its limp, dead feet touched the golden pool a shudder passed through the plant, and a bird somewhere far back in the forest cried out in horror. Quick as thought, a spasm of life shot up the tendrils, and like tongues of blue flame they closed round the victim, lapping his miserable body in their embrace. At the same time the petals began to rise, showing as they did so hard, leathery, unlovely outer rinds, and by the time the woodman was back at my side the flower was closed.

Closer and closer wound the blue tendrils; tighter and tighter closed the cruel petals with their iron grip, until at last we heard the ape's bones crackling like dry firewood; then next his head burst, his brains came oozing through the crevices, while blood and entrails followed them through every cranny, and the horrible mess with the overflow of the chalice curled down the stem in a hundred steaming rills, till at last the petals locked with an ugly snap upon their ghastly meal, and I turned away from the sight in dread and loathing.

That was plant Number One.

Plant Number Two was of milder disposition, and won a hearty laugh for my friendly woodman. In fact, being of a childlike nature, his success as a professor of botany quite pleased him, and not content with answering my questions, he set to work to find new vegetable surprises, greatly enjoying my wonder and the sense of importance it gave him.

In this way we came, later on in the day, to a spot where herbage was somewhat scantier, the grass coarse, and soil shallow. Here I espied a tree of small size, apparently withered, but still bearing a few parched leaves on its uppermost twigs.

"Now that," quoth the professor, "is a highly curious tree, and I should like you to make a close acquaintance with it. It grows from a seed in the course of a single springtime, perishes in the summer; but a few specimens stand throughout the winter, provided the situation is sheltered, as this one has done. If you will kindly go down and shake its stem I believe you will learn something interesting."

So, very willing to humour him, away I went to the tree, which was perfect in every detail, but apparently very dry, clasped it with both hands, and, pulling myself together, gave it a mighty shake. The result was instantaneous. The whole thing was nothing but a skin of dust, whence all fibre and sap had gone, and at my touch it dissolved into a cloud of powder, a huge puff of white dust which descended on me as though a couple of flour-bags had been inverted over my head; and as I staggered out sneezing and blinking, white as a miller from face to foot, the Martian burst into a wild, joyous peal of laughter that made the woods ring again. His merriment was so sincere I had not the heart to be angry, and soon laughed as loud as he did; though, for the future, I took his botanical essays with a little more caution.

Chapter 14

That woodman friend of mine proved so engaging it was difficult to get away, and thus when, dusk upon us, and my object still a long distance off, he asked me to spend the night at his hut, I gladly assented.

We soon reached the cabin where the man lived by himself whilst working in the forest. It was a picturesque little place on a tree-overhung lagoon, thatched, wattled, and all about were piles of a pleasant-scented bark, collected for the purpose of tanning hides, and I could not but marvel that such a familiar process should be practised identically on two sides of the universal ether. But as a matter of fact the similarity of many details of existence here and there was the most striking of the things I learned whilst in the red planet.

Within the hut stood a hearth in the centre of the floor, whereon a comfortable blaze soon sparkled, and upon the walls hung various implements, hides, and a store of dried fruits of various novel kinds. My host, when he had somewhat disdainfully watched me wash in a rill of water close by, suggested supper, and I agreed with heartiest good will.

"Nothing wonderful! Oh, Mr. Blue-coat!" he said, prancing about as he made his hospitable arrangements. "No fine meat or scented wine to unlock, one by one, all the doors of paradise, such as I have heard they have in lands beyond the sea; but fare good enough for plain men who eat but to live. So! reach me down yonder bunch of yellow aru fruit, and don't upset that calabash, for all my funniest stories lurk at the bottom of it."

I did as he bid, and soon we were squatting by the fire toasting arus on pointed sticks, the doorway closed with a wattle hurdle, and the black and gold firelight filling the hut with fantastic shadows. Then when the banana-like fruit was ready, the man fetched from a recess a loaf of bread savoured with the dust of dried and pounded fish, put the foresaid calabash of strong ale to warm, and down we sat to supper with real woodman appetites. Seldom have I enjoyed a meal so much, and when we had finished the fruit and the wheat cake my guide snatched up the great gourd of ale, and putting it to his lips called out:

"Here's to you, stranger; here's to your country; here's to your girl, if you have one, and death to your enemies!" Then he drank deep and long, and, passed the stuff to me.

"Here's to you, bully host, and the missus, and the children, if there are any, and more power to your elbow!"—the which gratified him greatly, though probably he had small idea of my meaning.

And right merry we were that evening. The host was a jolly good fellow, and his ale, with a pleasant savour of mint in it, was the heartiest drink I ever set lips to. We talked and laughed till the very jackals yapped in sympathy outside. And when he had told a score of wonderful wood stories as pungent of the life of these fairy forests as the aromatic scent of his bark-heaps outside, as iridescent with the colours of another world as the rainbow bubbles riding down his starlit rill, I took a turn, and told him of the commonplaces of my world so far away, whereat he laughed gloriously again. The greater the commonplace the larger his joy. The humblest story, hardly calculated to impress a griffin between watches on the main-deck, was a masterpiece of wit to that gentle savage; and when I "took off" the tricks and foibles of some of my superiors—Heaven forgive me for such treason!—he listened with the exquisite open-mouthed delight of one who wanders in a brand-new world of mirth.

We drank and laughed over that strong beer till the little owls outside raised their voice in combined accord, and then the woodman, shaking the last remnant of his sleepy wits together, and giving a reproachful look at me for finally passing him the gourd empty to the last drop, rose, threw a fur on a pile of dead grass at one side of the hut, and bid me sleep, "for his brain was giddy with the wonders of the incredible and ludicrous sphere which I had lately inhabited."

Slowly the fire died away; slowly the quivering gold and black arabesques on the walls merged in a red haze as the sticks dropped into tinder, and the great black outline of the hairy monster who had thrown himself down by the embers rose up the walls against that flush like the outline of a range of hills against a sunset glow. I listened drowsily for a space to his snoring and the laughing answer of the brook outside, and then that ambrosial sleep which is the gentle attendant of hardship and danger touched my tired eyelids, and I, too, slept.

My friend was glum the next morning, as they who stay over-long at the supper flagon are apt to be. He had been at work an hour on his bark-heaps when I came out into the open, and it was only by a good deal of diplomacy and some material help in sorting his faggots that he was got into a better frame of mind. I could not, however, trust his mood completely, and as I did not want to end so jovial a friendship with a quarrel, I hurried through our breakfast of dry bread, with hard-boiled lizard eggs, and then settling my reckoning with one of the brass buttons from my coat, which he immediately threaded, with every evidence of extreme gratification, on a string of trinkets hanging round his neck, asked him the way to Ar-hap's capital.

"Your way is easy, friend, as long as you keep to the straight path and have yonder two-humped mountain in front. To the left is the sea, and behind the hill runs the canal and road by which all traffic comes or goes to Ar-hap. But above all things pass not to the hills right, for no man goes there; there away the forests are thick as night, and in their perpetual shadows are the ruins of a Hither city, a haunted fairy town to which some travellers have been, but whence none ever returned alive."

"By the great Jove, that sounds promising! I would like to see that town if my errand were not so urgent."

But the old fellow shook his shaggy head and turned a shade yellower. "It is no place for decent folk," he growled. "I myself once passed within a mile of its outskirts at dusk, and saw the unholy little people's lanterned processions starting for the shrine of Queen Yang, who, tradition says, killed herself and a thousand babies with her when we took this land."

"My word, that was a holocaust! Couldn't I drop in there to lunch? It would make a fine paper for an antiquarian society."

Again the woodman frowned. "Do as I bid you, son. You are too young and green to go on ventures by yourself. Keep to the straight road: shun the swamps and the fairy forest, else will you never see Ar-hap."

"And as I have very urgent and very important business with him, comrade, no doubt your advice is good. I will call on Princess Yang some other day. And now goodbye! Rougher but friendlier shelter than you have given me no man could ask for. I am downright sorry to part with you in this lonely land. If ever we meet again—" but we never did! The honest old churl clasped me into his hairy bosom three times, stuffed my wallet with dry fruit and bread, and once more repeating his directions, sent me on my lonely way.

I confess I sighed while turning into the forest, and looked back more than once at his retreating form. The loneliness of my position, the hopelessness of my venture, welled up in my heart after that good comradeship, and when the hut was out of sight I went forward down the green grass road, chin on chest, for twenty minutes in the deepest dejection. But, thank Heaven, I was born with a tough spirit, and possess a mind which has learned in many fights to give brave counsel to my spirit, and thus presently I shook myself together, setting my face boldly to the quest and the day's work.

It was not so clear a morning as the previous one, and a steamy wind on what at sea I should have called the starboard bow, as I pressed forward to the distant hill, had a curiously subduing effect on my thoughts, and filled the forest glades with a tremulous unreality like to nothing on our earth, and distinctly embarrassing to a stranger in a strange land. Small birds in that quaint atmospheric haze looked like condors, butterflies like giant fowl, and the simplest objects of the forest like the imaginations of a disordered dream. Behind that gauzy hallucination a fine white mist came up, and the sun spread out flat and red in the sky, while the pent-in heat became almost unendurable.

Still I plodded on, growling to myself that in Christian latitudes all the evidences would have been held to betoken a storm before night, whatever they might do here, but for the most part lost in my own gloomy speculations. That was the more pity since, in thinking the walk over now, it seems to me that I passed many marvels, saw many glorious vistas in those nameless forests, many spreads of colour, many incidents that, could I but remember them more distinctly, would supply material for making my fortune as a descriptive traveller. But what would you? I have forgotten, and am too virtuous to draw on my imagination, as it is sometimes said other travellers have done when picturesque facts were deficient. Yes, I have forgotten all about that day, save that it was sultry hot, that I took off my coat and waistcoat to be cooler, carrying them, like the tramp I was, across my arm, and thus dishevelled passed some time in the afternoon an encampment of forest folk, wherefrom almost all the men were gone, and the women shy and surly.

In no very social humour myself, I walked round their woodland village, and on the outskirts, by a brook, just as I was wishing there were some one to eat my solitary lunch with, chanced upon a fellow busily engaged in hammering stones into weapons upon a flint anvil.

He was an ugly-looking individual at best, yet I was hard up for company, so I put my coat down, and, seating myself on a log opposite, proceeded to open my wallet, and take out the frugal stores the woodman had given me that morning.

The man was seated upon the ground holding a stone anvil between his feet, while with his hands he turned and chipped with great skill a spear-head he was making out of flint. It was about the only pastime he had, and his little yellow eyes gleamed with a craftsman's pleasure, his shaggy round shoulders were bent over the task, the chips flew in quick particles, and the wood echoed musically as the artificer watched the thing under his hands take form and fashion. Presently I spoke, and the worker looked up, not too pleased at being thus interrupted. But he was easy of propitiation, and over a handful of dried raisins communicative.

How, I asked, knowing a craftsman's craft is often nearest to his heart, how was it such things as that he chipped came to be thought of by him and his? Whereon the woodman, having spit out the raisin-stones and wiped his fingers on his fur, said in substance that the first weapon was fashioned when the earliest ape hurled the first stone in wrath.

"But, chum," I said, taking up his half-finished spear and touching the razor-fine edge with admiring caution, "from hurling the crude pebble to fashioning such as this is a long stride. Who first edged and pointed the primitive malice? What man with the soul of a thousand unborn fighters in him notched and sharpened your natural rock?"

Whereon the chipper grinned, and answered that, when the woodmen had found stones that would crack skulls, it came upon them presently that they would crack nuts as well. And cracking nuts between two stones one day a flint shattered, and there on the grass was the golden secret of the edge—the thing that has made man what he is.

"Yet again, good fellow," I queried, "even this happy chance only gives us a weapon, sharp, no doubt, and calculated to do a hundred services for any ten the original pebble could have done, but still unhandled, small in force, imperfect—now tell me, which of your amiable ancestors first put a handle to the fashioned flint, and how he thought of it?"

The workman had done his flake by now, and wrapping it in a bit of skin, put it carefully in his belt before turning to answer my question.

"Who made the first handle for the first flint, you of the many questions? She did—she, the Mother," he suddenly cried, patting the earth with his brown hand, and working himself up as he spoke, "made it in her heart for us her first-born. See, here is such as the first handled weapon that ever came out of darkness," and he snatched from the ground, where it had lain hidden under his fox-skin cloak, a heavy club. I saw in an instant how it was. The club had been a sapling, and the sapling's roots had grown about and circled with a splendid grip a lump of native flint. A woodman had pulled the sapling, found the flint, and fashioned the two in a moment of happy inspiration, the one to an axe-head and the other to a handle, as they lay Nature-welded!

"This, I say, is the first—the first!" screamed the old fellow as though I were contradicting him, thumping the ground with his weapon, and working himself up to a fury as its black magic entered his being. "This is the first: with this I slew Hetter and Gur, and those who plundered my hiding-places in the woods; with this I have killed a score of others, bursting their heads, and cracking their bones like dry sticks. With this— with this—" but here his rage rendered him inarticulate; he stammered and stuttered for a minute, and then as the killing fury settled on him his yellow teeth shut with a sudden snap, while through them his breath rattled like wind through dead pine branches in December, the sinews sat up on his hands as his fingers tightened upon the axe-heft like the roots of the same pines from the ground when winter rain has washed the soil from beneath them; his small eyes gleamed like baleful planets; every hair upon his shaggy back grew stiff and erect—another minute and my span were ended.

With a leap from where I sat I flew at that hairy beast, and sinking my fists deep in his throttle, shook him till his eyes blazed with delirious fires. We waltzed across the short greensward, and in and about the tree-trunks, shaking, pulling, and hitting as we went, till at last I felt the man's vigour dying within him; a little more shaking, a sudden twist, and he was lying on the ground before me, senseless and civil! That is the worst of some orators, I thought to myself, as I gloomily gathered up the scattered fragments of my lunch; they never know when they have said enough, and are too apt to be carried away by their own arguments.

That inhospitable village was left behind in full belief the mountain looming in the south could be reached before nightfall, while the road to its left would serve as a sure guide to food and shelter for the evening. But, as it turned out, the morning's haze developed a strong mist ere the afternoon was half gone, through which it was impossible to see more than twenty yards. My hill loomed gigantic for a time with a tantalising appearance of being only a mile or two ahead, then wavered, became visionary, and finally disappeared as completely as though the forest mist had drunk it up bodily.

There was still the road to guide me, a fairly well-beaten track twining through the glades; but even the best of highways are difficult in fog, and this one was complicated by various side paths, made probably by hunters or bark-cutters, and without compass or guide marks it was necessary to advance with extreme caution, or get helplessly mazed.

EDWIN L. ARNOLD

An hour's steady tramping brought me nowhere in particular, and stopping for a minute to consider, I picked a few wild fruit, such as my wood-cutter friend had eaten, from an overhanging bush, and in so doing slipped, the soil having now become damp, and in falling broke a branch off. The incident was only important from what follows. Picking myself up, perhaps a little shaken by the jolt, I set off again upon what seemed the plain road, and being by this time displeased by my surroundings, determined to make a push for "civilization" before the rapidly gathering darkness settled down.

Hands in pockets and collar up, I marched forward at a good round pace for an hour, constantly straining eyes for a sight of the hill and ears for some indications of living beings in the deathly hush of the shrouded woods, and at the end of that time, feeling sure habitations must now be near, arrived at what looked like a little open space, somehow seeming rather familiar in its vague outlines.

Where had I seen such a place before? Sauntering round the margin, a bush with a broken branch suddenly attracted my attention—a broken bush with a long slide in the mud below it, and the stamp of Navy boots in the soft turf! I glared at those signs for a moment, then with an exclamation of chagrin recognised them only too well—it was the bush whence I had picked the fruit, and the mark of my fall. An hour's hard walking round some accursed woodland track had brought me exactly back to the point I had started from—I was lost!

It really seemed to get twenty per cent darker as I made that abominable discovery, and the position dawned in all its uncomfortable intensity. There was nothing for it but to start off again, this time judging my direction only by a light breath of air drifting the mist tangles before it; and therein I made a great mistake, for the breeze had shifted several points from the quarter whence it blew in the morning.

Knowing nothing of this, I went forward with as much lightheartedness as could be managed, humming a song to myself, and carefully putting aside thoughts of warmth and supper, while the dusk increased and the great forest vegetation seemed to grow ranker and closer at every step.

Another disconcerting thing was that the ground sloped gradually downwards, not upwards as it should have done, till it seemed the path lay across the flats of a forest-covered plain, which did not conform to my wish of striking a road on the foot-hills of the mountain. However, I plodded on, drawing some small comfort from the fact that as darkness came the mist rose from the ground and appeared to condense in a ghostly curtain twenty feet overhead, where it hung between me and a clear night sky, presently illumined by starlight with the strangest effect.

Tired, footsore, and dejected, I struggled on a little further. Oh for a cab, I laughed bitterly to myself. Oh for even the humble necessary omnibus of civilisation. Oh for the humblest tuck-shop where a mug of hot coffee and a snack could be had by a homeless wanderer; and as I thought and plodded savagely on, collar up, hands in pockets, through the black tangles of that endless wood, suddenly the sound of wailing children caught my ear!

It was the softest, saddest music ever mortal listened to. It was as though scores of babes in pain were dropping to sleep on their mothers' breasts, and all hushing their sorrows with one accord in a common melancholy chorus. I stood spell-bound at that elfin wailing, the first sound to break the deathly stillness of the road for an hour or more, and my blood tingled as I listened to it. Nevertheless, here was what I was looking for; where there were weeping children there must be habitations, and shelter, and—splendid thought!—supper. Poor little babes! their crying was the deadliest, sweetest thing in sorrows I ever listened to. If it was cholic—why, I knew a little of medicine, and in gratitude for that prospective supper, I had a soul big enough to cure a thousand; and if they were in disgrace, and by some quaint Martian fashion had suffered simultaneous punishment for baby offences, I would plead for them.

In fact, I fairly set off at the run towards the sobbing, in the black, wet, night air ahead, and, tripping as I ran, looked down and saw in the filtering starlight that the forest grass had given place to an ancient roadway, paved with moss-grown flag-stones, such as they still used in Seth.

Without stopping to think what that might mean I hurried on, the wailing now right ahead, a tremulous tumult of gentle grief rising and falling on the night air like the sound of a sea after a storm; and so, presently, in a minute or two, came upon a ruined archway spanning the lonely road, held together by great masses of black-fingered creepers, gaunt and ghostly in the shadows, an extraordinary and unexpected vision; and as I stopped with a jerk under that forbidding gateway and glared at its tumbled masonry and great portals hanging rotten at their hinges, suddenly the truth flashed upon me. I had taken the forbidden road after all. I was in the ancient, ghost-haunted city of Queen Yang!

Chapter 15

The dark forest seemed to shut behind as I entered the gateway of the deserted Hither town, against which my wood-cutter friend had warned me, while inside the soft mist hung in the starlight like grey drapery over endless vistas of ruins. What was I to do? Without all was black and cheerless, inside there was at least shelter. Wet and cold, my courage was not to be put down by the stories of a silly savage; I would go on whatever happened. Besides, the soft sound of crying, now apparently all about, seemed companionable, and I had heard so much of ghosts of late, the sharp edge of fear at their presence was wearing off.

So in I went: up a broad, decayed street, its flagstones heaved everywhere by the roots of gnarled trees, and finding nothing save ruin, tried to rest under a wall. But the night air was chilly and the shelter poor, so out I came again, with the wailing in the shadows so close about now that I stopped, and mustering up courage called aloud:

"Hullo, you who weep there in the dark, are you living or dead?" And after a minute from the hollows of the empty hearths around came the sad little responsive echo:

"Are you living or dead?" It was very delusive and unsatisfactory, and I was wondering what to do next when a slant of warmer wind came up behind me under the mist, and immediately little tongues of blue flame blossomed without visible cause in every darksome crevice; pale flickers of miasmic light rising pallid from every lurking nook and corner in the black desolation as though a thousand lamps were lit by unseen fingers, and, knee high, floated out into the thoroughfare where they oscillated gently in airy grace, and then, forming into procession, began drifting before the tepid air towards the city centre. At once I thought of what the woodcutter had seen, but was too wet and sulky by this time to care. The fascination of the place was on me, and dropping into rear of the march, I went forward with it. By this time the wailing had stopped, though now and then it seemed a dark form moved in the empty doorways on either hand, while the mist, parting into gossamers before the wind, took marvellously human forms in every alley and lane we passed.

Thus I, a sodden giant, led by those elfin torches, paced through the city until we came to an open square with a great lumber of ruins in the centre all marred and spoiled by vegetation; and here the lights wavered, and went out by scores and hundreds, just as the petals drop from spent flowers, while it seemed, though it may have been only wind in the rank grass, that the air was full of most plaintive sighs as each little lamp slipped into oblivion.

The big pile was a mass of fallen masonry, which, from the broken pillars all about, might have been a palace or temple once. I pushed in, but it was as dark as Hades here, so, after struggling for a time in a labyrinth of chambers, chose a sandy recess, with some dry herbage by way of bedding in a corner, and there, thankful at least for shelter, my night's wanderings came to an end and I coiled myself down, ate a last handful of dry fruit, and, strange as it may seem, was soon sleeping peacefully.

I dreamed that night that a woman, with a face as white as ivory, came and bent over me. She led a babe by either hand, while behind her were scores of other ones, with lovely faces, but all as pale as the stars themselves, who looked and sighed, but said nothing, and when they had stared their fill, dropped out one by one, leaving a wonderful blank in the monotony where they had been; but beyond that dream nothing happened.

It was a fine morning when I woke again, and obviously broad day outside, the sunshine coming down through cracks in the old palace roof, and lying in golden pools on the floor with dazzling effect.

Rubbing my eyes and sitting up, it took me some time to get my senses together, and at first an uneasy feeling possessed me that I was somehow dematerialised and in an unreal world. But a twinge of cramp in my left arm, and a healthy sneeze, which frightened a score of bats overhead nearly out of their senses, was reassuring on this point, and rubbing away the cramp and staggering to my feet, I looked about at the strange surroundings. It was cavernous chaos on every side: magnificent architecture reduced to the confusion of a debris-heap, only the hollow chambers being here and there preserved by massive columns meeting overhead. Into these the yellow light filtered wherever a rent in a cupola or side-wall admitted it, and allured by the vision of corridors one beyond the other, I presently set off on a tour of discovery.

Twenty minutes' scrambling brought me to a place where the fallen jambs of a fine doorway lay so close together that there was barely room to pass between them. However, seeing light beyond, I squeezed through, and I found myself in the best-preserved chamber of all—a wide, roomy hall with a domed roof, a haze of mural paintings on the walls, and a marble floor nearly hidden in a century of fallen dust. I stumbled over something at the threshold, and picking it up, found it was a baby's skull! And there were more of them now that my eyes became accustomed to the light. The whole floor was mottled with them—scores and hundreds of bones and those poor little relics of humanity jutting out of the sand everywhere. In the hush of that great dead nursery the little white trophies seemed inexpressibly pathetic, and I should have turned back reverently from that chamber of forgotten sorrows but that something caught my eye in the centre of it.

It was an oblong pile of white stone, very ill-used and chipped, wrist-deep in dust, yet when a slant of light came in from above and fell straight upon it, the marble against the black gloom beyond blazed like living pearl. It was dazzling; and shading my eyes and going tenderly over through the poor dead babes, I looked, and there, full in the shine, lay a woman's skeleton, still wrapped in a robe of which little was left save the hard gold embroidery. Her brown hair, wonderful to say, still lay like lank, dead seaweed about her, and amongst it was a fillet crown of plain iron set with gems such as eye never looked upon before. There were not many, but enough to make the proud simplicity of that circlet glisten like a little band of fire—a gleaming halo on her dead forehead infinitely fascinating. At her sides were two other little bleached human flowers, and I stood before them for a long time in silent sympathy.

Could this be Queen Yang, of whom the woodcutter had told me? It must be—who else? And if it were, what strange chance had brought me here—a stranger, yet the first to come, since her sorrow, from her distant kindred? And if it were, then that fillet belonged of right to Heru, the last representative of her kind. Ought I not to take it to her rather than leave it as spoil to the first idle thief with pluck enough to deride the mysteries of the haunted city? Long time I thought over it in the faint, heavy atmosphere of that hall, and then very gently unwound the hair, lifted the circlet, and, scarcely knowing what I did, put it in my shoulder-bag.

After that I went more cheerfully into the outside sunshine, and setting my clothes to dry on a stone, took stock of the situation. The place was, perhaps, not quite so romantic by day as by night, and the scattered trees, matted by creepers, with which the whole were overgrown, prevented anything like an extensive view of the ruined city being obtained. But what gave me great satisfaction was to note over these trees to the eastward a two-humped mountain, not more than six or seven miles distant—the very one I had mislaid the day before. Here was reality and a chance of getting back to civilisation. I was as glad as if home were in sight, and not, perhaps, the less so because the hill meant villages and food; and you who have doubtless lunched well and lately will please bear in mind I had had nothing since breakfast the day before; and though this may look picturesque on paper, in practice it is a painful item in one's programme.

Well, I gave my damp clothes but a turn or two more in the sun, and then, arguing that from the bare ground where the forest ended half-way up the hill, a wide view would be obtained, hurried into my garments and set off thither right gleefully. A turn or two down the blank streets, now prosaic enough, an easy scramble through a gap in the crumbling battlements, and there was the open forest again, with a friendly path well marked by the passage of those wild animals who made the city their lair trending towards my landmark.

A light breakfast of soft green nuts, plucked on the way, and then the ground began to bend upwards and the woods to thin a little. With infinite ardour, just before midday, I scrambled on to a bare knoll on the very hillside, and fell exhausted before the top could be reached.

But what were hunger or fatigue to the satisfaction of that moment? There was the sea before me, the clear, strong, gracious sea, blue leagues of it, furrowed by the white ridges of some distant storm. I could smell the scent of it even here, and my sailor heart rose in pride at the companionship of that alien ocean. Lovely and blessed thing! how often have I turned from the shallow trivialities of the land and found consolation in the strength of your stately solitudes! How often have I turned from the tinselled presence of the shore, the infinite pretensions of dry land that make life a sorry, hectic sham, and found in the black bosom of the Great Mother solace and comfort! Dear, lovely sea, man— half of every sphere, as far removed in the sequence of your strong emotions from the painted fripperies of the woman-land as pole from pole—the grateful blessing of the humblest of your followers on you!

The mere sight of salt water did me good. Heaven knows our separation had not been long, and many an unkind slap has the Mother given me in the bygone; yet the mere sight of her was tonic, a lethe of troubles, a sedative for tired nerves; and I gazed that morning at the illimitable blue, the great, unfettered road to everywhere, the ever-varied, the immutable, the thing which was before everything and shall be last of all, in an ecstasy of affection.

EDWIN L. ARNOLD

There was also other satisfaction at hand. Not a mile away lay a well-defined road—doubtless the one spoken of by the wood-cutter—and where the track pointed to the seashore the low roofs and circling smoke of a Thither township showed.

There I went hot-footed, and, much too hungry to be nice in formality, swung up to the largest building on the waterside quay and demanded breakfast of the man who was lounging by its doorway chewing a honey reed. He looked me up and down without emotion, then, falling into the common mistake, said,

"This is not a hostel for ghosts, sir. We do not board and lodge phantoms here; this is a dry fish shop."

"Thrice blessed trade!" I answered. "Give me some dried fish, good fellow, or, for the matter of that, dried horse or dog, or anything mortal teeth can bite through, and I will show you my tastes are altogether mundane."

But he shook his head. "This is no place for the likes of you, who come, mayhap, from the city of Yang or some other abode of disembodied spirits—you, who come for mischief and pay harbourage with mischance—is it likely you could eat wholesome food?"

"Indeed I could, and plenty of it, seeing I have dined and breakfasted along the hedges with the blackbirds this two days. Look here, I will pay in advance. Will that get me a meal?" and, whipping out my knife, cut off another of my fast-receding coat buttons.

The man took it with great interest, as I hoped he would, the yellow metal being apparently a very scarce commodity in his part of the planet.

"Gold?" he asked.

"Well—ahem! I forgot to ask the man who sewed them on for me what they were exactly, but it looks like gold, doesn't it?"

"Yes," he answered, turning it to and fro admiringly in his hand, "you are the first ghost I ever knew to pay in advance, and plenty of them go to and fro through here. Such a pretty thing is well worth a meal—if, indeed, you can stomach our rough fare. Here, you woman within," he called to the lady whom I presume was his wife, "here is a gentleman from the nether regions who wants some breakfast and has paid in advance. Give him some of your best, for he has paid well."

"And what," said a female voice from inside, "what if I refused to serve another of these plaguy wanderers you are always foisting upon me?"

"Don't mind her tongue, sir. It's the worst part of her, though she is mighty proud of it. Go in and she will see you do not come out hungry," and the Thither man returned calmly to his honey stick.

"Come on, you Soul-with-a-man's-stomach," growled the woman, and too hungry to be particular about the tone of invitation, I strode into the parlour of that strange refreshment place. The woman was the first I had seen of the outer race, and better than might have been expected in appearance. Big, strong, and ruddy, she was a mental shock after the slender slips of girlhood on the far side of the water, half a dozen of whom she could have carried off without effort in her long arms. Yet there was about her the credential of rough health, the dignity of muscle, an upright carriage, an animal grace of movement, and withal a comely though strongly featured face, which pleased me at once, and later on I had great cause to remember her with gratitude. She eyed me sulkily for a minute, then her frown gradually softened, and the instinctive love of the woman for the supernatural mastered her other feelings.

"Is that how you looked in another world?" she asked.

"Yes, exactly, cap to boots. What do you think of the attire, ma'am?"

"Not much," replied the good woman frankly. "It could not have been becoming even when new, and you appear as though you had taken a muddy road since then. What did you die of?"

"I will tell you so much as this, madam—that what I am like to die of now is hunger, plain, unvarnished hunger, so, in Heaven's name, get out what you have and let me fall-to, for my last meal was yesterday morning."

Whereat, with a shrug of her shoulders at the eccentricities of nether folk, the woman went to the rear of the house, and presently came back with a meal which showed her husband had done scant justice to the establishment by calling it a dry fish shop. It is true, fish supplied the staple of the repast, as was inevitable in a seaport, but, like all Martian fish, it was of ambrosial kind, with a savour about it of wine and sunshine such as no fish on our side of space can boast of. Then there were cakes, steaming and hot, vegetables which fitted into the previous course with exquisite nicety, and, lastly, a wooden tankard of the invariable Thither beer to finish off. Such a meal as a hungry man might consider himself fortunate to meet with any day.

The woman watched me eat with much satisfaction, and when I had answered a score of artless questions about my previous state, or present condition and prospects, more or less to her satisfaction, she supplied me in turn with some information which was really valuable to me just then.

First I learned that Ar-hap's men, with the abducted Heru, had passed through this very port two days before, and by this time were probably in the main town, which, it appeared, was only about twelve hours' rowing up the salt-water estuary outside. Here was news! Heru, the prize and object of my wild adventure, close at hand and well. It brought a whole new train of thoughts, for the last few days had been so full of the stress of travel, the bare, hard necessity of getting forward, that the object of my quest, illogical as it may seem, had gone into the background before these things. And here again, as I finished the last cake and drank down to the bottom of the ale tankard, the extreme folly of the venture came upon me, the madness of venturing single-handed into the den of the Wood King. What had I to hope for? What chance, however remote, was there of successfully wresting that blooming prize from the arms of her captor? Force was out of the question; stealth was utterly impractical; as for cajolery, apparently the sole remaining means of winning back the Princess—why, one might as well try the persuasion of a penny flute upon a hungry eagle as seek to rouse Ar-hap's sympathies for bereaved Hath in that way. Surely to go forward would mean my own certain destruction, with no advantage, no help to Heru; and if I was ever to turn back or stop in the idle quest, here was the place and time. My Hither friends were behind the sea; to them I could return before it was too late, and here were the rough but honest Thither folk, who would doubtless let me live amongst them if that was to be my fate. One or other alternative were better than going to torture and death.

"You seem to take the fate of that Hither girl of yours mightily to heart, stranger," quoth my hostess, with a touch of feminine jealousy, as she watched my hesitation. "Do you know anything of her?"

"Yes," I answered gloomily. "I have seen her once or twice away in Seth."

"Ah, that reminds me! When they brought her up here from the boats to dry her wet clothes, she cried and called in her grief for just such a one as you, saying he alone who struck down our men at her feast could rescue her—"

"What! Heru here in this room but yesterday! How did she look? Was she hurt? How had they treated her?"

My eagerness gave me away. The woman looked at me through her half-shut eyes a space, and then said, "Oh! sits the wind in *that* quarter? So you can love as well as eat. I must say you are well-conditioned for a spirit."

I got up and walked about the room a space, then, feeling very friendless, and knowing no woman was ever born who was not interested in another woman's loves, I boldly drew my hostess aside and told her about Heru, and that I was in pursuit of her, dwelling on the girl's gentle helplessness, my own hare-brained adventure, and frankly asking what sort of a sovereign Ar-hap was, what the customs of his court might be, and whether she could suggest any means, temporal or spiritual, by which he might be moved to give back Heru to her kindred.

Nor was my confidence misplaced. The woman, as I guessed, was touched somewhere back in her female heart by my melting love-tale, by my anxiety and Heru's peril. Besides, a ghost in search of a fairy lady—and such the slender folk of Seth were still considered to be by the race which had supplanted them—this was romance indeed. To be brief, that good woman proved invaluable.

She told me, firstly, that Ar-hap was believed to be away at war, "weekending" as was his custom, amongst rebellious tribes, and by starting at once up the water, I should very probably get to the town before he did. Secondly, she thought if I kept clear of private brawls there was little chance of my receiving injury, from the people at all events, as they were accustomed to strange visitors, and civil enough until they were fired by war. "Sickle cold, sword hot," was one of their proverbs, meaning thereby that in peaceful times they were lambs, however lionlike they might be in contest.

This was reassuring, but as to recovering the lady, that was another matter over which the good woman shook her head. It was ill coming between Ar-hap and his tribute, she said; still, if I wanted to see Heru once again, this was my opportunity, and, for the rest, that chance, which often favours the enamoured, must be my help.

Briefly, though I should probably have gone forward in any case out of sheer obstinacy, had it been to certain destruction, this better aspect of the situation hastened my resolution. I thanked the woman for help, and then the man outside was called in to advise as to the best and speediest way of getting within earshot of his hairy sovereignty, the monarch of Thitherland.

Chapter 16

The Martian told me of a merchant boat with ten rowers which was going up to the capital in a couple of hours, and as the skipper was a friend of his they would no doubt take me as supercargo, thereby saving the necessity of passenger fees, which was obviously a consideration with me. It was not altogether a romantic approach to the dungeon of an imprisoned beauty, but it was practical, which is often better if not so pleasant. So the offer was gladly closed with, and curling myself in a rug of foxskins, for I was tired with much walking, sailors never being good foot-gangers, I slept soundly fill they came to tell me it was time to go on board.

The vessel was more like a canal barge than anything else, lean and long, with the cargo piled in a ridge down the centre as farmers store their winter turnips, the rowers sitting on either side of this plying oars like dessert-spoons with long handles, while they chanted a monotonous cadence of monosyllables:

> *Oh, ho, oh,*
> *Oh, ho, oh,*
> *How high, how high.*

and then again after a pause—

> *How high, how high*
> *Oh, ho, oh,*
> *Oh, ho, oh.*

the which was infinitely sleep-provoking if not a refrain of a high intellectual order.

I shut my eyes as we pulled away from the wharfs of that nameless emporium and picked a passage through a crowd of quaint shipping, wondering where I was, and asking myself whether I was mentally rising equal to my extraordinary surroundings, whether I adequately appreciated the immensity of my remove from those other seas on which I had last travelled, tiller-ropes in hand, piloting a captain's galley from a wharf. Good heavens, what would my comrades on my ship say if they could see me now steering a load of hairy savages up one of those waterways which our biggest telescopes magnify but to the thickness of an indication? No, I was not rising equal to the occasion, and could not. The human mind is of but limited capacity after all, and such freaks of fortune are beyond its conception. I knew I was where I was, but I knew I should probably never get the chance of telling of it, and that no one would ever believe me if I did, and I resigned myself to the inevitable with sullen acquiescence, smothering the wonder that might have been overwhelming in passing interests of the moment.

There is little to record of that voyage. We passed through a fleet of Ar-hap's warships, empty and at anchor in double line, serviceable half-decked cutters, built of solid timber, not pumpkin rind it was pleasant to notice, and then the town dropped away as we proceeded up a stream about as broad as the Hudson at its widest, and profusely studded with islands. This water was bitterly salt and joined another sea on the other side of the Martian continent. Yet it had a pronounced flow against us eastward, this tide running for three spring months and being followed, I learned, as ocean temperatures varied, by a flow in the opposite direction throughout the summer.

Just at present the current was so strong eastwards, the moisture beaded upon my rowers' tawny hides as they struggled against it, and their melancholy song dawdled in "linked sweetness long drawn out," while the swing of their oars grew longer and longer. Truly it was very hot, far hotter than was usual for the season, these men declared, and possibly this robbed me of my wonted energy, and you, gentle reader, of a description of all the strange things we passed upon that highway.

Suffice it to say we spent a scorching afternoon, the greater part of a stifling night moored under a mud-bank with a grove of trees on top from which gigantic fire-flies hung as though the place were illuminated for a garden fete, and then, rowing on again in the comparatively cool hours before dawn, turned into a backwater at cock-crow.

The skipper of our cargo boat roused me just as we turned, putting under my sleepy nostrils a handful of toasted beans on a leaf, and a small cup full of something that was not coffee, but smelt as good as that matutinal beverage always does to the tired traveller.

Over our prow was an immense arch of foliage, and underneath a long arcade of cool black shadows, sheltering still water, till water and shadow suddenly ended a quarter of a mile down in a patch of brilliant colour. It was as peaceful as could be in the first morning light, and to me over all there was the inexpressible attraction of the unknown.

As our boat slipped silently forward up this leafy lane, a thin white "feather" in her mouth alone breaking the steely surface of the stream, the men rested from their work and began, as sailors will, to put on their shore-going clothes, the while they chatted in low tones over the profits of the voyage. Overhead flying squirrels were flitting to and fro like bats, or shelling fruit whereof the husks fell with a pleasant splash about us, and on one bank a couple of early mothers were washing their babies, whose smothered protests were almost the only sound in this morning world.

Another silent dip or two of the oars and the colour ahead crystallised into a town. If I said it was like an African village on a large scale, I should probably give you the best description in the fewest words. From the very water's edge up to the crown of a low hill inland, extended a mass of huts and wooden buildings, embowered and partly hidden in bright green foliage, with here and there patches of millet, or some such food plant, and the flowers that grow everywhere so abundantly in this country. It was all Arcadian and peaceful enough at the moment, and as we drew near the men were just coming out to the quays along the harbour front, the streets filling and the town waking to busy life.

A turn to the left through a watergate defended by towers of wood and mud, and we were in the city harbour itself; boats of many kinds moored on every side; quaint craft from the gulfs and bays of Nowhere, full of unheard-of merchandise, and manned by strange-faced crews, every vessel a romance of nameless seas, an epitome of an undiscovered world, and every moment the scene grew busier as the breakfast smoke arose, and wharf and gangway set to work upon the day's labours.

Our boat—loaded, as it turned out, with spoil from Seth—was run to a place of honour at the bottom of the town square, and was an object of much curiosity to a small crowd which speedily collected and lent a hand with the mooring ropes, the while chatting excitedly with the crew about further tribute and the latest news from overseas. At the same time a swarthy barbarian, whose trappings showed him to be some sort of functionary, came down to our "captain," much wagging of heads and counting of notched sticks taking place between them.

I, indeed, was apparently the least interesting item of the cargo, and this was embarrassing. No hero likes to be neglected, it is fatal to his part. I had said my prayers and steeled myself to all sorts of fine endurance on the way up, and here, when it came to the crisis, no one was anxious to play the necessary villain. They just helped me ashore civilly enough, the captain nodded his head at me, muttering something in an indifferent tone to the functionary about a ghost who had wandered overseas and begged a passage up the canal; the group about the quay stared a little, but that was all.

Once I remember seeing a squatting, life-size heathen idol hoisted from a vessel's hold and deposited on a sugar-box on a New York quay. Some ribald passer-by put a battered felt hat upon Vishnu's sacred curls, and there the poor image sat, an alien in an indifferent land, a sack across its shoulders, a "billycock" upon its head, and honoured at most with a passing stare. I thought of that lonely image as almost as lonely I stood on the Thither men's quay, without the support of friends or heroics, wondering what to do next.

However, a cheerful disposition is sometimes better than a banking account, and not having the one I cultivated the other, sunning myself amongst the bales for a time, and then, since none seemed interested in me, wandered off into the town, partly to satisfy my curiosity, and partly in the vague hope of ascertaining if my princess was really here, and, if possible, getting sight of her.

Meanwhile it turned hot with a supernatural, heavy sort of heat altogether, I overheard passersby exclaiming, out of the common, and after wandering for an hour through gardens and endless streets of thatched huts, I was glad enough to throw myself down in the shadow of some trees on the outskirts of the great central pile of buildings, a whole village in itself of beam-built towers and dwelling-place, suggesting by its superior size that it might actually be Ar-hap's palace.

Hotter and hotter it grew, while a curious secondary sunrise in the west, the like of which I never saw before seemed to add to the heat, and heavier and heavier my eyelids, till I dozed at last, and finally slept uncomfortably for a time.

Rousing up suddenly, imagine my surprise to see sitting, chin on knees, about a yard away, a slender girlish figure, infinitely out of place in that world of rough barbarians. Was it possible? Was I dreaming? No, there was no doubt about it, she was a girl of the Hither folk, slim and pretty, but with a wonderfully sad look in her gazelle eyes, and scarcely a sign of the indolent happiness of Seth in the pale little face regarding me so fixedly.

"Good gracious, miss," I said, still rubbing my eyes and doubting my senses, "have you dropped from the skies? You are the very last person I expected to see in this barbarian place."

EDWIN L. ARNOLD

"And you too, sir. Oh, it is lovely to see one so newly from home, and free-seeming—not a slave."

"How did you know I was from Seth?"

"Oh, that was easy enough," and with a little laugh she pointed to a pebble lying between us, on which was a piece of battered sweetmeat in a perforated bamboo box. Poor An had given me something just like that in a playful mood, and I had kept it in my pocket for her sake, being, as you will have doubtless observed, a sentimental young man, and now I clapped my hand where it should have been, but it was gone.

"Yes," said my new friend, "that is yours. I smelt the sweetmeat coming up the hill, and crossed the grass until I found you here asleep. Oh, it was lovely! I took it from your pocket, and white Seth rose up before my swimming eyes, even at the scent of it. I am Si, well named, for that in our land means sadness, Si, the daughter of Prince Hath's chief sweetmeat-maker, so I should know something of such stuff. May I, please, nibble a little piece?"

"Eat it all, my lass, and welcome. How came you here? But I can guess. Do not answer if you would rather not."

"Ay, but I will. It is not every day I can speak to ears so friendly as yours. I am a slave, chosen for my luckless beauty as last year's tribute to Ar-hap."

"And now?"

"And now the slave of Ar-hap's horse-keeper, set aside to make room for a fresher face."

"And do you know whose face that is?"

"Not I, a hapless maid sent into this land of horrors, to bear ignominy and stripes, to eat coarse food and do coarse work, the miserable plaything of some brute in semi-human form, with but the one consolation of dying early as we tribute-women always die. Poor comrade in exile, I only know her as yet by sympathy."

"What if I said it was Heru, the princess?"

The Martian girl sprang to her feet, and clasping her hands exclaimed,

"Heru, the Slender! Then the end comes, for it is written in our books that the last tribute is paid when the best is paid. Oh, how splendid if she gave herself of free will to this slavery to end it once for all. Was it so?"

"I think, Si, your princess could not have known of that tradition; she did not come willingly. Besides, I am come to fetch her back, if it may be, and that spoils the look of sacrifice."

"You to fetch her back, and from Ar-hap's arms? My word, Sir Spirit, you must know some potent charms; or, what is less likely, my countrymen must have amazingly improved in pluck since I left them. Have you a great army at hand?"

But I only shook my head, and, touching my sword, said that here was the only army coming to rescue Heru. Whereon the lady replied that she thought my valour did me more honour than my discretion. How did I propose to take the princess from her captors?

"To tell the truth, damsel, that is a matter which will have to be left to your invention, or the kindness of such as you. I am here on a hare-brained errand, playing knight-errant in a way that shocks my common sense. But since the matter has gone so far I will see it through, or die in the attempt. Your bully lord shall either give me Heru, stock, lock, and block, or hang me from a yard-arm. But I would rather have the lady. Come, you will help me; and, as a beginning, if she is in yonder shanty get me speech with her."

Poor Si's eyes dilated at the peril of the suggestion, and I saw the sluggish Martian nature at war against her better feelings. But presently the latter conquered. "I will try," she said. "What matter a few stripes more or less?" pointing to her rosy shoulders where red scars crisscross upon one another showed how the Martian girls fared in Ar-hap's palace when their novelty wore off. "I will try to help you; and if they kill me for it—why, that will not matter much." And forthwith in that blazing forenoon under the flickering shadow of the trees we put our heads together to see what we might do for Heru.

It was not much for the moment. Try what we would that afternoon, I could not persuade those who had charge of the princess to let me even approach her place of imprisonment, but Si, as a woman, was more successful, actually seeing her for a few moments, and managed to whisper in her ear that I had come, the Spirit-with-the-gold-buttons-down-his front, afterwards describing to me in flowing Martian imagery—but doubtless not more highly coloured than poor Heru's emotion warranted—how delightedly that lady had received the news.

Si also did me another service, presenting me to the porter's wife, who kept a kind of boarding-house at the gates of Ar-hap's palace for gentlemen and ladies with grievances. I had heard of lobbying before, and the presentation of petitions, though I had never indulged myself in the pastime; but the crowd of petitioners here, with petitions as

EDWIN L. ARNOLD

wild and picturesque as their own motley appearances, was surely the strangest that ever gathered round a seat of supreme authority.

Si whispered in the ear of that good woman the nature of my errand, with doubtless some blandishment of her own; and my errand being one so much above the vulgar and so nearly touching the sovereign, I was at once accorded a separate room in the gate-house, whence I could look down in comparative peace on the common herd of suitors, and listen to the buzz of their invective as they practised speeches which I calculated it would take Ar-hap all the rest of his reign to listen to, without allowing him any time for pronouncing verdicts on them.

Here I made myself comfortable, and awaited the return of the sovereign as placidly as might be. Meanwhile fate was playing into my feeble hands.

I have said it was hot weather. At first this seemed but an outcome of the Martian climate, but as the hours went by the heat developed to an incredible extent. Also that red glare previously noted in the west grew in intensity, till, as the hours slipped by, all the town was staring at it in panting horror. I have seen a prairie on fire, luckily from the far side of a comfortably broad river, and have ridden through a pine-forest when every tree for miles was an uplifted torch, and pungent yellow smoke rolled down each corrie side in grey rivers crested with dancing flame. But that Martian glare was more sombre and terrible than either.

"What is it?" I asked of poor Si, who came out gasping to speak to me by the gate-house.

"None of us know, and unless the gods these Thither folk believe in are angry, and intend to destroy the world with yonder red sword in the sky, I cannot guess. Perhaps," she added, with a sudden flash of inspiration, "it comes by your machinations for Heru's help."

"No!"

"If not by your wish, then, in the name of all you love, set your wish against it. If you know any incantations suitable for the occasion, oh, practise them now at once, for look, even the very grass is withering; birds are dropping from trees; fishes, horribly bloated, are beginning to float down the steaming rills; and I, with all others, have a nameless dread upon me."

Hotter and hotter it grew, until about sunset the red blaze upon the sky slowly opened, and showed us for about half an hour, through the opening a lurid, flame-coloured meteor far out in space beyond; then the cleft closed again, and through that abominable red curtain came the very breath of Hades.

What was really happening I am not astronomer enough to say, though on cooler consideration I have come to the conclusion that our planet, in going out to its summer pastures in the remoter fields of space, had somehow come across a wandering lesser world and got pretty well singed in passing. This is purely my own opinion, and I have not yet submitted it to the kindly authorities of the Lick Observatory for verification. All I can say for certain is that in an incredibly short space of time the face of the country changed from green to sear, flowers drooped; streams (there were not many in the neighbourhood apparently) dried up; fishes died; a mighty thirst there was nothing to quench settled down on man and beast, and we all felt that unless Providence listened to the prayers and imprecations which the whole town set to work with frantic zeal to hurl at it, or that abominable comet in the sky sheered off on another tack with the least possible delay, we should all be reduced to cinders in a very brief space of time.

Chapter 17

The evening of the second day had already come, when Ar-hap arrived home after weekending amongst a tribe of rebellious subjects. But any imposing State entry which might have been intended was rendered impossible by the heat and the threat of that baleful world in the western sky.

It was a lurid but disordered spectacle which I witnessed from my room in the gate-house just after nightfall. The returning army had apparently fallen away exhausted on its march through the town; only some three hundred of the bodyguard straggled up the hill, limp and sweating, behind a group of pennons, in the midst of which rode a horseman whose commanding presence and splendid war harness impressed me, though I could not make out his features; a wild, impressionist scene of black outlines, tossing headgear, and spears glittering and vanishing in front of the red glare in the sky, but nothing more. Even the dry throats of the suitors in the courtyard hardly mustered a husky cry of welcome as the cavalcade trooped into the enclosure, and then the shadows enfolded them up in silence, and, too hot and listless to care much what the morrow brought forth, I threw myself on the bare floor, tossing and turning in a vain endeavour to sleep until dawn came once more.

A thin mist which fell with daybreak drew a veil over the horrible glare in the west for an hour or two, and taking advantage of the slight alleviation of heat, I rose and went into the gardens to enjoy a dip in a pool, making, with its surrounding jungle of flowers, one of the pleasantest things about the wood-king's forest citadel. The very earth seemed scorched and baking underfoot—and the pool was gone! It had run as dry as a limekiln; nothing remained of the pretty fall which had fed it but a miserable trickle of drops from the cascade above. Down beyond the town shone a gleam of water where the bitter canal steamed and simmered in the first grey of the morning, but up here six months of scorching drought could not have worked more havoc. The very leaves were dropping from the trees, and the luxuriant growths of the day before looked as though a simoon had played upon them.

I staggered back in disgust, and found some show of official activity about the palace. It was the king's custom, it appeared, to hear petitions and redress wrongs as soon after his return as possible, but today the ceremony was to be cut short as his majesty was going out with all his court to a neighbouring mountain to "pray away the comet," which by this time was causing dire alarm all through the city.

"Heaven's own particular blessing on his prayers, my friend," I said to the man who told me this. "Unless his majesty's orisons are fruitful, we shall all be cooked like baked potatoes before nightfall, and though I have faced many kinds of death, that is not the one I would choose by preference. Is there a chance of myself being heard at the throne? Your peculiar climate tempts me to hurry up with my business and begone if I may."

"Not only may you be heard, sir, but you are summoned. The king has heard of you somehow, and sent me to find and bring you into his presence at once."

"So be it," I said, too hot to care what happened. "I have no levee dress with me. I lost my luggage check some time ago, but if you will wait outside I will be with you in a moment."

Hastily tidying myself up, and giving my hair a comb, as though just off to see Mr. Secretary for the Navy, or on the way to get a senator to push a new patent medicine for me, I rejoined my guide outside, and together we crossed the wide courtyard, entered the great log-built portals of Ar-hap's house, and immediately afterwards found ourselves in a vast hall dimly lit by rays coming in through square spaces under the eaves, and crowded on both sides with guards, courtiers, and supplicants. The heat was tremendous, the odour of Thither men and the ill-dressed hides they wore almost overpowering. Yet little I recked for either, for there at the top of the room, seated on a dais made of rough-hewn wood inlet with gold and covered with splendid furs, was Ar-hap himself.

A fine fellow, swarthy, huge, and hairy, at any other time or place I could have given him due admiration as an admirable example of the savage on the borderland of grace and culture, but now I only glanced at him, and then to where at his side a girl was crouching, a gem of human loveliness against that dusky setting. It was Heru, my ravished princess, and, still clad in her diaphanous Hither robes, her face white with anxiety, her eyes bright as stars, the embodiment of helpless, flowery beauty, my heart turned over at sight of her.

Poor girl! When she saw me stride into the hall she rose swiftly from Ar-hap's side, clasped her pretty hands, and giving a cry of joy would have rushed towards me, but the king laid a mighty paw upon her, under which she subsided with a shiver as though the touch had blanched all the life within.

"Good morning, your majesty," I said, walking boldly up to the lower step of the dais.

"Good morning, most singular-looking vagrant from the Unknown," answered the monarch. "In what way can I be of service to you?"

"I have come about that girl," I said, nodding to where Heru lay blossoming in the hot gloom like some night-flowering bud. "I do not know whether your majesty is aware how she came here, but it is a highly discreditable incident in what is doubtless your otherwise blameless reign. Some rough scullions intrusted with the duty of collecting your majesty's customs asked Prince Hath of the Hither people to point out the most attractive young person at his wedding feast, and the prince indicated that lady there at your side. It was a dirty trick, and all the worse because it was inspired by malice, which is the meanest of all weaknesses. I had the pleasure of knocking down some of your majesty's representatives, but they stole the girl away while I slept, and, briefly, I have come to fetch her back."

The monarch had followed my speech, the longest ever made in my life, with fierce, blinking eyes, and when it stopped looked at poor shrinking Heru as though for explanation, then round the circle of his awestruck courtiers, and reading dismay at my boldness in their faces, burst into a guttural laugh.

"I suppose you have the great and puissant Hither nation behind you in this request, Mr. Spirit?"

"No, I came alone, hoping to find justice here, and, if not, then prepared to do all I could to make your majesty curse the day your servants maltreated my friends."

"Tall words, stranger! May I ask what you propose to do if Ar-hap, in his own palace, amongst his people and soldiers, refuses to disgorge a pretty prize at the bidding of one shabby interloper—muddy and friendless?"

"What should I do?"

"Yes," said the king, with a haughty frown. "What would you do?"

I do not know what prompted the reply. For a moment I was completely at a loss what to say to this very obvious question, and then all on a sudden, remembering they held me to be some kind of disembodied spirit, by a happy inspiration, fixing my eyes grimly on the king, I answered,

"What would I do? Why, *I would haunt you!*"

It may not seem a great stroke of genius here, but the effect on the Martian was instantaneous. He sat straight up, his hands tightened, his eyes dilated, and then fidgeting uneasily, after a minute he beckoned to an over-dressed individual, whom Heru afterwards told me was the Court necromancer, and began whispering in his ear.

After a minute's consultation he turned again, a rather frightened civility struggling in his face with anger, and said, "We have no wish, of course, stranger, to offend you or those who had the honour of your patronage. Perhaps the princess here was a little roughly handled, and, I confess, if she were altogether as reluctant as she seems, a lesser maid would have done as well. I could have wooed this one in Seth, where I may shortly come, and our espousals would possibly have lent, in the eyes of your friends, quite a cheerful aspect to my arrival. But my ambassadors have had no great schooling in diplomacy; they have brought Princess Heru here, and how can I hand her over to one I know nothing of? How do I know you are a ghost, after all? How do I know you have anything but a rusty sword and much impertinence to back your astounding claim?"

"Oh, let it be just as you like," I said, calmly shelling and eating a nut I had picked up. "Only if you do not give the maid back, why, then—" And I stopped as though the sequel were too painful to put into words.

Again that superstitious monarch of a land thronged with malicious spirits called up his magician, and, after they had consulted a moment, turned more cheerfully to me.

"Look here, Mister-from-Nowhere, if you are really a spirit, and have the power to hurt as you say, you will have the power also to go and come between the living and the dead, between the present and the past. Now I will set you an errand, and give you five minutes to do it in."

"Five minutes!" I exclaimed in incautious alarm.

"Five minutes," said the monarch savagely. "And if in that time the errand is not done, I shall hold you to be an impostor, an impudent thief from some scoundrel tribe of this world of mine, and will make of you an example which shall keep men's ears tingling for a century or two."

Poor Heru dropped in a limp and lovely heap at that dire threat, while I am bound to say I felt somewhat uncomfortable, not unnaturally when all the circumstances are considered, but contented myself with remarking, with as much bravado as could be managed,

"And now to the errand, Ar-hap. What can I do for your majesty?"

EDWIN L. ARNOLD

The king consulted with the rogue at his elbow, and then nodding and chuckling in expectancy of his triumph, addressed me.

"Listen," he cried, smiting a huge hairy hand upon his knee, "listen, and do or die. My magician tells me it is recorded in his books that once, some five thousand years ago, when this land belonged to the Hither people, there lived here a king. It is a pity he died, for he seems to have been a jovial old fellow; but he did die, and, according to their custom, they floated him down the stream that flows to the regions of eternal ice, where doubtless he is at this present moment, caked up with ten million of his subjects. Now just go and find that sovereign for me, oh you bold-tongued dweller in other worlds!"

"And if I go how am I to know your ancient king, as you say, amongst ten million others?"

"That is easy enough," quoth Ar-hap lightly. "You have only to pass to and fro through the ice mountains, opening the mouths of the dead men and women you meet, and when you come to a middle-sized man with a fillet on his head and a jaw mended with gold, that will be he whom you look for. Bring me that fillet here within five minutes and the maid is yours."

I started, and stared hard in amazement. Was this a dream? Was the royal savage in front playing with me? By what incredible chance had he hit upon the very errand I could answer to best, the very trophy I had brought away from the grim valley of ice and death, and had still in my shoulder-bag? No, he was not playing; he was staring hard in turn, joying in my apparent confusion, and clearly thinking he had cornered me beyond hope of redemption.

"Surely your mightiness is not daunted by so simple a task," scowled the sovereign, playing with the hilt of his huge hunting-knife, "and all amongst your friends' kindred too. On a hot day like this it ought to be a pleasant saunter for a spirit such as yourself."

"Not daunted," I answered coldly, turning on my heels towards the door, "only marvelling that your majesty's skull and your necromancer's could not between them have devised a harder task."

Out into the courtyard I went, with my heart beating finely in spite of my assumed indifference; got the bag from a peg in my sleeping-room, and was back before the log throne ere four minutes were gone.

"The old Hither king's compliments to your majesty," I said, bowing, while a deathly hush fell on all the assembly, "and he says though your ancestors little liked to hear his voice while alive, he says he has no objection to giving you some jaw now he is dead," and I threw down on the floor the golden circlet of the frozen king.

Ar-hap's eyes almost started from his head as, with his courtiers, he glared in silent amazement at that shining thing while the great drops of fear and perspiration trickled down his forehead. As for poor Heru, she rose like a spirit behind them, gazed at the jaw-bone of her mythical ancestor, and then suddenly realising my errand was done and she apparently free, held out her hands, and, with a tremulous cry, would have come to me.

But Ar-hap was too quick for her. All the black savage blood swelled into his veins as he swept her away with one great arm, and then with his foot gave the luckless jaw a kick that sent it glittering and spinning through the far doorway out into the sunshine.

"Sit down," he roared, "you brazen wench, who are so eager to leave a king's side for a nameless vagrant's care! And you, sir," turning to me, and fairly trembling with rage and dread, "I will not gainsay that you have done the errand set you, but it might this once be chance that got you that cursed token, some one happy turn of luck. I will not yield my prize on one throw of the dice. Another task you must do. Once might be chance, but such chance comes not twice."

"You swore to give me the maid this time."

"And why should I keep my word to a half-proved spirit such as you?"

"There are some particularly good reasons why you should," I said, striking an attitude which I had once seen a music-hall dramatist take when he was going to blast somebody's future—a stick with a star on top of it in his hand and forty lines of blank verse in his mouth.

The king writhed, and begged me with a sign to desist.

"We have no wish to anger you. Do us this other task and none will doubt that you are a potent spirit, and even I, Ar-hap, will listen to you."

"Well, then," I answered sulkily, "what is it to be this time?"

After a minute's consultation, and speaking slowly as though conscious of how much hung on his words, the king said,

"Listen! My soothsayer tells me that somewhere there is a city lost in a forest, and a temple lost in the city, and a tomb lost in the temple; a city of ghosts and djins given over to bad spirits, wherefore all human men shun it by day and night. And on the tomb is she who was once queen there, and by her lies her crown. Quick! oh you to whom all distances are nothing, and who see, by your finer essence, into all times and places. Away to that city! Jostle the memories of the unclean things

EDWIN L. ARNOLD

that hide in its shadows; ask which amongst them knows where dead Queen Yang still lies in dusty state. Get guides amongst your comrade ghosts. Find Queen Yang, and bring me here in five minutes the bloody circlet from her hair."

Then, and then for the first time, I believed the planet was haunted indeed, and I myself unknowingly under some strange and watchful influence. Spirits, demons! Oh! what but some incomprehensible power, some unseen influence shaping my efforts to its ends, could have moved that hairy barbarian to play a second time into my hands like this, to choose from the endless records of his world the second of the two incidents I had touched in hasty travel through it? I was almost overcome for a minute; then, pulling myself together, strode forward fiercely, and, speaking so that all could hear me, cried, "Base king, who neither knows the capacities of a spirit nor has learned as yet to dread its anger, see! your commission is executed in a thought, just as your punishment might be. Heru, come here." And when the girl, speechless with amazement, had risen and slipped over to me, I straightened her pretty hair from her forehead, and then, in a way which would make my fortune if I could repeat it at a conjuror's table, whipped poor Yang's gemmy crown from my pocket, flashed its baleful splendour in the eyes of the courtiers, and placed it on the tresses of the first royal lady who had worn it since its rightful owner died a hundred years before.

A heavy silence fell on the hall as I finished, and nothing was heard for a time save Heru sobbing on my breast and a thirsty baby somewhere outside calling to its mother for the water that was not to be had. But presently on those sounds came the fall of anxious feet, and a messenger, entering the doorway, approached the throne, laid himself out flat twice, after which obeisance he proceeded to remind the king of the morning's ceremonial on a distant hill to "pray away the comet," telling his majesty that all was ready and the procession anxiously awaiting him.

Whereon Ar-hap, obviously very well content to change the subject, rose, and, coming down from the dais, gave me his hand. He was a fine fellow, as I have said, strong and bold, and had not behaved badly for an autocrat, so that I gripped his mighty fist with great pleasure.

"I cannot deny, stranger," he said, "that you have done all that has been asked of you, and the maid is fairly yours. Yet before you take away the prize I must have some assurance of what you yourself will do with her. Therefore, for the moment, until this horrible thing in the sky which threatens my people with destruction has gone, let it be truce between us—you to your lodgings, and the princess back, unharmed, amongst my women till we meet again."

"But—"

"No, no," said the king, waving his hand. "Be content with your advantage. And now to business more important than ten thousand silly wenches," and gathering up his robes over his splendid war-gear the wood king stalked haughtily from the hall.

Chapter 18

Hotter and hotter grew that stifling spell, more and more languid man and beast, drier and drier the parching earth.

All the water gave out on the morning after I had bearded Ar-hap in his den, and our strength went with it. No earthly heat was ever like it, and it drank our vitality up from every pore. Water there was down below in the bitter, streaming gulf, but so noisome that we dared not even bathe there; here there was none but the faintest trickle. All discipline was at an end; all desire save such as was born of thirst. Heru I saw as often as I wished as she lay gasping, with poor Si at her feet, in the women's verandah; but the heat was so tremendous that I gazed at her with lack-lustre eyes, staggering to and fro amongst the courtyard shadows, without nerve to plot her rescue or strength to carry out anything my mind might have conceived.

We prayed for rain and respite. Ar-hap had prayed with a wealth of picturesque ceremonial. We had all prayed and cursed by turns, but still the heavens would not relent, and the rain came not.

At last the stifling heat and vapour reached an almost intolerable pitch. The earth reeked with unwholesome humours no common summer could draw from it, the air was sulphurous and heavy, while overhead the sky seemed a tawny dome, from edge to edge of angry clouds, parting now and then to let us see the red disc threatening us.

Hour after hour slipped by until, when evening was upon us, the clouds drew together, and thunder, with a continuous low rumble, began to rock from sky to sky. Fitful showers of rain, odorous and heavy, but unsatisfying, fell, and birds and beasts of the woodlands came slinking in to our streets and courtyards. Ever since the sky first darkened our own animals had become strangely familiar, and now here were these wild things of the woods slinking in for companionship, sagheaded and frightened. To me especially they came, until that last evening as I staggered dying about the streets or sat staring into the remorseless sky from the steps of Heru's prison house, all sorts of beasts drew softly in and crowded about, whether I sat or moved, all asking for the hope I had not to give them.

At another time this might have been embarrassing; then it seemed pure commonplace. It was a sight to see them slink in between the useless showers, which fell like hot tears upon us—sleek panthers with lolling tongues; russet-red wood dogs; bears and sloths from the dark arcades of the remote forests, all casting themselves down gasping in the palace shadows; strange deer, who staggered to the garden plots and lay there heaving their lives out; mighty boars, who came from the river marshes and silently nozzled a place amongst their enemies to die in! Even the wolves came off the hills, and, with bloodshot eyes and tongues that dripped foam, flung themselves down in my shadow.

All along the tall stockades apes sat sad and listless, and on the roof-ridges storks were dying. Over the branches of the trees, whose leaves were as thin as though we had had a six months' drought, the toucans and Martian parrots hung limp and fashionless like gaudy rags, and in the courtyard ground the corn-rats came up from their tunnels in the scorching earth to die, squeaking in scores along under the walls.

Our common sorrow made us as sociable as though I were Noah, and Ar-hap's palace mound another Ararat. Hour after hour I sat amongst all these lesser beasts in the hot darkness, waiting for the end. Every now and then the heavy clouds parted, changing the gloom to sudden fiery daylight as the great red eye in the west looked upon us through the crevice, and, taking advantage of those gleams, I would reel across to where, under a spout leading from a dried rivulet, I had placed a cup to collect the slow and tepid drops that were all now coming down the reed for Heru. And as I went back each time with that sickly spoonful at the bottom of the vessel all the dying beasts lifted their heads and watched—the thirsty wolves shambling after me; the boars half sat up and grunted plaintively; the panthers, too weak to rise, beat the dusty ground with their tails; and from the portico the blue storks, with trailing wings, croaked husky greeting.

But slower and slower came the dripping water, more and more intolerable the heat. At last I could stand it no longer. What purpose did it serve to lay gasping like this, dying cruelly without a hope of rescue, when a shorter way was at my side? I had not drank for a day and a half. I was past active reviling; my head swam; my reason was clouded. No! I would not stand it any longer. Once more I would take Heru and poor Si the cup that was but a mockery after all, then fix my sword into the ground and try what next the Fates had in store for me.

So once again the leathern mug was fetched and carried through the prostrate guards to where the Martian girl lay, like a withered flower, upon her couch. Once again I moistened those fair lips, while my own tongue was black and swollen in my throat, then told Si, who had had

none all the afternoon, to drink half and leave half for
put her aching lips to the cup and tilted it a little, then pa
mistress. And Heru drank it all, and Si cried a few hot tears
hands, *for she had taken none*, and she knew it was her life!

Again picking a way through the courtyard, scarce noticing r.
beasts lifted their heads as I passed, I went instinctively, cup in har
the well, and then hesitated. Was I a coward to leave Heru so? Ou,
I not to stay and see it out to the bitter end? Well, I would compoun
with Fate. I would give the malicious gods one more chance. I would
put the cup down again, and until seven drops had fallen into it I would
wait. That there might be no mistake about it, no sooner was the mug
in place under the nozzle wherefrom the moisture beads collected and
fell with infinite slowness, than my sword, on which I meant to throw
myself, was bared and the hilt forced into a gaping crack in the ground,
and sullenly contented to leave my fate so, I sat down beside it.

I turned grimly to the spout and saw the first drop fall, then another,
and another later on, but still no help came. There was a long rift in the
clouds now, and a glare like that from an open furnace door was upon
me. I had noticed when I came to the spring how the comet which was
killing us hung poised exactly upon the point of a distant hill. If he had
passed his horrible meridian, if he was going from us, if he sunk but a
hair's breadth before that seventh drop should fall, I could tell it would
mean salvation.

But the fourth drop fell, and he was big as ever. The fifth drop
fell, and a hot, pleasing nose was thrust into my hand, and looking
down I saw a grey wolf had dragged herself across the court and was
asking with eloquent eyes for the help I could not give. The sixth drop
gathered, and fell; already the seventh was like a seedling pearl in its
place. The dying wolf yanked affectionately at my hand, but I put her
by and undid my tunic. Big and bright that drop hung to the spout lip;
another minute and it would fall. A beautiful drop, I laughed, peering
closely at it, many-coloured, prismatic, flushing red and pink, a tiny
living ruby, hanging by a touch to the green rim above; enough! enough!
The quiver of an eyelash would unhinge it now; and angry with the life
I already felt was behind me, and turning in defiant expectation to the
new to come, I rose, saw the red gleam of my sword jutting like a fiery
spear from the cracking soil where I had planted it, then looked once
more at the drop and glanced for the last time at the sullen red terror
on the hill.

es dazed, my senses reeling? I said a space ago that the
exactly on the mountain-top and if it sunk a hair's breadth
e it; and now, why, there *was* a flaw in its lower margin, a
of the great red foot that before had been round and perfect.
my smarting eyes away a minute,—saw the seventh drop fall
melodious tingle into the cup, then back again,—there was no
ake—the truant fire was a fraction less, it had shrunk a fraction
hind the hill even since I looked, and thereon all my life ran back
into its channels, the world danced before me, and "Heru!" I shouted
hoarsely, reeling back towards the palace, "Heru, 'tis well; the worst is
past!"

But the little princess was unconscious, and at her feet was poor
Si, quite dead, still reclining with her head in her hands just as I had
left her. Then my own senses gave out, and dropping down by them I
remembered no more.

I must have lain there an hour or two, for when consciousness
came again it was night—black, cool, profound night, with an inky
sky low down upon the tree-tops, and out of it such a glorious deluge
of rain descending swiftly and silently as filled my veins even to listen
to. Eagerly I shuffled away to the porch steps, down them into the
swimming courtyard, and ankle-deep in the glorious flood, set to work
lapping furiously at the first puddle, drinking with gasps of pleasure,
gasping and drinking again, feeling my body filling out like the thirsty
steaming earth below me. Then, as I still drank insatiably, there came a
gleam of lightning out of the gloom overhead, a brilliant yellow blaze,
and by it I saw a few yards away a panther drinking at the same pool as
myself, his gleaming eyes low down like mine upon the water, and by
his side two apes, the black water running in at their gaping mouths,
while out beyond were more pools, more drinking animals. Everything
was drinking. I saw their outlined forms, the gleam shining on wet
skins as though they were cut out in silver against the darkness, each
beast steaming like a volcano as the Heaven-sent rain smoked from his
fevered hide, all drinking for their lives, heedless of aught else—and
then came the thunder.

It ran across the cloudy vault as though the very sky were being
ripped apart, rolling in mighty echoes here and there before it died
away. As it stopped, the rain also fell less heavily for a minute, and
as I lay with my face low down I heard the low, contented lapping
of numberless tongues unceasing, insatiable. Then came the lightning

EDWIN L. ARNOLD

again, lighting up everything as though it were daytime. The twin black apes were still drinking, but the panther across the puddle had had enough; I saw him lift his grateful head up to the flare; saw the limp red tongue licking the black nose, the green eyes shining like opals, the water dripping in threads of diamonds from the hairy tag under his chin and every tuft upon his chest—then darkness again.

To and fro the green blaze rocked between the thunder crashes. It struck a house a hundred yards away, stripping every shingle from the roof better than a master builder could in a week. It fell a minute after on a tall tree by the courtyard gate, and as the trunk burst into white splinters I saw every leaf upon the feathery top turn light side up against the violet reflection in the sky beyond, and then the whole mass came down to earth with a thud that crushed the courtyard palings into nothing for twenty yards and shook me even across the square.

Another time I might have stopped to marvel or to watch, as I have often watched with sympathetic pleasure, the gods thus at play; but tonight there were other things on hand. When I had drunk, I picked up an earthen crock, filled it, and went to Heru. It was a rough drinking-vessel for those dainty lips, and an indifferent draught, being as much mud as aught else, but its effect was wonderful. At the first touch of that turgid stuff a shiver of delight passed through the drowsy lady. At the second she gave a sigh, and her hand tightened on my arm. I fetched another crockful, and by the flickering light rocking to and fro in the sky, took her head upon my shoulder, like a prodigal new come into riches, squandering the stuff, giving her to drink and bathing face and neck till presently, to my delight, the princess's eyes opened. Then she sat up, and taking the basin from me drank as never lady drank before, and soon was almost herself again.

I went out into the portico, there snuffing the deep, strong breath of the fragrant black earth receiving back into its gaping self what the last few days had taken from it, while quick succeeding thoughts of escape and flight passed across my brain. All through the fiery time we had just had the chance of escaping with the fair booty yonder had been present. Without her, flight would have been easy enough, but that was not worth considering for a moment. With her it was more difficult, yet, as I had watched the woodmen, accustomed to cool forest shades, faint under the fiery glare of the world above, to make a dash for liberty seemed each hour more easy. I had seen the men in the streets drop one by one, and the spears fall from the hands of guards about the pallisades; I had seen messengers who came to and fro collapse before their errands were accomplished, and the forest women, who were Heru's gaolers, groan and drop across the thresholds of her prison, until at length the way was clear—a babe might have taken what he would from that half-scorched town and asked no man's leave. Yet what did it avail me? Heru was helpless, my own spirit burnt in a nerveless frame, and so we stayed.

But with rain strength came back to both of us. The guards, lying about like black logs, were only slowly returning to consciousness; the town still slept, and darkness favoured; before they missed us in the morning light we might be far on the way back to Seth—a dangerous way truly, but we were like to tread a rougher one if we stayed. In fact, directly my strength returned with the cooler air, I made up my mind to the venture and went to Heru, who by this time was much recovered. To her I whispered my plot, and that gentle lady, as was only natural, trembled at its dangers. But I put it to her that no time could be better than the present: the storm was going over; morning would "line the black mantle of the night with a pink dawn of promise"; before any one stirred we might be far off, shaping a course by our luck and the stars for her kindred, at whose name she sighed. If we stayed, I argued, and the king changed his mind, then death for me, and for Heru the arms of that surly monarch, and all the rest of her life caged in these pallisades amongst the uncouth forms about us.

The lady gave a frightened little shiver at the picture, but after a moment, laying her head upon my shoulder, answered, "Oh, my guardian spirit and helper in adversity, I too have thought of tomorrow, and doubt whether that horror, that great swine who has me, will not invent an excuse for keeping me. Therefore, though the forest roads are dreadful, and Seth very far away, I will come; I give myself into your hands. Do what you will with me."

"Then the sooner the better, princess. How soon can you be prepared?"

She smiled, and stooping picked up her slippers, saying as she did so, "I am ready!"

There were no arrangements to be made. Every instant was of value. So, to be brief, I threw a dark cloak over the damsel's shoulders, for indeed she was clad in little more than her loveliness and the gauziest filaments of a Hither girl's underwear, and hand in hand led her down the log steps, over the splashing, ankle-deep courtyard, and into the shadows of the gateway beyond.

Down the slope we went; along towards the harbour, through a score of deserted lanes where nothing was to be heard but the roar of rain and the lapping of men and beasts, drinking in the shadows as though they never would stop, and so we came at last unmolested to the wharf. There I hid royal Seth between two piles of merchandise, and went to look for a boat suitable to our needs. There were plenty of small craft moored to rings along the quay, and selecting a canoe—it was no time to stand on niceties of property—easily managed by a single paddle, I brought it round to the steps, put in a fresh water-pot, and went for the princess.

With her safely stowed in the prow, a helpless, sodden little morsel of feminine loveliness, things began to appear more hopeful and an escape down to blue water, my only idea, for the first time possible. Yet I must needs go and well nigh spoil everything by over-solicitude for my charge.

Had we pushed off at once there can be no doubt my credit as a spirit would have been established for all time in the Thither capital, and the belief universally held that Heru had been wafted away by my enchantment to the regions of the unknown. The idea would have gradually grown into a tradition, receiving embellishments in succeeding generations, until little wood children at their mother's knees came to listen in awe to the story of how, once upon a time, the Sun-god loved a beautiful maiden, and drove his fiery chariot across the black night-fields to her prison door, scorching to death all who strove to gainsay him. How she flew into his arms and drove away before all men's eyes, in his red car, into the west, and was never seen again—the foresaid Sun-god being I, Gulliver Jones, a much under-paid lieutenant in the glorious United States navy, with a packet of overdue tailors' bills in my pocket, and nothing lovable about me save a partiality for meddling with other people's affairs.

This is how it might have been, but I spoiled a pretty fairy story and changed the whole course of Martian history by going back at that moment in search of a wrap for my prize. Right on top of the steps was a man with a lantern, and half a glance showed me it was the harbour master met with on my first landing.

"Good evening," he said suspiciously. "May I ask what you are doing on the quay at such an hour as this?"

"Doing? Oh, nothing in particular, just going out for a little fishing."

"And your companion the lady—is she too fond of fishing?"

I swore between my teeth, but could not prevent the fellow walking to the quay edge and casting his light full upon the figure of the girl below. I hate people who interfere with other people's business!

"Unless I am very much mistaken your fishing friend is the Hither woman brought here a few days ago as tribute to Ar-hap."

"Well," I answered, getting into a nice temper, for I had been very much harrassed of late, "put it at that. What would you do if it were so?"

"Call up my rain-drunk guards, and give you in charge as a thief caught meddling with the king's property."

"Thanks, but as my interviews with Ar-hap have already begun to grow tedious, we will settle this little matter here between ourselves at once." And without more to-do I closed with him. There was a brief scuffle and then I got in a blow upon his jaw which sent the harbour master flying back head over heels amongst the sugar bales and potatoes.

Without waiting to see how he fared I ran down the steps, jumped on board, loosened the rope, and pushed out into the river. But my heart was angry and sore, for I knew, as turned out to be the case, that our secret was one no more; in a short time we should have the savage king in pursuit, and now there was nothing for it but headlong flight with only a small chance of getting away to distant Seth.

Luckily the harbour master lay insensible until he was found at dawn, so that we had a good start, and the moment the canoe passed from the arcade-like approach to the town the current swung her head automatically seaward, and away we went down stream at a pace once more filling me with hope.

Chapter 19

All went well and we fled down the bitter stream of the Mart____ at a pace leaving me little to do but guide our course just c_ snags and promontories on the port shore. Just before dawn, how____ with a thin mist on the water and flocks of a flamingo-like bird croaki__ as they flew southward overhead, we were nearly captured again.

Drifting silently down on a rocky island, I was having a drink at the water-pitcher at the moment, while Heru, her hair beaded with prismatic moisture and looking more ethereal than ever, sat in the bows timorously inhaling the breath of freedom, when all on a sudden voices invisible in the mist, came round a corner. It was one of Ar-hap's war-canoes toiling up-stream. Heru and I ducked down into the haze like dab-chicks and held our breath.

Straight on towards us came the toiling ship, the dip of oars resonant in the hollow fog and a ripple babbling on her cutwater plainly discernible.

> *Oh, oh!*
> *Hoo, hoo!*
> *How high, how high!"*

sounded the sleepy song of the rowers till they were looming right abreast and we could smell their damp hides in the morning air. Then they stopped suddenly and some one asked,

"Is there not something like a boat away on the right?"

"It is nothing," said another, "but the lees of last night's beer curdling in your stupid brain."

"But I saw it move."

"That must have been in dreams."

"What is all that talking about?" growled a sleepy voice of authority from the stern.

"Bow man, sir, says he can see a boat."

"And what does it matter if he can? Are we to delay every time that lazy ruffian spying a shadow makes it an excuse to stop to yawn and scratch? Go on, you plankful of lubbers, or I'll give you something worth thinking about!" And joyfully, oh, so joyfully, we heard the sullen dip of oars commence again.

...ore happened after that till the sun at length shone on the
...r town at the estuary mouth, making the masts of fishing
...ering there like a golden reed-bed against the cool, clean blue
...a beyond.

...ght glad we were to see it, and keeping now in shadow of the
...s, made all haste while light was faint and mist hung about to reach
...e town, finally pushing through the boats and gaining a safe hiding-
place without hostile notice before it was clear daylight.

Covering Heru up and knowing well all our chances of escape lay
in expedition, I went at once, in pursuance of a plan made during the
night, to the good dame at what, for lack of a better name, must still
continue to be called the fish-shop, and finding her alone, frankly told
her the salient points of my story. When she learned I had "robbed
the lion of his prey" and taken his new wife singlehanded from the
dreaded Ar-hap her astonishment was unbounded. Nothing would do
but she must look upon the princess, so back we went to the hiding-
place, and when Heru knew that on this woman depended our lives she
stepped ashore, taking the rugged Martian hand in her dainty fingers
and begging her help so sweetly that my own heart was moved, and,
thrusting hands in pocket, I went aside, leaving those two to settle it in
their own female way.

And when I looked back in five minutes, royal Seth had her
arms round the woman's neck, kissing the homely cheeks with more
than imperial fervour, so I knew all was well thus far, and stopped
expectorating at the little fishes in the water below and went over to
them. It was time! We had hardly spoken together a minute when a
couple of war-canoes filled with men appeared round the nearest
promontory, coming down the swift water with arrow-like rapidity.

"Quick!" said the fishwife, "or we are all lost. Into your canoe and
paddle up this creek. It runs out to the sea behind the town, and at the
bar is my man's fishing-boat amongst many others. Lie hidden there
till he comes if you value your lives." So in we got, and while that good
Samaritan went back to her house we cautiously paddled through a
deserted backwater to where it presently turned through low sandbanks
to the gulf. There were the boats, and we hid the canoe and lay down
amongst them till, soon after, a man, easily recognised as the husband
of our friend, came sauntering down from the village.

At first he was sullen, not unreasonably alarmed at the danger into
which his good woman was running him. But when he set eyes on Heru

he softened immediately. Probably that thick-bodied fellow had n
seen so much female loveliness in so small a bulk in all his life, ɛ
being a man, he surrendered at discretion.

"In with you, then," he growled, "since I must needs risk my neck fo.
a pair of runaways who better deserve to be hung than I do. In with you
both into this fishing-cobble of mine, and I will cover you with nets
while I go for a mast and sail, and mind you lie as still as logs. The town
is already full of soldiers looking for you, and it will be short shrift for
us all if you are seen."

Well aware of the fact and now in the hands of destiny, the princess
and I lay down as bidden in the prow, and the man covered us lightly
over with one of those fine meshed seines used by these people to catch
the little fish I had breakfasted on more than once.

Materially I could have enjoyed the half-hour which followed, since
such rest after exertion was welcome, the sun warm, the lapping of sea
on shingle infinitely soothing, and, above all, Heru was in my arms!
How sweet and childlike she was! I could feel her little heart beating
through her scanty clothing, while every now and then she turned her
gazelle eyes to mine with a trust and admiration infinitely alluring. Yes!
as far as that went I could have lain there with that slip of maiden
royalty for ever, but the fascination of the moment was marred by the
thought of our danger. What was to prevent these new friends giving
us away? They knew we had no money to recompense them for the risk
they were running. They were poor, and a splendid reward, wealth itself
to them, would doubtless be theirs if they betrayed us even by a look.
Yet somehow I trusted them as I have trusted the poor before with the
happiest results, and telling myself this and comforting Heru, I listened
and waited.

Minute by minute went by. It seemed an age since the fisherman had
gone, but presently the sound of voices interrupted the sea's murmur.
Cautiously stealing a glance through a chink imagine my feelings on
perceiving half a dozen of Ar-hap's soldiers coming down the beach
straight towards us! Then my heart was bitter within me, and I tasted
of defeat, even with Heru in my arms. Luckily even in that moment
of agony I kept still, and another peep showed the men were now
wandering about rather aimlessly. Perhaps after all they did not know
of our nearness? Then they took to horseplay, as idle soldiers will even in
Mars, pelting each other with bits of wood and dead fish, and thereon
I breathed again.

earer they came and nearer, my heart beating fast as they strolled ongst the boats until they were actually "larking" round the one next ours. A minute or two of this, and another footstep crunched on the ebbles, a quick, nervous one, which my instinct told me was that of our returning friend.

"Hullo old sprat-catcher! Going for a sail?" called out a soldier, and I knew that the group were all round our boat, Heru trembling so violently in my breast that I thought she would make the vessel shake.

"Yes," said the man gruffly.

"Let's go with him," cried several voices. "Here, old dried haddock, will you take us if we help haul your nets for you?"

"No, I won't. Your ugly faces would frighten all the fish out of the sea."

"And yours, you old chunk of dried mahogany, is meant to attract them no doubt."

"Let's tie him to a post and go fishing in his boat ourselves," some one suggested. Meanwhile two of them began rocking the cobble violently from side to side. This was awful, and every moment I expected the net and the sail which our friend had thrown down unceremoniously upon us would roll off.

"Oh, stop that," said the Martian, who was no doubt quite as well aware of the danger as we were. "The tide's full, the shoals are in the bay—stop your nonsense, and help me launch like good fellows."

"Well, take two of us, then. We will sit on this heap of nets as quiet as mice, and stand you a drink when we get back."

"No, not one of you," quoth the plucky fellow, "and here's my staff in my hand, and if you don't leave my gear alone I will crack some of your ugly heads."

"That's a pity," I thought to myself, "for if they take to fighting it will be six to one—long odds against our chances." There was indeed a scuffle, and then a yell of pain, as though a soldier had been hit across the knuckles; but in a minute the best disposed called out, "Oh, cease your fun, boys, and let the fellow get off if he wants to. You know the fleet will be down directly, and Ar-hap has promised something worth having to the man who can find that lost bit of crackling of his. It's my opinion she's in the town, and I for one would rather look for her than go haddock fishing any day."

"Right you are, mates," said our friend with visible relief. "And, what's more, if you help me launch this boat and then go to my missus and tell her what you've done, she'll understand, and give you the biggest pumpkinful of beer in the place. Ah, she will understand, and bless your soft hearts and heads while you drink it—she's a cute one is my missus."

"And aren't you afraid to leave her with us?"

"Not I, my daisy, unless it were that a sight of your pretty face might give her hysterics. Now lend a hand, your accursed chatter has already cost me half an hour of the best fishing time."

"In with you, old buck!" shouted the soldiers; I felt the fisherman step in, as a matter of fact he stepped in on to my toes; a dozen hands were on the gunwales: six soldier yells resounded, it seemed, in my very ears: there was the grit and rush of pebbles under the keel: a sudden lurch up of the bows, which brought the fairy lady's honey-scented lips to mine, and then the gentle lapping of deep blue waters underneath us!

There is little more to be said of that voyage. We pulled until out of sight of the town, then hoisted sail, and, with a fair wind, held upon one tack until we made an island where there was a small colony of Hither folk.

Here our friend turned back. I gave him another gold button from my coat, and the princess a kiss upon either cheek, which he seemed to like even more than the button. It was small payment, but the best we had. Doubtless he got safely home, and I can but hope that Providence somehow or other paid him and his wife for a good deed bravely done.

Those islanders in turn lent us another boat, with a guide, who had business in the Hither capital, and on the evening of the second day, the direct route being very short in comparison, we were under the crumbling marble walls of Seth.

Chapter 20

It was like turning into a hothouse from a keen winter walk, our arrival at the beautiful but nerveless city after my life amongst the woodmen.

As for the people, they were delighted to have their princess back, but with the delight of children, fawning about her, singing, clapping hands, yet asking no questions as to where she had been, showing no appreciation of our adventures—a serious offence in my eyes—and, perhaps most important of all, no understanding of what I may call the political bearings of Heru's restoration, and how far their arch enemies beyond the sea might be inclined to attempt her recovery.

They were just delighted to have the princess back, and that was the end of it. Theirs was the joy of a vast nursery let loose. Flower processions were organised, garlands woven by the mile, a general order issued that the nation might stay up for an hour after bedtime, and in the vortex of that gentle rejoicing Heru was taken from me, and I saw her no more, till there happened the wildest scene of all you have shared with me so patiently.

Overlooked, unthanked, I turned sulky, and when this mood, one I can never maintain for long, wore off, I threw myself into the dissipation about me with angry zeal. I am frankly ashamed of the confession, but I was "a sailor ashore," and can only claim the indulgences proper to the situation. I laughed, danced, drank, through the night; I drank deep of a dozen rosy ways to forgetfulness, till my mind was a great confusion, full of flitting pictures of loveliness, till life itself was an illusive pantomime, and my will but thistle-down on the folly of the moment. I drank with those gentle roisterers all through their starlit night, and if we stopped when morning came it was more from weariness than virtue. Then the yellow-robed slaves gave us the wine of recovery—alas! my faithful An was not amongst them—and all through the day we lay about in sodden happiness.

Towards nightfall I was myself again, not unfortunately with the headache well earned, but sufficiently remorseful to be in a vein to make good resolutions for the future.

In this mood I mingled with a happy crowd, all purposeless and cheerful as usual, but before long began to feel the influence of one of those drifts, a universal turning in one direction, as seaweed turns

when the tide changes, so characteristic of Martia
a lovely soft velvet dusk, but not dark yet, and I sai
fairy at my side:

"Whither away, comrade? It is not eight bells yet. Su
going to be put to bed so early as this?"

"No," said that smiling individual, "it is the princess. We
to listen to Princess Heru in the palace square. She reads the g
the terrace again tonight, to see if omens are propitious for her ma.
She *must* marry, and you know the ceremony has been unavoida
postponed so far."

"Unavoidably postponed?" Yes, Heaven wotted I was aware of the
fact. And was Heru going to marry black Hath in such a hurry? And
after all I had done for her? It was scarcely decent, and I tried to rouse
myself to rage over it, but somehow the seductive Martian contentment
with any fate was getting into my veins. I was not yet altogether sunk
in their slothful acceptance of the inevitable, but there was not the
slightest doubt the hot red blood in me was turning to vapid stuff
such as did duty for the article in their veins. I mustered up a half-
hearted frown at this unwelcome intelligence, turning with it on my
face towards the slave girl; but she had slipped away into the throng,
so the frown evaporated, and shrugging my shoulders I said to myself,
"What does it matter? There are twenty others will do as well for me. If
not one, why then obviously another, 'tis the only rational way to think,
and at all events there is the magic globe. That may tell us something."
And slipping my arm round the waist of the first disengaged girl—we
were not then, mind you, in Atlantic City—I kissed her dimpling cheek
unreproached, and gaily followed in the drift of humanity, trending
with a low hum of pleasure towards the great white terraces under the
palace porch.

How well I knew them! It was just such an evening Heru had
consulted Fate in the same place once before; how much had happened
since then! But there was little time or inclination to think of those
things now. The whole phantom city's population had drifted to one
common centre. The crumbling seaward ramparts were all deserted; no
soldier watch was kept to note if angry woodmen came from over seas;
a soft wind blew in from off the brine, but told no tales; the streets were
empty, and, when as we waited far away in the southern sky the earth
planet presently got up, by its light Heru, herself again, came tripping
down the steps to read her fate.

other magic globe under a shroud on a tripod for
the charmed circle upon the terrace, and I was close
princess did not see me.

weird, fantastic dance commenced, the princess working
om the drowsiest undulations to a hurricane of emotion.
stopped close by the orb, and seized the corner of the web
it. We saw the globe begin to beam with veiled magnificence
touch.

Not an eye wavered, not a thought wandered from her in all that
silent multitude. It was a moment of the keenest suspense, and just
when it was at its height there came a strange sound of hurrying feet
behind the outermost crowd, a murmur such as a great pack of wolves
might make rushing through snow, while a soft long wail went up from
the darkness.

Whether Heru understood it or not I cannot say, but she hesitated a
moment, then swept the cloth from the orb of her fate.

And as its ghostly, self-emitting light beamed up in the darkness
with weird brilliancy, there by it, in gold and furs and war panoply, huge,
fierce, and lowering, stood—*Ar-hap himself!*

Ay, and behind him, towering over the crouching Martians, blocking
every outlet and street, were scores and hundreds of his men. Never was
surprise so utter, ambush more complete. Even I was transfixed with
astonishment, staring with open-mouthed horror at the splendid figure
of the barbarian king as he stood aglitter in the ruddy light, scowling
defiance at the throng around him. So silently had he come on his
errand of vengeance it was difficult to believe he was a reality, and not
some clever piece of stageplay, some vision conjured up by Martian
necromancy.

But he was good reality. In a minute comedy turned to tragedy. Ar-
hap gave a sign with his hand, whereon all his men set up a terrible
warcry, the like of which Seth had not heard for very long, and as
far as I could make out in the half light began hacking and hewing
my luckless friends with all their might. Meanwhile the king made at
Heru, feeling sure of her this time, and doubtless intending to make
her taste his vengeance to the dregs; and seeing her handled like that,
and hearing her plaintive cries, wrath took the place of stupid surprise
in me. I was on my feet in a second, across the intervening space, and
with all my force gave the king a blow upon the jaw which sent even
him staggering backwards. Before I could close again, so swift was

EDWIN L. ARNOLD

the sequence of events in those flying minutes, a wild mob or
victims and executioners in one disordered throng, was betwe
How the king fared I know not, nor stopped to ask, but half drag,
half carrying Heru through the shrieking mob, got her up the par
steps and in at the great doors, which a couple of yellow-clad slav.
more frightened of the barbarians than thoughtful of the crowd
without, promptly clapped to, and shot the bolts. Thus we were safe
for a moment, and putting the princess on a couch, I ran up a short
flight of stairs and looked out of a front window to see if there were a
chance of succouring those in the palace square. But it was all hopeless
chaos with the town already beginning to burn and not a show of fight
anywhere which I could join.

I glared out on that infernal tumult for a moment or two in an agony
of impotent rage, then turned towards the harbour and saw in the shine
of the burning town below the ancient battlements and towers of Seth
begin to gleam out, like a splendid frost work of living metal clear-cut
against the smooth, black night behind, and never a show of resistance
there either. Ay, and by this time Ar-hap's men were battering in our
gates with a big beam, and somehow, I do not know how it happened,
the palace itself away on the right, where the dry-as-dust library lay,
was also beginning to burn.

It was hopeless outside, and nothing to be done but to save Heru,
so down I went, and, with the slaves, carried her away from the hall
through a vestibule or two, and into an anteroom, where some yellow-
girt individuals were already engaged in the suggestive work of tying
up palace plate in bundles, amongst other things, alas! the great gold
love-bowl from which—oh! so long ago—I had drawn Heru's marriage
billet. These individuals told me in tremulous accents they had got a
boat on a secret waterway behind the palace whence flight to the main
river and so, far away inland, to another smaller but more peaceful city
of their race would be quite practical; and joyfully hearing this news, I
handed over to them the princess while I went to look for Hath.

And the search was not long. Dashing into the banquet-hall, still
littered with the remains of a feast, and looking down its deserted
vistas, there at the farther end, on his throne, clad in the sombre
garments he affected, chin on hand, sedate in royal melancholy,
listening unmoved to the sack of his town outside, sat the prince
himself. Strange, gloomy man, the great dead intelligence of his race
shining in his face as weird and out of place as a lonely sea beacon

nothing before the glow of sunrise, never had he appeared so
ious as at that moment. Even in the heat of excitement I stared
n in amazement, wishing in a hasty thought the confusion of the
few weeks had given me opportunity to penetrate the recesses of
s mind, and therefrom retell you things better worth listening to
than all the incident of my adventures. But now there was no time to
think, scarce time to act.

"Hath!" I cried, rushing over to him, "wake up, your majesty. The
Thither men are outside, killing and burning!"

"I know it."

"And the palace is on fire. You can smell the reek even here."

"Yes."

"Then what are you going to do?"

"Nothing."

"My word, that is a fine proposition for a prince! If you care nothing
for town or palace perhaps you will bestir yourself for Princess Heru."

A faint glimmer of interest rose upon the alabaster calm of his face
at that name, but it faded instantly, and he said quietly,

"The slaves will save her. She will live. I looked into the book of her
fate yesterday. She will escape, and forget, and sit at another marriage
feast, and be a mother, and give the people yet one more prince to keep
the faint glimmer of our ancestry alive. I am content."

"But, d—it, man, I am not! I take a deal more interest in the young
lady than you seem to, and have scoured half this precious planet of yours
on her account, and will be hanged if I sit idly twiddling my thumbs
while her pretty skin is in danger." But Hath was lost in contemplation
of his shoe-strings.

"Come, sir," I said, shaking his majesty by the shoulder, "don't be
down on your luck. There has been some rivalry between us, but never
mind about that just now. The princess wants you. I am going to save
both her and you, you must come with her."

"No."

"But you *shall* come."

"No!"

By this time the palace was blazing like a bonfire and the uproar
outside was terrible. What was I to do? As I hesitated the arras
at the further end of the hall was swept aside, a disordered mob of
slaves bearing bundles and dragging Heru with them rushing down
to the door near us. As Heru was carried swiftly by she stretched her

milk-white arms towards the prince and turned her face, lovely as convolvulus flower even in its pallor, upon him.

It was a heart-moving appeal from a woman with the heart of a child, and Hath rose to his feet while for a moment there shone a look of responsible manhood in his eyes. But it faded quickly; he bowed slowly as though he had received an address of condolence on the condition of his empire, and the next moment the frightened slaves, stumbling under their burdens, had swept poor Heru through the doorway.

I glanced savagely round at the curling smoke overhead, the red tendrils of fire climbing up a distant wall, and there on a table by us was a half-finished flask of the lovely tinted wine of forgetfulness. If Hath would not come sober perhaps he might come drunk.

"Here," I cried, "drink to tomorrow, your majesty, a sovereign toast in all ages, and better luck next time with these hairy gentlemen battering at your majesty's doors," and splashing out a goblet full of the stuff I handed it to him.

He took it and looked rather lovingly into the limpid pool, then deliberately poured it on the step in front of him, and throwing the cup away said pleasantly,

"Not tonight, good comrade; tonight I drink a deeper draught of oblivion than that,—and here come my cup-bearers."

Even while he spoke the palace gates had given way; there was a horrible medley of shrieks and cries, a quick sound of running feet; then again the arras lifted and in poured a horde of Ar-hap's men-at-arms. The moment they caught sight of us about a dozen of them, armed with bows, drew the thick hide strings to their ears and down the hall came a ravening flight of shafts. One went through my cap, two stuck quivering in the throne, and one, winged with owl feather, caught black Hath full in the bosom.

He had stood out boldly at the first coming of that onset, arms crossed on breast, chin up, and looking more of a gentleman than I had ever seen him look before; and now, stricken, he smiled gravely, then without flinching, and still eyeing his enemies with gentle calm, his knees unlocked, his frame trembled, then down he went headlong, his red blood running forth in rivulets amongst the wine of oblivion he had just poured out.

There was no time for sentiment. I shrugged my shoulders, and turning on my heels, with the woodmen close after me, sprang through the near doorway. Where was Heru? I flew down the corridor by which

seemed she had retreated, and then, hesitating a moment where it
divided in two, took the left one. This to my chagrin presently began
to trend upwards, whereas I knew Heru was making for the river down
below.

But it was impossible to go back, and whenever I stopped in those
deserted passages I could hear the wolflike patter of men's feet upon my
trail. On again into the stony labyrinths of the old palace, ever upwards,
in spite of my desire to go down, until at last, the pursuers off the track
for a moment, I came to a north window in the palace wall, and, hot
and breathless, stayed to look out.

All was peace here; the sky a lovely lavender, a promise of coming
morning in it, and a gold-spangled curtain of stars out yonder on the
horizon. Not a soul moved. Below appeared a sheer drop of a hundred
feet into a moat winding through thickets of heavy-scented convolvulus
flowers to the waterways beyond. And as I looked a skiff with half a
dozen rowers came swiftly out of the darkness of the wall and passed
like a shadow amongst the thickets. In the prow was all Hath's wedding
plate, and in the stern, a faint vision of unconscious loveliness, lay Heru!

Before I could lift a finger or call out, even if I had had a mind to do
so, the shadow had gone round a bend, and a shout within the palace
told me I was sighted again.

On once more, hotly pursued, until the last corridor ended in two
doors leading into a half-lit gallery with open windows at the further
end. There was a wilderness of lumber down the sides of the great garret,
and now I come to think of it more calmly I imagine it was Hath's
Lost Property Office, the vast receptacle where his slaves deposited
everything lazy Martians forgot or left about in their daily life. At that
moment it only represented a last refuge, and into it I dashed, swung
the doors to and fastened them just as the foremost of Ar-hap's men
hurled themselves upon the barrier from outside.

There I was like a rat in a trap, and like a rat I made up my mind
to fight savagely to the end, without for a moment deceiving myself
as to what that end must be. Even up there the horrible roar of
destruction was plainly audible as the barbarians sacked and burned
the ancient town, and I was glad from the bottom of my heart my poor
little princess was safely out of it. Nor did I bear her or hers the least
resentment for making off while there was yet time and leaving me to
my fate—anything else would have been contrary to Martian nature.
Doubtless she would get away, as Hath had said, and elsewhere drop a

few pearly tears and then over her sugar-candy and lo
with happy completeness—most blessed gift! And .
foresaid barbarians were battering on my doors, while ove
choking smoke was pouring in in ever-increasing volumes.

In burst the first panel, then another, and I could see thr
gaps a medley of tossing weapons and wild faces without. Shor
for me if they came through, so in the obstinacy of desperation
to work to pile old furniture and dry goods against the barricade. A
as they yelled and hammered outside I screamed back defiance from
within, sweating, tugging, and hauling with the strength of ten men,
piling up the old Martian lumber against the opening till, so fierce was
the attack outside, little was left of the original doorway and nothing
between me and the besiegers but a rampart of broken woodwork half
seen in a smother of smoke and flames.

Still they came on, thrusting spears and javelins through every
crevice and my strength began to go. I threw two tables into a gap,
and brained a besieger with a sweetmeat-seller's block and smothered
another, and overturned a great chest against my barricade; but what
was the purpose of it all? They were fifty to one and my rampart quaked
before them. The smoke was stifling, and the pains of dissolution in my
heart. They burst in and clambered up the rampart like black ants. I
looked round for still one more thing to hurl into the breach. My eyes
lit on a roll of carpet: I seized it by one corner meaning to drag it to the
doorway, and it came undone at a touch.

That strange, that incredible pattern! Where in all the vicissitudes
of a chequered career had I seen such a one before? I stared at it in
amazement under the very spears of the woodmen in the red glare of
Hath's burning palace. Then all on a sudden it burst upon me that *it
was the accursed rug*, the very one which in response to a careless wish
had swept me out of my own dear world, and forced me to take as wild
a journey into space as ever fell to a man's lot since the universe was
made!

And in another second it occurred to me that if it had brought me
hither it might take me hence. It was but a chance, yet worth trying
when all other chances were against me. As Ar-hap's men came
shouting over the barricade I threw myself down upon that incredible
carpet and cried from the bottom of my heart,

"I wish—I wish I were in New York!"

Yes!

. thrilling suspense and then the corners lifted as
ᵹ breeze were playing upon them. Another moment
curled over like an incoming surge. One swift glance I
ᵐoke and flames, the glittering spears and angry faces, and
upon fold, a stifling, all-enveloping embrace, a lift, a sense of
ᵤuman speed—and then forgetfulness.

ᵗhen I came to, as reporters say, I was aware the rug had ejected
on solid ground and disappeared, forever. Where was I! It was cool,
ᵈamp, and muddy. There were some iron railings close at hand and a
street lamp overhead. These things showed clearly to me, sitting on a
doorstep under that light, head in hand, amazed and giddy—so amazed
that when slowly the recognition came of the incredible fact my wish
was gratified and I was home again, the stupendous incident scarcely
appealed to my tingling senses more than one of the many others I had
lately undergone.

Very slowly I rose to my feet, and as like a discreditable reveller as
could be, climbed the steps. The front door was open, and entering the
oh, so familiar hall a sound of voices in my sitting-room on the right
caught my ear.

"Oh no, Mrs. Brown," said one, which I recognised at once as my
Polly's, "he is dead for certain, and my heart is breaking. He would
never, never have left me so long without writing if he had been alive,"
and then came a great sound of sobbing.

"Bless your kind heart, miss," said the voice of my landlady in reply,
"but you don't know as much about young gentlemen as I do. It is not
likely, if he has gone off on the razzle-dazzle, as I am sure he has, he
is going to write every post and tell you about it. Now you go off to
your ma at the hotel like a dear, and forget all about him till he comes
back—that's *my* advice."

"I cannot, I cannot, Mrs. Brown. I cannot rest by day or sleep by
night for thinking of him; for wondering why he went away so suddenly,
and for hungering for news of him. Oh, I am miserable. Gully! Gully!
Come to me," and then there were sounds of troubled footsteps pacing
to and fro and of a woman's grief.

That was more than I could stand. I flung the door open, and, dirty,
dishevelled, with unsteady steps, advanced into the room.

"Ahem!" coughed Mrs. Brown, "just as I expected!"

But I had no eyes for her. "Polly! Polly!" I cried, and that dear girl,
after a startled scream and a glance to make sure it was indeed the

EDWIN L. ARNOLD

recovered prodigal, rushed over and threw all her weight ot comfortable womanhood into my arms, and the moment ɪ into a passion of happy tears down my collar.

"Humph!" quoth the landlady, "that is not what *brown* gets w. forgets his self. No, not by any means."

But she was a good old soul at heart, and, seeing how matters stɔ with a parting glance of scorn in my direction and a toss of her hea went out of the room, and closed the door behind her.

Need I tell in detail what followed? Polly behaved like an angel, and when in answer to her gentle reproaches I told her the outlines of my marvellous story she almost believed me! Over there on the writing-desk lay a whole row of the unopened letters she had showered upon me during my absence, and amongst them an official one. We went and opened it together, and it was an intimation of my promotion, a much better "step" than I had ever dared to hope for.

Holding that missive in my hand a thought suddenly occurred to me.

"Polly dear, this letter makes me able to maintain you as you ought to be maintained, and there is still a fortnight of vacation for me. Polly, will you marry me tomorrow?"

"No, certainly not, sir."

"Then will you marry me on Monday?"

"Do you truly, truly want me to?"

"Truly, truly."

"Then, yes," and the dear girl again came blushing into my arms.

While we were thus the door opened, and in came her parents who were staying at a neighbouring hotel while inquiries were made as to my mysterious absence. Not unnaturally my appearance went a long way to confirm suspicions such as Mrs. Brown had confessed to, and, after they had given me cold salutations, Polly's mother, fixing gold glasses on the bridge of her nose and eyeing me haughtily therefrom, observed,

"And now that you *are* safely at home again, Lieutenant Gulliver Jones, I think I will take my daughter away with me. Tomorrow her father will ascertain the true state of her feelings after this unpleasant experience, and subsequently he will no doubt communicate with you on the subject." This very icily.

But I was too happy to be lightly put down.

"My dear madam," I replied, "I am happy to be able to save her father that trouble. I have already communicated with this young lady as to

...er feelings, and as an outcome I am delighted to be able to ... are to be married on Monday."

...es, Mother, it is true, and if you do not want to make me the ...iserable of girls again you will not be unkind to us."

... brief, that sweet champion spoke so prettily and smoothed things ...everly that I was "forgiven," and later on in the evening allowed to ...cort Polly back to her hotel.

"And oh!" she said, in her charmingly enthusiastic way when we were saying goodnight, "you shall write a book about that extraordinary story you told me just now. Only you must promise me one thing."

"What is it?"

"To leave out all about Heru—I don't like that part at all." This with the prettiest little pout.

"But, Polly dear, see how important she was to the narrative. I cannot quite do that."

"Then you will say as little as you can about her?"

"No more than the story compels me to."

"And you are quite sure you like me much the best, and will not go after her again?"

"Quite sure."

The compact was sealed in the most approved fashion; and here, indulgent reader, is the artless narrative that resulted—an incident so incredible in this prosaic latter-day world that I dare not ask you to believe, and must humbly content myself with hoping that if I fail to convince yet I may at least claim the consolation of having amused you.

A Note About the Author

ᴸester Arnold (1857–1935) was a British author and journalist father, Edwin Arnold, was one of the first popularizers of Eastern ᴸght in the UK. The author is best known for his novels, *Phra the* ᴸenician and especially *Gulliver of Mars*, which is often held as the ᴸrst true planetary romance and a likely influence on the Mars novels of Edgar Rice Burroughs.

A Note from the Publisher

Spanning many genres, from non-fiction essays to literature classics to children's books and lyric poetry, Mint Edition books showcase the master works of our time in a modern new package. The text is freshly typeset, is clean and easy to read, and features a new note about the author in each volume. Many books also include exclusive new introductory material. Every book boasts a striking new cover, which makes it as appropriate for collecting as it is for gift giving. Mint Edition books are only printed when a reader orders them, so natural resources are not wasted. We're proud that our books are never manufactured in excess and exist only in the exact quantity they need to be read and enjoyed.

bookfinity™

Discover more of your favorite classics with Bookfinity™.

- Track your reading with custom book lists.
- Get great book recommendations for your personalized Reader Type.
- Add reviews for your favorite books.
- AND MUCH MORE!

Visit **bookfinity.com** and take the fun Reader Type quiz to get started.

Enjoy our classic and modern companion pairings!

Classic & Modern